THE NERD

The Nerd

Giles K Caperton

R

Rambunctious Books

You're not going to like me. It's not your fault, it's mine. I try, I do *really* try, but I make terrible first impressions, and even if I get off to an OK start it's only a matter of time before I slip up and my actual personality leaks out and that invariably ruins everything. So I'm under no illusion that this is going to make me any friends.

Equally, I know there's no hope of salvaging my professional reputation. I fell so far and so publicly from grace that no matter what I say now, no matter the evidence I present, the story that people will always remember is the one about the nerd whose incompetence allowed a hacker to make off with millions. The clout I had in the world I moved in (which, I mean, I don't want to brag but it used to be substantial) is forever gone.

It's just...

I think what it *is* is that if the whole world is going to despise me, I'd rather believe they at least despised the real me, not the version of me that got plastered all over the Internet in the aftermath of it all. Even though I know it won't change anything, I want to get down in writing what actually happened, who I actually am, and what I actually did, and let myself be judged for that.

So this isn't really a story about some high-tech heist, or about the missing £7.4 million, or even about what happened to poor Moritz Ortlauf.

This is a story about *me*.

1

It was the morning of the day when everything started to go wrong, and a bloated pink blob loomed out at me through the steamy haze, resolving itself, as I approached the bathroom mirror, into my reflection. Squinting slightly, because I didn't have my lenses in yet, I peered at the inevitable, disappointing form before me: a huge, blotchy lump of flesh, with too much hair on its shoulders, too little on its scalp, piggy eyes, a bulbous nose, and a BMI of 65.

(Yes, 65. Yes, the healthy range is 20 to 24.9. Yes, that means if you cut me in half straight down my spine, both halves of me would still be clinically obese. You're put off already, aren't you? I told you you wouldn't like me.)

I've always had a very strong sense that the outer surfaces of my body aren't really *me*. They're just cladding around a more essential part that starts a couple of inches behind my eyes. I *loathe* my cladding. If I could separate my conscious mind from the body that carries it around I would do so in a heartbeat. The dystopian future in which we're all brains in jars with plugs sticking out of our cerebellums, communing majestically with the machines, is emphatically OK by me.

Anyway, I try not to think about my body most of the time, but a moment of post-shower moping is something of a morning ritual for me. And on that morning I moped for slightly longer than usual, because I was dimly aware I had just forgotten something. I was holding out a forlorn hope that if I stayed still and waited long enough, the lost idea might somehow wander back into my head.

To explain what the idea was, I need to talk about cupcakes.

Imagine, if you will, that you're my teammate at work, and it's your birthday, and, as per unofficial office policy, you've brought in a tray of cupcakes for the team to mark the occasion. You set them down in the kitchenette upon arrival, then head to your desk. Ten minutes later you return to brew your first cuppa of the day, and you notice to your horror that all the cakes have already been eaten. The kitchen is empty apart from yours truly, who is washing his hands at the sink.

"Colin, you didn't... you didn't eat *all* the cupcakes, did you?" you inquire, your affected nonchalance masking a very real concern.

Now, I want you to imagine two possible scenarios here. The first is that I turn around slowly, a mildly questioning look on my face, and say, simply and openly: "No." In this case, you could continue to consider me a suspect, but you might equally conclude that I probably wasn't the phantom cupcake-scoffer. You couldn't be sure either way.

But now imagine a second scenario, where no sooner is the question past your lips than I spin round and blurt out an abrupt and hurried "No!".

Bet your list of suspects just narrowed, didn't it?

The key thing is this: In the second scenario, you've learnt something extra, not from the content of what I've said, but rather *how* I've said it, and specifically, by paying attention to the timing of my response. More than that, what you've learnt is something that I've actively tried to hide from you.

Now, one final step: Imagine that, instead of being a colleague, I'm a computer. And imagine that the piece of information I'm trying to hide is not *whether I've eaten the cupcakes* but rather, say, *whether the master password for the international banking system begins with the letter J.*

In this final scenario, by asking me, a computer, a question and paying close attention to how quickly I respond, you are technically conducting what's known in the trade as a 'side channel timing attack'. Congratulations! You're a hacker now. Please use your new-found powers responsibly.

Anyway, while I was in the shower, I had had the beginnings of a thought about how some software I had written at work was theoretically susceptible to something vaguely along those lines. Problematically though, because I'm never really awake until at least half way through my morning ablutions, I hadn't managed to consciously articulate any of the details before my thoughts were interrupted by the shower head, which treated me to one of its occasional five-second bursts of ice-cold spray. I yelped and nearly fell over, steadying myself at the last second by pawing at the shower curtain, and yanking one end off its hooks in the process. By the time I'd recovered my composure the thought about a hack had sunk back into my subconscious. I was just left with a vague worry that somewhere, at some point, I'd written a programme that might not be entirely up to the job, in a way that was potentially significant. Which was rather mortifying, because this is the *exact* sort of mistake that I'm paid quite a lot of money not to make.

Staring at the mirror wasn't helping retrieve the lost insight. I shook my head dolefully at my reflection. I needed to fix my bloody shower. The problem was, I didn't understand anything about how showers worked, and the thought of letting a plumber, a *stranger*, into the bathroom in my flat (my most private place within my most private place!) was horrifying. Plus all the local plumbers' websites I could find made you give out your phone number when you contacted them so that they could call you back, and I hate phone calls.

I promised myself that if it got worse I'd get it fixed, and resigned myself to the occasional ice-blast in the meantime. I fumbled my lenses in, squeezed into some clothes, and headed through to the kitchen for breakfast.

*

Breakfast should be a good time of day for me. I'm *into* breakfast, conceptually. My ideal morning meal is actually several meals. In a perfect world it would feature something meaty and salty like sausages and bacon, something sweet, like maybe jam on toast, and something satisfyingly hefty like por-ridge drowned in golden syrup, all served up one after the other.

However.

Big Sis says I mustn't eat like that at breakfast. Big Sis says it's important I get enough fibre. And Big Sis is very good at making me feel bad if I don't do what she asks.

So my breakfast each day is a bowl of bran flakes. But, be-cause I can't stand the taste of bran flakes, I mix in those dried marshmallow pieces, the type that they put in American cereal (and which you can bulk-buy online in five kilogram bags), in a ratio approaching one-to-one. And I wash away any lin-gering bran-y aftertaste with a pint of coke. That way I am technically doing what Big Sis commands, but without mak-ing myself miserable in the process.

I know. My eating habits are cartoonishly gross. It's not ok to have coke and marshmallows for breakfast. I *know*. But we don't all have a choice in these things. Trade-offs must be made.

Anyway, that morning I was half way through my cereal when my phone buzzed. My heart sank. It was an email from Mum. No message, just a link to an article in the Telegraph and a '*Sent from my iPad beside the pool in sunny Limassol!* sig-nature. The article was, surprise, surprise, about some new 'scientific discovery' around weight loss. It hurts every time. I winced, closed the tab and archived the email. Mum can send me as much pseudo-science pseudo-journalism as an expression of her disapproval as she likes. That's her prerogative. I can disregard it. That's mine.

Breakfast done, I tossed bowl, cup and spoon into the dishwasher, donned my jacket, shovelled some snacks into my rucksack, and started my pre-flight checks for leaving home. Windows: closed. Bathroom and kitchen taps: off. Big power strip that powers my computer: off. Lights: off. Gas hobs: definitely off. Thermostat: turned down just in case there's a power cut that resets the timer thereby leaving the heating off all day. Internet-connected smoke alarm: functioning, synced to the app on my phone, and currently reporting zero atmospheric carbon monoxide. Satisfied that everything was ready, I headed for the door.

This was one of the harder parts of my day. The outside world has always been a difficult place for me, and leaving my flat takes an effort of will every time. Each morning before work I stand for a little while, my hand on the inside surface of my door, waiting to build up the courage to leave. Some days it takes just a few seconds, some days it takes quarter of an hour. Today it took four and a half minutes (not counting the additional time I wasted retrieving my keys which I'd unintentionally left in the kitchen). Marginally longer than average, which I put down to lingering distress from yet another attempt by Mum to meddle in my life. Not long enough that I needed to be on the alert for signs of an impending panic attack over the course of the day. Not quite perfectly emotionally stable, but good enough.

*

I played the Gabardine Suit Game at the bus stop. Big Sis taught it to me as a teenager. (She, always the artsy one of the family, had been *heavily* into Simon & Garfunkel at the time, and apparently it's named after a line from one of their songs.) The idea is simple: whenever you're out in public, pick the closest person to you and assume that they are a thief, spy, or generally malicious agent. Try to work out the most plausible way that they could rob, defraud or otherwise harm you. Then plan how you would foil them.

Big Sis introduced it to help me with my shyness. The idea was that if I was scared of someone, I should think about the worst thing they could possibly do and work out how to cope with that, and then I wouldn't be frightened any more. In practice it didn't actually fix the shyness, but it was curiously addictive, and for a while I used to play it religiously with my other sibling, Little Sis (back in the days when we spoke to each other), whenever we were out in public. She grew out of it, but somehow I never could.

There was a woman standing near me with a heavy coat folded over her arm, meaning I couldn't see her hands. This suggested to me that she was holding a knife, and was angling to get close enough to surreptitiously stab me in the groin and then whisk herself away, unsuspected, as I collapsed. To fend her off I'd need to keep my rucksack between my body and her blade, but it might be better to yank her coat away preemptively so that her knife was exposed and she, uncovered, was forced to beat a retreat.

Next to her was a teenager of ambiguous gender playing on their phone. Their attack vector was less clear. Perhaps they were subtly trying to take photos of me as part of a complex identity fraud scheme. Maybe they needed a face shot in the hope that they could steal my phone and use the photo to get round the facial recognition lock. I made sure not to look directly in their direction.

As it happened, both the teenager and the woman with the coat got onto the 176 when it rolled up, meaning that I had the stop to myself by the time my bus, the 149, arrived. It was empty enough that I had plenty of choices about where to sit. Normally, sitting down on public transport means you have to worry that someone will get on who needs the seat more than you, and that you won't notice them, and then you'll be the berk who didn't give up their seat. Or worse, that someone who doesn't need the seat but *looks* like they do will get on and you'll offer them your seat and they'll be offended because you've implied that they're old or so fat they look pregnant or something, and then you'll be the berk who offended a stranger.

(Yes, I've thought about this a lot. The idea of being called out for doing something socially unacceptable on public transport is the sort of thing that regularly stops me sleeping at night.)

Anyway, I've found a solution: people who need a seat on the bus because they are too infirm to stand are also invariably too infirm to make it up the stairs, so if I sit upstairs I never have to worry about giving up my seat to someone else. I can close my eyes, listen to something on my phone (I alternate between extremely high-brow podcasts about cryptography, and extremely low-brow schlock fantasy audiobooks), and pretend I'm in a quiet white room by myself.

And yes, I do fit on the upstairs seats of a London bus. Just.

*

If you don't work in tech you probably won't have heard of Paladin, my employer. Despite being a big deal in the tech world they're almost unheard of among the general public. We keep businesses safe from hackers, and we do it very well, but said businesses don't like owning up to needing protection from that sort of threat. It's the type of subject that makes investors and clients jittery, so everyone prefers it if we keep a low profile.

Paladin's headquarters are strategically situated in Finsbury Square in London, just near enough to the City to suggest that they're serious players in the world of corporate services, and just close enough to Silicon Roundabout to pretend that they're part of the trendy tech scene. This duality has led to some mild absurdities, not least of which is the dress code. Men are expected to wear formal shirts every day, but you're allowed and even encouraged to completely conceal the shirt under a company-branded hoodie. This, frankly, sucks for me as, for whatever reason, I sweat way more in a shirt than a t-

shirt, and I'm sure my co-workers notice the smell. I do sometimes wear a hoodie to try to conceal it, but the hoodies are so
thick that I end up sweating, and smelling, even more.

Anyway, by the time my bus dropped me off in Finsbury
Square it was still ten to nine, so I took the opportunity to
drop into the hipster coffee-cum-cycle shop next to the office.
I go in there two or three times a week, and I always order the
same thing, but they never give any sign of recognising me,
and I've never dared ask for 'the usual'. So instead I waited my
turn, and then gave the bearded, tattooed, artisan barista my
order, and then gave it to him again when he didn't hear me
the first time.

Oh, yes, something else you should know about me: I've
got a mild stammer, and I'm so self-conscious about my voice
that I've become a terrible mumbler. It's self-defeating, of
course. No one hears me the first time, so I end up having
to repeat myself, sometimes twice, which just draws out the
whole ordeal, but at this point I'm past hoping that I can
change. I mumble my way through life, and if you've ever had
to take my order in a restaurant, or deal with me in a post office or bank, I apologise for the frustration I must have caused
you.

At 8:57 I walked in through the office doors, clutching my
hard-won latte and feeling more or less ready to face the day.
I had no idea that I'd already made the mistake that would cost
me my job. Did you spot it?

2

I wasn't always fat. When I was a child I was chubby, to be sure, but I wasn't... *this.* I was, however, awkward and shy, and with hindsight I was always pretty weird, so I didn't have friends at school. But I did have an older sister who looked out for me, a younger sister who worshipped the ground I trod on, and a mother who was at least well-meaning, if inconsistent. But life could certainly have been a whole lot worse, all things considered.

Then when I was fifteen, I nearly killed Little Sis. She survived, but was permanently disabled. I'm not ready to talk about the specifics quite yet, but suffice it to say that in the process of me ruining her life, several extreme personal failings of mine were laid acutely bare, and we all realised that I wasn't cut out for dealing with real people in the real world.

I had to seek, therefore, an alternative form of existence. I found myself drawn to computers: I liked the way they were logical, predictable, controllable. Obviously, they can't replace some of the emotional aspects of human interaction, but I discovered that food was, to a certain extent, an effective substitute for that. The weight gain was an unfortunate side effect, but I was able to shape my life such that I had very few requirements concerning my own physical ability.

Discovering programming started me down a pathway that I would follow without deviation for the next 20 years. I didn't go to university, instead using my portfolio of personal projects to land a junior role with a software agency, which led to another job with a bigger agency in London that had a focus on information security or 'infosec' (a fancy term for trying to keep computers safe from hackers), which eventually led to a coveted job at Paladin, the big dog in the industry. Paladin was the elite brand: in a world where everyone gets hacked eventually, they were unique in that no system of theirs had ever been successfully targeted. They were known as the best of the best, and I managed to walk into an Enterprise Security Architect role, with commensurate salary and, for the first time in my life, prestige.

I loved that job from the moment I started on my first day. Don't get me wrong, the first day was also *awful*: endless conversations with friendly HR people who I struggled to make eye contact with, a thousand awkward introductions, and the constant fear of doing something wrong and making a bad impression on my new colleagues.

But *on day one* they had me start work designing a whole security system for a new client, from scratch, with carte blanche to do it however I wanted. All I had to do was write a five-page document with accompanying summary slide deck justifying my choices. It was heavenly. (And yes, I'm aware of how ridiculous that must sound to a normal person.)

In time I was assigned a permanent team, and got to know everyone in it well enough that I didn't choke on 'Good morning', and even managed to make small talk with some of them on good days. I didn't make *friends* with anyone, of course, but that was all right. I had regular contact with Big Sis to stop me spiralling in on myself. I wasn't exactly happy, but things were stable. And stability is more or less the best that I can realistically aspire to.

*

"Fucking Todd, man. I'm calling him, right now."

"To say what?"

"To tell him he's a fucking idiot."

"Why?"

"Because he's a fucking idiot! He wants to disable two-factor auth in the new version of Labyrinth."

"You're kidding me. I went over this with him on Friday."

"Well he must have had a fucking crazy weekend, because this is what he sent through last night."

"Let me see... ok... Oh good grief. That man has a mind like a... Look, at this stage would it be the end of the world to give him what he wants?"

"Oh fuck, really? Fucking *really*? Colin, I need you to come here right now and sort this bullshit out, because I tell you man, any more of it and I quit, I quit right here."

Rémy (the sweary one) was in one of his regular tussles with Kayla when I arrived in the Bunker (the widely used but unofficial name for my team's dingy, subterranean workspace). Rémy was the junior developer on my team, but he never let his inexperience hold him back from expressing an opinion. In an office environment where bad language was normally not tolerated, he managed to get away with using 'fuck' in every second sentence when he was angry. I suspected this was mostly because somehow it sounded more eloquent in his thick Marseille accent.

Kayla gave me a weary look. I understood: if Rémy was this riled by 9am, the Bunker would be a tiring place to spend the day. I dropped my rucksack on my chair, walked over to Rémy's desk and squinted at his screen, where the latest email from Todd Nash of Maison de Gauguin was on display.

"You see, man? Kayla is being as stupid as Todd right now."

Rémy was right, in one sense. I won't bore you with the details, but what Todd was asking for was a huge step backwards, security-wise, and there was no way we should be entertaining it. But it wasn't Kayla's fault that she didn't understand. She was the account manager for our team, and she had no formal technical training, nor an intuitive grasp of how security works. But now I had to point out to her why Todd's suggestion was indefensible, and I really didn't want to do it in a way that hurt her feelings. I always worried I came across as condescending when I explained tech stuff to her, which was the last thing I wanted to do.

"Uh…" I started.

This was hard. People were hard. I suddenly wanted a snack.

"Never mind," said Kayla lightly. "I trust you. I'll just... I'll just talk him out of it. Again."

Rémy rolled his eyes as I tried to hide my relief.

"Director of Digital. He's their Director of fucking Digital and he doesn't even get how passwords work. You know what, I'm scared. I am scared of how much stupidity there is in the world. It really worries me, you know?"

He jabbed a finger in Kayla's direction and smiled wryly.

"And you nearly sided with Todd on this one. You've gotta make sure you can tell the difference between the idiots and the... the us. If Todd tells you something and I tell you he's a fucking idiot, you've gotta believe me. I need a cigarette. Look at me, it's only 9 o'clock and already I need a fucking cigarette break. It's gonna be a long day, man."

Rémy stalked out, leaving me alone in the Bunker with Kayla, who shook her head.

"That boy has a lot of anger, and I'm not sure he always remembers which way he's trying to point it."

I agreed with her, but I couldn't think of anything to say about it, so I just raised my eyebrows and nodded in what I hoped was a sympathetic-looking way.

Rémy always overreacted to things, but I had long since come to the conclusion that Todd Nash really was an idiot. The Maison de Gauguin contract was, by and large, a source of real pleasure for me, but it came with a Todd-shaped fly in the ointment.

If you haven't already heard of Maison de Gauguin, or MDG, what you need to know is that as an organisation they positioned themselves somewhere between an art auctioneer and a private members' club. The company was built around the insight that there is a certain sort of super-rich individual who, while they want to buy art because it gives them something to brag about, tends not to actually know anything *about* art, not to particularly enjoy visiting galleries, and not to want to come within ten miles of real artists (who can apparently be a prickly bunch). Maison de Gauguin allows them to skip all that, by putting together a service that makes art buying glamorous and fun. When a piece from a particularly trendy former Saatchi protégé comes up for sale, they will arrange a Dubai pool party for their multi-millionaire members. Over a long boozy weekend, they will encourage bids without harping on too much about the actual art or artist or any of that boring stuff. When the champagne hangovers clear a few days later, one hedonistically over-indulgent plutocrat will realise they've forked out a few tens of millions for something that'll probably sit in storage and never be seen by them again.

We, of course, never got to experience that side of MDG. We got to experience Todd Nash, their Digital Director. His unsuitability for the job was matched only by his blindness to his own inadequacies. The fact that in conversation he occasionally got confused about the difference between a website and an email didn't deter him in the slightest from making arbitrary decisions about the technology that his company used to facilitate their multi-million pound art deals.

Paladin's contract with MDG accounted for most of my team's output for the past year, and the system for making and receiving payments we had built for them – called Labyrinth – was my baby. It was quite possibly my proudest achievement. We were now in discussion with them about a newer, better version, which would involve a raft of new features – hence the stream of 'helpful' thoughts coming in from Todd.

*

With Rémy briefly out of the way, Kayla and I settled down at our desks, and all was quiet until Debi arrived, in conversation with Bled. Bled greeted me with a lazy nod. His glassy smile and slow speech gave the impression of someone who didn't care very much what was going on around them, and had earned him a reputation as a laid-back slacker (although in actual fact he worked hard and cared a lot). I liked him, largely because once you got to know him, he was predictable, reliable, and therefore *manageable*, even by someone like me.

Debi, on the other hand, was a rarity: A female coder who worked in infosec. Now look, I'm not going to bore you with a history of how and why we've ended up in a world where there are so few women who code. I'm just going to state the obvious and regrettable fact that in software development as a whole, women make up no more than 10% of the workforce, and they are even more rare in the field of information security.

So Debi was unusual. But then again, Debi was unusual. She wore chunky black boots, black jeans, black chokers and black long-sleeve t-shirts with logos of bands with names like Sepulchrist and Necronomicon on them. Curls of tattoos peeked out at her wrists and neck that hinted tantalisingly at inky swirls extending across her whole torso. Her naturally dark complexion was made to seem lighter by contrast with her dyed-black hair and black cherry lipstick. As far as I could tell she'd been dressing that way since she was a teenager, and, rather wonderfully, nothing about growing up, getting a mortgage or rearing children had in any way caused her to tone down her style. As with Rémy and swearing, Debi ignored rules about dress code so completely and so comfortably that I don't think it occurred to anyone that there was something wrong about her being the only one wearing full goth gear in an office stuffed with branded hoodies and shirts.

"Morning, Colin! Got some top goss for you: Priyanka just signed J-Chem as a client!" she announced excitedly. "Big contract too – they want us to build them a brand spanking new accounting system."

"That's great," I replied warmly. I liked it when Debi acted pleased to see me.

"It would be... except that she managed to convince them that for 'security' reasons they needed the entire thing to use Burncoin."

I frowned.

"Why on earth would they need–"

"Oh but it's *so secure!*" Debi squealed, doing her best impression of Priyanka, our effervescent head of sales. "And of course, you must be aware that no less an institution than *Maison de Gauguin* has adopted it for all their transactions? That makes it just the most sexy tech since the Bluetooth-powered dildo."

It took me a few seconds to recover from hearing Debi use the words 'sexy' and 'dildo', so I'll take this opportunity to explain a little bit about what she was talking about. J-Chem were a big account that we had been chasing for a while, and it sounded like Priyanka had just closed the deal, by convincing them that we could make their new system use a cryptocurrency called Burncoin.

Don't worry, I'm not about to start waffling on about blockchains or any other crypto guff. If you don't know about cryptocurrencies, all I need to tell you is that they're magic internet money. They come in various different flavours, and for a time Burncoin was a very popular option because (and this is the only detail you need to remember) it is completely untraceable, making it hugely popular with rich people's accountants, who are keen to keep their clients' transactions hidden from the prying eyes of tax inspectors around the world. We had built Labyrinth for MDG to facilitate payments in Burncoin, and now apparently J-Chem, bewitched by MDG's glamour, wanted something similar.

Debi's news caused quite a stir among my team. Well, I say mine, but while I'm the technical lead, mercifully I'm not supposed to actually *lead* them – that responsibility falls to patient, hard-working, Canadian Kayla. In other teams the architect is fully in charge, but in my case everyone silently agreed that my forte is computers, not people, so Kayla was brought in to do all the messy human-focussed stuff. Like every team at Paladin we were officially named after a type of sword – 'Foil' in our case – but at some point Priyanka decided to nickname us the Bunker Buddies, and it caught on.

Anyway, for the first twenty minutes of the morning, the Bunker Buddies merrily rowed about the merits and pitfalls of Burncoin until Rémy returned from his cigarette break and, to spare us all *his* two cents on the matter, Kayla gently suggested we settle down to work.

*

The morning passed without incident. In between mundane tasks, I spent some time on the #riddles channel on our team's group chat. We set each other brainteasers, and had an informal weekly competition where you got points for solving puzzles or setting ones that other people couldn't solve. I almost always got more right than anyone else, but two weeks in every three I didn't let myself announce all of my right answers, because it was no fun for everyone else if I won all the time. This was my week for winning, though, so I breezed through a couple of cryptic crossword clues Kayla had thrown in, and narrowly avoided being tripped up by Rémy's latest picture puzzle. I realised I was rushing it because what I really wanted was to have another crack at Debi's submission from the day before. She had a knack of coming up with what I considered *proper* riddles, and I always enjoyed them. Her latest was a real poser:

The crypt is empty except for a treasure chest. The chest is closed, locked, and indestructible, and cannot be opened without the key. The thief enters the crypt empty-handed, and leaves with one item of treasure in his hand. How?

Debi always made you think laterally. I briefly considered whether the treasure in question was going to be something like 'knowledge', but that seemed far-fetched. Of course, there were endless solutions that technically worked – the thief could have entered the crypt with a jewel in his mouth, or a key between his buttocks, for example – but that wasn't going to be the *right* answer. Knowing Debi, it would be something satisfying. I couldn't spot it immediately, but that was fine. I was (perhaps arrogantly) pretty confident no one else was going to get it before me, so I had until the end of the week to work it out at my leisure.

At lunchtime I nipped out to the McDonald's around the corner. I'd been going there for years, but I was still surreptitious about it. You're not supposed to eat at McDonald's if you work in a tech company in London. You're supposed to go to trendy ramen bars, or eat falafel wraps from street markets, or chug meal-replacement protein smoothies. But, much as I wish it were otherwise, I don't like any of those things. I like warm, unchallenging burgers in comforting, clothy buns with crispy, salty fries. I like the way that the meat, the bread, the milkshakes and the chicken nuggets all have fundamentally the same texture. I like the way that I know exactly what each mouthful will be like before it goes in. I don't, however, like being thought of as the office fat man who only eats at McDonald's, so I always sit upstairs where I won't be spotted by co-workers passing by on the street.

My favourite table was free, to my delight. It's a good table – right up in the corner, so that you can sit with your back to the wall with the whole room in your field of view. Crucially, while you're sat there, no one can see your phone screen, which meant that while I was eating I could safely check the my personal Gmail account. I am a very, *very* private person, and am not prepared to risk the possibility of anyone – colleagues, family or total strangers – seeing the contents of my personal emails. Emails like the one currently sitting in my inbox telling me I had a new message from HarlequinCyanide waiting for me on AltMatch.

So... I suppose now it's time for me to talk about my love life.

Don't get your hopes up. You're not about to discover that I'm secretly a prolific womaniser. I'm still a reclusive, social disaster. Sex isn't something that happens to people like me. But while relationships in the traditional sense may be out, that doesn't mean I don't crave intimacy and companionship. I'm haunted by loneliness just like everyone else. I've just had to be a bit creative with how I scratch that itch.

AltMatch is one of a host of dating websites run by a company called XOX Connections, which range from vanilla sites like Amanda's List, which is a fairly straightforward clone of match.com, to super-niche ones like Sportscar Soulmates and even Amputee Connections. AltMatch is their long-standing offering for people who don't really fit anywhere else: the weirdos, freaks and nerds. It was *Visigoth* magazine's official "Best place to find love if you're a non-conformist" back in 2011, apparently. Unlike the generation of dating apps that sprang up after it that constantly push you towards real-world meetings with a view to falling in love and/or getting laid, AltMatch is an online-first community, facilitating private, entirely internet-based communication between compatible strangers. So if you're like me in that (a) you never want to actually *meet* the people you meet and (b) you have a thing for piercings, tattoos and dyed hair, it ticks quite a lot of boxes.

(Before you say anything about that last bit, yes, fine, I thought Debi was stunning and awesome and smelt intoxicating, and I spent more time that I liked to admit browsing her Facebook photos, but no, I was never in love with her or anything like that. She had a husband and two children, and of course there was no question that she'd be interested in me. I just experienced quite... *complex* emotional resonances when I was around her.)

Other people go on dates, hook up with strangers in bars, or... I don't know, go on long walks in the countryside with their soulmates or something. I chatted to fellow recluses on

AltMatch. It wasn't much of a love life, but it was the closest I could get.

And now my heart was trilling because I had a message back from HarlequinCyanide. Her profile was enigmatic: a close-up picture of a mascara'd eye in a dark room with a curl of blue hair looping down into shot. The interests she listed were generic (reading, baking, and tea) and unrevealing. But her username, a reference to a very weird but rather good Japanese anime series, had piqued my interest. I'd sent a message congratulating her on her taste. She messaged back, and we'd chatted about the show, and TV more generally, over the space of a few weeks. Then she'd gone quiet, and I, disappointed, had made myself forget about her. Until now.

The message read:

Hey, sorry for the silence. I had a bit of a bad week and needed to disconnect for a bit. But I'm back! Anyway... you said you know about cryptocurrencies, right? Honestly... should I be, like, buying Bitcoins? Or how about this Burncoin thing I keep hearing about? Is it, like, a sensible investment, or is it a scam? I don't want to get shafted. Or at least, not like that (BTW I can't BELIEVE they don't let me put emojis on here – I could really use a sticking-out-tongue-while-winking-smiley right about now!!) X HQCN

I decided not to reply immediately. My first instinct was to give a detailed answer about whether cryptocurrencies were best thought of as a fiat currency, an investment instrument, or an exercise in hype and sophistry, and if this were a conversation in real life that's exactly what I would have ended up saying, and only realised too late just how boring I was being. That was the beauty of messaging on AltMatch. I could take the time to override my god-awful social instincts. In the meantime it was just nice to feel that someone in the universe had reached out and made contact. That felt warm and comforting.

3

The rest of the day was uneventful. At the end of the afternoon Debi rounded up the team to go to the pub. The Bunker Buddies have all long since learned to stop asking me to join them for that sort of thing, which is great because it spares me the embarrassment of trying to come up with an excuse to say no.

Look. I Do Not Socialise. I spend my evenings alone in my flat. I love my flat. Mostly because of the reliable absence of people in it. It's not that I don't like people. I like them a lot, and I wish I could spend more time around them. It's just that whenever I *do* spend time around people I always fuck it up and make it awkward and they don't enjoy it and I end up miserable. So I spare everyone the unpleasantness, and spend my time in more solitary pursuits.

Besides, I technically had a prior engagement: It was a Wednesday night, and that meant it was nearly time for my weekly phone call with Big Sis. So I quietly packed up my things and left.

*

Coming home to my flat is one of the great pleasures in my life. The feeling of release once the third lock clicks into place is blissful. The horrors and stresses of the outside world stay politely outside on my doorstep, and within I can revel in the sensation of being completely in control once more. I can sit in front of my very carefully chosen PC in my very carefully chosen ergonomic chair, positioned exactly how I like it, enjoying the quiet hum of my very carefully chosen air conditioning unit that keeps the temperature exactly where I want it to be, and allow myself to slob out without any concern for how I might appear to other people.

That evening when I got home I followed my standard Wednesday routine, putting a big tray of frozen roasties in the oven and scooping some Bisto into a jug before commencing an inventory of my kitchen supplies.

Here's the thing: I'm certainly not an adventurous eater. Mostly I like eating the same stuff on a regular basis, and that stuff normally takes the form of cook-from-frozen carbohydrates and processed meats. I buy in bulk, and store everything in a large chest freezer which I replenish weekly. That bit is simple.

What makes it complicated are the cravings. I like to think I'm relatively self-aware, certainly enough so to know that for me food is both a shield from, and a proxy for, conventional emotional states. That is how I arranged my life when it became clear that I couldn't cope with doing things the normal way. But, just as emotions are complicated, unpredictable things, so too are my appetites. Some days the meal planner says pizza but what I *need* is pasta. I know better than to try to defy these alimentary imperatives. Financially this is not a problem (the salary they offered when I joined Paladin was more than enough to accommodate my lifestyle, and besides, they keep giving me raises), but keeping my kitchen well-stocked enough to accommodate whatever cravings I might suddenly experience requires a certain level of time investment, and twice a week I assess my supplies and root out expired foods.

Today I discovered that my Pot Noodle supplies were getting low, the fresh pesto in the fridge was too close to end of life for comfort, and, most alarmingly, the chocolate cupboard was almost entirely devoid of mini eggs. I chucked the pesto in the bin and added all three items to my next online shop order.

Stocks thus reviewed to my satisfaction, I could relax, and take a moment to myself on the sofa to rally my spirits enough to dial my sister.

What you need to know is that Big Sis isn't like me in any way: I'm big; she's not. I can't cope; she can. I'm a nerd; she's an actor. A good one too. She was currently in the middle of a nine month contract in the West End, which was more glamorous than it sounded, because she only had one actual line, so she spent most of her time sitting in a dressing room backstage, reading books, doing crosswords and, on Wednesday nights, speaking to me on the phone.

"Hey Boy."

"Hey Big Sis."

"Now, before I forget, I've made you a dentist appointment."

"I don't need–"

"Yes you do. It's been years since your last check-up, but more importantly I think you need to see the hygienist. Your teeth are getting yellow. Are you flossing?"

"Yes I'm flossing," I lied. "And my teeth aren't –"

"Yes they *are*," she said brusquely. "I noticed last time I came round. I pick up on these things. It's my job."

I had an urge to point out that it really wasn't, but I bit my tongue. As distressing as it was to have her fuss over my dental health in such detail, the idea of having to ring up the dentist to make an appointment *myself* was more distressing still.

Big Sis looked out for me. She always had, ever since as kids it became clear that Mum wasn't really up to the task. Then, after the Incident, when it also became painfully apparent that I wasn't a complete enough human being to be able to cope with the real world, she took on the bits of life I couldn't handle, and had been shouldering that burden ever since. And she'd sacrificed a lot to do it: when her agent tried to get her out to LA for "pilot season" fifteen years previously she had politely declined. Her official reason was that there was a fringe show she wanted to do because she thought it might tour, but really I knew it was because she knew she couldn't help me if she got a long-running gig in the US.

"Anyway," she continued, "how's everything?"

"Meh. Mum sent me another judgy weight loss article."

"Oh, sorry, I should have warned you she was going to do that."

"You spoke to her?"

"She drunk-dialled me last night," said Big Sis,. "I think she and Terry are in the middle of another of their silent fights, and its brought on another crisis of conscience about us. She tried to talk me into moving to Cyprus again."

"Oh for God's sake–" I began, angrily.

"She was just drunk."

"Then why was she still on at me the next morning?" I muttered.

"Well, what was in the article? Maybe it'd be worth–"

"No," I said firmly, or rather, as firmly as I ever got, which was not very. As far as I was concerned Big Sis had free rein to meddle in every part of my life apart from the eating. She had other opinions. Hence our awkward compromise re fibre at breakfast.

After a brief, ever-so-slightly tense pause she shrugged.

"Alright. So what have you been up to?"

"I..." I cast around for something I could say. My life was so routine that it was hard to fulfil Big Sis's constant requests for *news*.

I decided to risk a topic I didn't often bring up.

"I've started chatting to someone new online. A woman."

Big Sis made a pained sound.

"I wish you wouldn't. Every time you end up with all the heartache of a real relationship with none of the benefits. You'll make yourself miserable over her, and then it'll end, and that'll make you miserable too. This online stuff is the worst of both worlds, and it's not *real*. I wish you'd try actually dating people in real life."

I bristled.

"I can't–" I started to reply, angrily.

"You *can* though. Look, I *know* how hard it is for you. Ok? You know I know. I'm not asking you to suddenly be... normal. But even you can have something more than make-believe with internet strangers. And sure, dating apps are great. I mean, come on, everyone I know is on Tinder. But you have to take the plunge at some point and *meet* people. I think you'd actually do really well at it. Once you get past the... you know... underneath it all you're *so* nice, you're a genius, obviously, you're really funny sometimes..."

I was too cross to listen as Big Sis reeled off a list of laughably inaccurate compliments. Even though she knew all about my failings, and in fact was the one person I was comfortable talking about them to in depth, she still saw what was left of me through a ridiculously rose-tinted lense. That was presumably the reason she hadn't given up on me after all this time. And, as I was never entirely immune to flattery, it was also one of the reasons why I enjoyed her company. When she wasn't needling me about my love life, that is.

I finally got her off the topic of me, and we spent another half hour or so nattering about not much in particular while I retrieved and ate my potatoes and gravy. She told me a little bit about her latest auditions, and her ongoing tryst with her beautiful-but-dim flatmate Ruby. Big Sis is essentially the only person in the world I've got the hang of *chatting* to, and I will concede it's a nice thing to do every so often.

At about 8 o'clock Big Sis had to start getting into costume and makeup to deliver her one line, so we finished up.

"Don't forget your dentist appointment."

"I won't."

"And I'm serious – you need to stop the virtual relationships. They just make you miserable."

I grunted.

"And look out for a parcel – I've ordered you some more pants from that site."

"I don't need –"

"When was the last time you bought any yourself?"

Touché.

"Goodbye, Sis."

"Goodbye, Boy."

*

My familial obligations discharged, I put my gravy-smeared plate back in the kitchen and settled down at my computer. My first port of call was Humanalog. It's a news site that claims to add human interest to tech stories, by going digging into profiles of the people involved in big events in the global technology scene. What that actually means is that basically it's a bunch of gossip and speculation that verges on the libellous. Compared to the dry, comparative impartiality of typical tech news sites it's utterly addictive, albeit a guilty pleasure.

But there was nothing much new on there since yesterday: they tend to go only for long reads and big scoops, and some days they don't have much to say.

Ordinarily at that point I would spend 20 minutes browsing for a show to watch, before settling down for a night of spuds and streaming. But tonight there was something niggling at me, and I needed to address it before I could let myself zone out. I picked myself up out of my chair and headed to the place where I always do my best and most serious thinking: the toilet.

The thing was, it had really stung when Big Sis was so casually dismissive about online relationships. I had had to fight an urge to bring up my chat history with HarlequinCyanide right there, to somehow prove that this was a real person I was making a real connection with. Big Sis was wrong to dismiss it all as fake, and I felt belittled when she did.

But, real or not, she was fundamentally right: it always did make me miserable in the end. Only last year, after nine months of being close with 404_girl_not_found came to an end, I'd taken a week's sick leave. I'd told everyone I had the flu, and tried to believe it myself, but in truth I was just really, really, incapacitatingly sad for a while.

I was time to face facts. Big Sis knew what was best for me, and I couldn't afford to unsettle the careful equilibrium I had created in my life. I needed to come off AltMatch, and give up on HarlequinCyanide before things got serious. It would hurt, but that in itself was proof positive that it needed doing, before I let myself go any further down this road.

Thus resolved, I finished up in the bathroom and made my way back to the kitchen, trying hard not to feel sorry for myself. I rooted through my cupboards until I found a bag of long-life croissants and worked my way resolutely through those. They were a little bit dry, so I allowed myself to sluice a little golden syrup on each one, just enough to counteract the dryness, and then a little bit more to make them interesting. I've found that most baked goods can be improved through the judicious application of golden syrup, and if that disgusts you then so be it. When the bag was empty I felt a little bit better, and I plopped myself down in my chair and spent the rest of the evening defiantly binge-watching TV sci-fi.

By the time I went to bed, a little before one in the morning, I had convinced myself I was in a good mood. I had made a sensible decision, and Big Sis would be proud of me. Tomorrow I would message HarlequinCyanide and tell her I was quitting AltMatch, and that would be that. My unhealthy yearning for her quirky charm was already fading. I didn't need heartache. I had my life in order. I had my job, and that was enough for me. Everything was stable. Everything was under control.

*

Although, of course, it wasn't. Because half an hour later Kayla called to tell me that Labyrinth – my baby, the fruit of over a year's labour, the most secure software I had ever designed – had just been hacked, and the thieves were making off with nearly seven and a half million pounds; taking my career and by extension my whole life with them.

4

The reason I could never be a hacker is that the best way to hack a system isn't to go after the tech; it's to go after the people. It's not that tech is invulnerable. Quite the opposite. *Any* piece of software will have weak points, because software is built by humans, and humans (myself emphatically included) are just too floppy-brained to think through every logical eventuality in advance. It's just that tech is *inflexible*, and so too are the bugs and loopholes in it. Imagine you're making your way through a maze, and you find a small hole that's opened up in one of the walls. You can try to cheat by squeezing through it, but unless you're spectacularly lucky the hole won't lead you to the exit. It'll probably just lead you to another part of the maze. Most of the time, that's what it's like when hackers find vulnerabilities in software.

Humans, on the other hand, are endlessly flexible. They are creative, multi-talented and adaptable, and as such they are the best tool a hacker could ask for. Consider, for example, one of Paladin's clients, a chain of gyms who paid us to audit their security. Sabre team spent a week running through the standard checks and found nothing particularly alarming about the client's IT systems. So, as much out of boredom as for any other reason, Sabre's team lead, Marco Posnett, came up with what would forever after be known internally as 'The Posnett Gambit'. He put on a cheap suit with a lanyard attached to a generic-looking ID badge, and on a quiet weekday afternoon he took a train to Birmingham, walked in to the reception of one of the two branches of the gym just outside the city centre, and said something along the lines of, "Hi! I've just come up from central office. Stephen's got me doing unannounced security audits on every branch – would you believe you're my fifth stop of the day? It's these new government regulations. Anyway, I'm sorry to be a pain, but I'm going to need to be shown your safe and anywhere that you store documents."

Within three minutes he had been given unsupervised access to a safe containing over £1000 in cash, valuables worth a similar amount, and a couple of financial reports filled with *highly* sensitive information. He repeated this exercise in three different branches, each time with similar results, and *at no point* did anyone bother checking whether he was supposed to be there.

The Posnett Gambit worked then, and it's worked every time we've used it since. It's a great way to scare executives into buying very expensive training courses from us. The reason it works so well is that in general, people just want to be helpful. Give them a plausible justification and they'll do whatever you ask. This is what's known in the trade as 'social engineering'.

Knowing this, when Maison de Gauguin had come to us the previous year and asked us to build some ultra-secure cryptocurrency payment software, I was charged with designing a system that was social engineering-proof, one that was so secure that misguided staff couldn't give away secret information even if they wanted to. It was a herculean task, but I did what I could, and when Labyrinth launched I was very proud of the end result. It would be *very* hard for a MDG employee to get social engineered into compromising their payment system, because no one, not even Todd, had enough access to the system to do anything more than they were supposed to.

*

"They got social engineered," came Kayla's voice down the phone.

"How?" I responded, still blearily trying to shake off a turbulent dream about getting lost backstage at Big Sis's theatre.

"Don't know. Todd was the one who contacted me, and... well he wasn't making *total* sense. I just reached their office, but so far I'm still struggling to get anyone to explain. I should have called you earlier."

"Ok. Ok. Uh... what do we do?"

Half awake and disoriented, I was feeling completely nonplussed. I'd never been in a situation like this before. This sort of thing just didn't *happen* at Paladin.

"I'm going to need you on-site with me. There's a taxi on its way to you, it's probably ten minutes away. Oh Jesus I'm going to need some coffee." She dropped her voice to a whisper. "Some of these people... they make *Todd* seem smart."

"Ok... ok. I'll be there as soon as I can."

"Great. The cab has your number, they'll call you when they're outside and they know where to go from there. I'll see you soon. Bye"

"Bye."

I lay in bed for a few seconds, trying to process what I'd just been told. A paralysing panic was bubbling up from my gut, of a quality and magnitude I'd not experienced since Thessaloniki, two decades ago. Slowly the enormity of what had just happened dawned on me. My system, my responsibility, my baby, had just been hacked.

How do you always manage to get everything so wrong, Colin?

Oh God. I had fucked up. I had made a multi-million pound fuck-up. I was going to be fired, I was going to be sued, I was going to be prosecuted...

I lay there, paralysed by an overwhelming whirl of muggy half-thoughts, until my phone buzzed in my hand: a notification that a grey Prius driven by a Bassan was just arriving on my road. Shit. I should have been getting ready.

I yanked on some clothes, thumbed in my lenses, and gathered up a laptop, some cables and a few other bits of kit, fielding increasingly agitated phone calls from Bassan as I did so. Yes, I was definitely still coming. Yes, I was happy for him to

THE NERD | 41

set the meter running. Sorry, I would try to speak up. No, I wasn't on the street yet.

There was no time for my pre-flight checks, and no time to carefully gather up the willpower to leave the flat. Instead I let the wave of adrenaline carry me out the door and down to the street.

*

The eerie calm of a quiet car sliding through deserted, street-lit London roads in the middle of the night was in stark contrast to the tumultuous panic I kept experiencing in the back seat. This had never happened before. Yes, I had written code with bugs in it. Yes, systems I'd made had been targeted by hackers before. But never before had I or *anyone* at Paladin built a system that had suffered a serious breach, let alone one that involved theft on such a large scale. I had allowed myself to believe that it was never going to happen to me. That it could never. That I was too good.

I had been an arrogant fucking idiot.

Maison de Gauguin HQ was down in Wimbledon, which meant there was plenty of time to kill in the car. Mercifully Bassan wasn't the chatty type. I spent the time reading the Labyrinth documentation (most of which I'd written), trying to re-familiarise myself with every detail of how it worked. But I couldn't focus over the deafening roaring in my ears, the bitter thudding in my chest, and the constant inner monologue that wouldn't shut up, chanting "I fucked up, I fucked up, I fucked up…"

And behind it all was another thought, one whose presence I was ashamed to acknowledge but nevertheless one that wouldn't leave me alone: At some point Mum was going to hear about this, and I'd have to sit through hours of phone time with her painstakingly *not mentioning it,* the insinuations dripping like poison off the edges of every pregnant pause. The idea that I'd have to acknowledge to her yet another thing that I couldn't get right was almost too much to bear.

Eventually we pulled in to a car park outside an art deco-styled warehouse, bulked out by a few glass and steel extensions. It looked like every light in the building was switched on, and there were a dozen cars in the car park.

I got out of the taxi, after a brief exchange with Bassan where I tried to convey to him that yes, this was a business trip and should be charged to our company account, and no, I didn't want a receipt. Then I got *back* into the taxi to retrieve the laptop I'd nearly forgotten on the back seat. Finally, I was ready, and walked up to the front entrance and through the door into reception.

5

There's a certain smell that you sometimes get in the foyers of trendy buildings. I think, although I'm not sure, that in particular it's ones where there are those expensive 'reclaimed' floorboards, which is why it correlates with trendiness. I don't know the first thing about fragrances or anything like that, but in an uneducated way I've been wondering about it, off and on, for years. The best I can come up with is that maybe it emerges when the chemical smell of the cleaning products used by professionals on old wood flooring gets deliberately covered up by some sort of fancy air freshener to try to reduce its harshness. I've encountered that particular smell a few times in my adult life, and it always stands out when I do. The reason, of course, that I notice it is that I first smelled it in the foyer of the Optima Physiotherapy Clinic. After the Incident, Little Sis was for a time a private inpatient there, where a specialist tried in vain to help her regain the use of the left side of her body. She stayed for what felt like a year, but must in actual fact have only been a few months. It was down near Brighton, so we would only visit at weekends, Big Sis and I. (Mum spent most of the week there, and gave herself the weekend off.) Little Sis was never ready for us when we first arrived, so we'd glumly wait in the reception, listening to the radio playing behind the desk, looking at the pictures on the wall. Smelling that smell.

*

The MDG reception was deserted. I hovered uncomfortably for a little bit, shifting my weight on the creaking wooden floorboards. Would I get in trouble for just wandering in uninvited? Or would I get in trouble for dawdling here instead of being more proactive? I was too flustered to think straight. I was doing everything wrong. I needed Kayla to tell me what to do.

As I reached for my phone to call her, I heard voices coming from the corridor that led away from the reception area.

"...not very helpful."

That was a woman's voice. It sounded tetchy.

"Right, right, sure," came a reply, "but all I'm saying is I've got fifty of my team sat upstairs and they don't know what to do. Now obviously they're coming to me right now, but I'd have thought it would be more appropriate for them to be getting some, y'know, guidance from... well, from you."

The second voice I knew well: Maison de Gauguin's Digital Director, Todd Nash.

"Then I would suggest that they *guide* themselves home to bed," the woman retorted. "Frankly, *I* should be in bed. Look, if your boss had gone through anything like the normal channels we'd have told him very clearly that we don't need to start dusting for fingerprints and putting up barrier tape –"

"No, but surely you should at least be taking statements from people like, I dunno, me, and –"

"It's the middle of the night! Why would I take statements now, when everyone is half-awake and no one even knows what's going on? I'm here essentially as a courtesy, to explain the situation in person, and what I am trying to... Who are you?"

Todd and the woman had rounded a corner and had caught sight of me. He was a small man, with spiky hair and freckled skin that was oddly shiny. He was dressed in various trendy shades of black. The woman was tall, with long loops of braided hair. She was perhaps in her early forties, with high, arching eyebrows above large, cold eyes. Her clothes were smart but dishevelled, and she had very obviously been asleep recently. She was waving an accusing hand in my direction.

"I, uh..."

"Oh for God's sake," said the woman, turning back to Todd, "You left the doors unlocked and no one at the front desk? You really will have a burglary at this rate."

"Whoops! I'll get Yoo-Jin to come down in a sec. Hi Colin! Er... this is Colin. Colin, this is, um, Sargea–"

"Detective Inspector Susan Otembi," the woman interjected, putting just a *tiny* bit of extra emphasis on her title. Todd appeared not to notice.

"Colin's from Paladin. He built Labyrinth."

Todd clapped me gently on the shoulder, and I immediately embarrassed myself.

Here's the thing: I'm not one for physical contact. At all. Most of the time when someone touches me through my clothes I flinch, and in the rare situations when someone puts their hand on my bare skin it produces a sensation that's exactly as unpleasant as physical pain, although it's not quite the same thing. When people discover this they often conclude that I must be autistic. I'm not, though, and no, for the record I'm not remotely Aspergic either. I'm just wired up a bit wrong, physiologically. Some people respond to physical contact with a wash of oxytocin and warm feelings. I get a bad case of the ouchy-flinchies.

So in what was an already stressful situation, Todd's unexpected hand on me caused me to conduct a sort of full-body shudder, just as Otembi's stern gaze was fully on me.

"UhhhHHN....ughhhh," I gurgled, involuntarily.

Otembi looked at me coolly for a second, and then, with a minute shake of her head, turned back to Todd.

"Well. *This* is the man who's supposed to be here. Send *everyone* home, other than the people he asks for."

"Oh," said Todd, frowning. "Really?"

"This is what I have been trying to tell you. In a situation like this, the first thing that needs to happen – the only thing that needs to happen as a matter of urgency – is for a competent IT bod, one who understands the affected system, to take initial action to prevent any further breach, and get comprehensive copies of all relevant data. That's it. That's all.

"Now," she continued, turning to me, "I'm assuming you're competent?"

"Uh..." I said. I didn't feel very competent at that point.

"Oh God, look, I *really* need you to tell me you're competent so that I can go home. Qualifications: You've got CISSP? CISMP? Something?"

"Uh, yes, uh... both. Yes." I stuttered.

Otembi briefly closed her eyes as though offering a quick prayer of thanks.

"Perfect. Alright, and the American lady upstairs, she's a colleague of yours, is she?"

"Yeah, uh, she's Canadi–"

"Good. Well she seems to be fairly compos mentis, and she has my card. I suggest that you liaise with me via her. Does that work?"

I nodded. It suited me fine, and I could see why this woman would prefer to deal with Kayla than me.

"Perfect. Then let's all touch base in the morning. So: the correct people are here, responsibilities are understood, and lines of communication have been established. I am going back to bed."

And with that she stomped abruptly out the door.

"Oh," said Todd, sounding somewhat disappointed. "Well that's a bit... well."

He turned to me, brightening.

"So, you're in charge of the investigation, then. How do you want to get started?"

I swallowed hard, feeling the panic rising anew in my chest. I dearly wanted to eat something, but I hadn't brought any food with me.

"Uh..."

My brain still didn't seem to be working. It felt like I was stuck in neutral, and no matter how hard I pressed down on the accelerator the engine wouldn't start... doing whatever engines do. Spinning? I didn't know. I'd never learnt to drive. At Mum's cruel insistence I'd had one driving lesson aged eighteen, and it was a disaster. I'd been too nervous to be able to speak to the instructor, and after an hour of me perspiring in silence he'd got impatient and asked if I wanted to go home, but by that point I'd sweated so much into the seat that I didn't want to get out in case he saw the wet patch I'd made, so I...

"Shall we... find Kayla perhaps?" prompted Todd, distracting me from my tailspin.

I nodded, gratefully.

We took the lift up to the first floor in awkward silence. Mercifully, as we emerged from the lift I saw Kayla stepping out of a meeting room. She saw me and gave a small wave.

"I'm just going to grab Yoo-Jin, get her to sort out having someone on reception," murmured Todd, wandering off in the other direction.

"Hey Colin," said Kayla.

"H-hey. Uh, what's..."

"Going on? Oh my goodness, it's a –" she lowered her voice " – it's a complete shit-show. They kept trying to call the police, literally *while* I was walking them through the incident response strategy, you know the one with the whole PR piece about not calling the police yet? Anyway, I thought I'd won that argument but it turned out Gavin, the chairman, rang someone high up in the Met, the commissioner or someone, and insisted they send someone. So this woman turned up –"

Kayla fished a card out of her pocket that read:

Detective Inspector Susan Otembi, Corporate Liaison, Metropolitan Police Cyber Crime Unit (MPCCU)

"– and boy does she not want to be here."

"I met her. She, uh, s-she left."

"Oh. Good. I mean, she knew her stuff, but I think there was a real danger she was going to punch someone. Meanwhile literally the whole office is crammed into the big conference room, apart from..."

She jerked her head back in the direction of the room she had come from.

"Actually, if you don't mind jumping in, I think you'd better speak to him. He was the, you know, the mark."

"Uh...?"

"You know, the mark. The stooge. The one they social engineered."

"Oh."

"They've had him sitting by himself in that room, not telling him anything. By the time I found him he was hysterical, I've basically been trying to calm him down for the past hour. Um, I think he's ok now but just... be gentle?"

Oh no. 'Soft skills'. I decided to keep my mouth firmly shut.

Kayla led me into the meeting room, where a man was slumped down in his chair, facing away from the door.

"So this is Mo. Mo, this is Colin. He's our tech lead, and he's going to get to the bottom of what happened. Would you mind... telling him what you told me? About the phone call?"

The man turned to face us, wearing the most baleful expression I think I have ever seen. He was young – perhaps early twenties – with floppy hair, thick glasses and trendy stubble. He had a light, clear voice with some sort of European lilt to it, maybe German.

"Hello," he began. "I'm... I'm so sorry. I really – I mean I *really* screwed up. I was stupid, so stupid –"

"That's ok. Just tell Colin what happened."

"Of course. Sorry. I... I was on reception. I got a phone call. He said he was from Paladin, and they were doing a 'server patch'? Or I think it was something like that. I recognised the name Paladin, and I knew you do IT for us. I've only been here a few weeks, so I don't.... Well, he said he needed to get something done by 6 o'clock otherwise the system would reset. I mean, of course, he was just making it all up, but it sounded so believable to me, and I... thought I was being helpful. I said sure, I could help, so he had me open up a program, the, you know, the black box, with the white text, is it called a terminal? Anyway, he had me type some stuff in – it was gibberish to me, but he talked me through it – and then some more stuff appeared on screen and he had me read it to him – it was a bunch of random numbers and letters – and then he had me type a few more words and then he hung up. That was it. I really didn't think I could have done anything wrong. It was only when Todd sent the emails that I realised they were hackers and… I was such an idiot, I didn't even own up to it straight away. I just felt so, so *stupid*, and… I just… sat there, wishing… wishing I'd been smart enough to…"

He tailed off, and began to tear up. I nearly said something. I could feel the words trying to form in my throat. I wanted to explain that it wasn't his fault, he wasn't *supposed* to be smart enough, it wasn't his job. That it was my job to be smart enough to have designed a system to accommodate his stupidity, anyone's stupidity, and that I was the one who had failed. Thankfully, I only got as far as saying "Uh" before Kayla cut me off, and said, soothingly.

"It's ok, Mo. I'm sure it'll be ok. You made an honest mistake."

That was, even I could see, a better way of putting it.

She turned to me. "So… that sounds like they got him to read them the master password, right? The, what's it called, private key? And once they got that, they could transfer money wherever they wanted?"

"Uh, yeah," I mumbled uncomfortably. "But… there's, uh, no way it should have been possible for an employee to make the private key appear on screen, no matter what commands they put in. The… the whole point was to keep it completely sealed off from other systems."

"Yeah," said Kayla. "That's what I thought. So… Mo, can you remember what commands it was he had you type?"

Mo looked like the sky had fallen on his head.

"I don't... I don't remember. It was all gobbledygook, you know? Maybe four different sort of words, joined up with, you know, slashes, dashes, that sort of thing."

"It'd be really helpful if you could remember any specific bits."

"Well... oh! Right at the end there was the word 'history'. I remember that bit. He said it was something to do with saving the details for later. It was the word history and then a couple of other characters, I think."

"Er... Was it a dash and then the letter 'c'?" I suggested, my heart sinking.

"Yes, that was it!"

Kayla turned to me, her expression hopeful. I shook my head.

"That's the, uh, command to clear the records of all the other commands you just entered. He sort of... got you to cover some tracks for him."

Mo's face crumpled, and he looked like he was about to cry again.

"Do you remember anything else?" Kayla urged. "Anything else at all?"

"I'm sorry, I don't."

"Ok, well, never mind. If anything comes to you, let us know. Colin, I know you said it shouldn't be possible for someone to get to the private key that way, but..." she shrugged.

"I know," I nodded. "It really sounds like that's what happened. But it doesn't... sound right..."

I tailed off, lamely. I just couldn't see how our system could be brought down by a few commands tapped into a reception computer.

"Well, of course we'll have to investigate all the options," said Kayla. "Maybe –"

She was interrupted by the return of Todd Nash.

"So, how's it going?" he asked brightly.

"Well, it's early days, but Mo has been really helpful. We're just working out the next steps."

"Ok, great. Quick q, then: Would it be alright if a couple of the staff went home?"

Kayla looked a little flustered. "I... I don't know, Todd. I don't really understand why they're all here in the first place."

"Well, we thought it would be sensible to get them all here, you know, in case you or the police wanted to interview them. Better safe than sorry."

"Well... I'm sure you can send them home now. It sounds like Mo was the one who knew the most about it, and he's told us everything he knows."

"Ok, great. And I suppose you'll want a statement from me as well."

"Uh, I mean we're not really taking statements per se, but –"

"Well, I thought it would be sensible given that, you know, I'm the Digital Director."

Kayla's face twitched perceptibly, but her voice remained level. "Sure thing. Uh, Mo, why don't you go home and get some rest?"

Mo slunk out of his chair. "You're sure I can't do anything more? I just feel... really awful about this whole thing."

"No, you're good for now. Just let us know if you remember any more details. And don't worry, ok? It'll be fine."

Mo gave a sad little smile and let himself out. Todd went over and leaned up on the conference table.

"Are you going to record it then?"

Wordlessly, and with a carefully neutral expression, Kayla took her phone from her pocket and opened a dictaphone app, then set it down on the table.

"Ok, so, what do you want to know?"

"Well... you said you wanted to give a statement," prompted Kayla.

"Ok sure, but I didn't know if there was anywhere particular you wanted to begin."

"Maybe... maybe just tell me what happened today?"

Todd smiled. "Good idea. Ok, so. It was mostly quite a normal day. We were doing a debrief on the Abu Dhabi event – did I tell you about that? It was off the chain. Anyway, I completely forgot about the payment for the Nua Nigel piece."

"I'm sorry, the what?"

"Nua Nigel. He's a painter, very high profile. We found him a buyer for Hash-Four-Six – it's this piece he did, it's hard to describe but it's absolutely... yeah. Anyway, today was the day of the incoming transfer, but we're all a bit dazed after Abu Dhabi, and I completely forgot that the money was coming in until we got the phone call from Lena, she's the buyer, saying she'd sent it. So that was great, and we have a thing we do with champagne and cupcakes every time we receive a payment, and that was fun. But then at about home time, another email came through saying the money had left our account again. I thought 'that's a bit weird', because we weren't supposed to complete the sale for another week, so I thought I'd look into it in the morning.

"But *then* Rachel – have you met Rachel? She's our comms and social manager, she's great – Rachel emailed me saying she'd got a weird mention on Twitter from someone called My Little Pony or something, and she just picked up on it because it mentioned the £7.4m, and the price isn't supposed to be public yet – she had a whole press release ready about it for later – and that was the thing that *really* set alarm bells ringing. Tell, you what, let me see if..."

He fumbled his phone out of his pocket and pulled up a tweet from a user called Pony Club Comms with the username *@pc1184*. It read:

What's that? Someone hacked @MDeGauguin to the tune of £7.4m? I wonder who... #PonyClub

"I mean, that seems pretty significant, doesn't it? Anyway, a few calls later and we established that the money *definitely* shouldn't have left our account yet. So I got Yoo-Jin to drive back into the office – she only lives round the corner so it's no biggie – and she logged into Labyrinth and confirmed that the money wasn't there anymore. I sent a couple of emails round the office asking if anyone knew anything at all, and when Mo rang me and said about his phone call, we put two and two together and realised we'd been hacked. At that point we decided to move quickly so we called everyone back into the office and I rang you."

He gave a little shrug.

"Will that do?"

Kayla nodded. "Thanks Todd. That's... some helpful context."

"So, what next?"

Kayla looked at me.

"Uh... could we... could we look at Labyrinth?" I said, hesitantly.

Todd nodded sagely, then led us out of the meeting room, down a couple of corridors to an open space with a few tables scattered around, monitors and keyboards on each. Todd leant over in front of one, woke it up, and after a few false starts pulled up the Labyrinth home screen. He had just completed the rigmarole of logging in when his phone rang.

"Oh hold up, it's Gavin. I'd better give him an update. Go ahead, look around."

He sauntered off, phone pressed to his head, as I took over the mouse. I realised that merely being sat in front of a screen was having a calming influence on me. I was fractionally less far from my comfort zone now.

Labyrinth looked more or less like any banking website. The main feature on screen was a summary of Maison du Gauguin's Burncoin 'wallet' – the equivalent of a current account. Currently, and unpromisingly, the balance of the account was currently showing as being 0.01 Burncoins, worth approximately £2.40.

"So, uh, I'm guessing the 0.01 is just the leftover from some previous transaction. If there was a £7m deposit today then the wallet that should have about... thirty thousand Burncoins in it."

I noticed I was back to being able to do basic mental arithmetic, which was a start, at least.

"Show me the transaction history for the wallet?" asked Kayla.

I clicked the appropriate menu option.

"Huh," said Kayla. "There should be an inbound and an outbound transaction there, right?"

"Uh, yes. We'd expect a deposit in the morning, and then a withdrawal by the hackers in the evening. But it looks like there's been no activity all week. Maybe... maybe no money came in in the first place and it's all a misunderstanding?" I said hopefully. But even as I said it, I knew what Kayla's response would be.

"It'd be nice, but then how do you explain the notification emails, the buyer confirming they'd sent the money, the message from the hackers, the –"

"I... yep," I said, my heart sinking. "But... the thing is, if they managed not only to take out the money but also wipe Labyrinth's records of deposits and withdrawals that means they didn't just hack the system, uh, they completely *owned* it."

As I processed this unpleasant thought, Todd reappeared.

"Any progress?"

"We're just trying to rule out a few basics," Kayla replied. "You said you'd confirmed the money had arrived this afternoon?"

"Look, I just know what your system tells me. The website said that thirty-something thousand Burncoins had come in. Or was it forty-something? Anyway, it was there on the website. I've no way of knowing if that was true."

I rubbed at my eyes with thumb and forefinger. At least my brain was beginning to unfreeze enough that a few common-sense basics were beginning to occur to me.

"I'll, uh, go down to the servers in the basement and start analysing the logs. Maybe in the morning we can get someone else out here to give me a –"

"Let's not set up camp if we can help it," Kayla cut me off. "It's incredibly late, we're all tired, and I'd rather we came at this with the freshest eyes possible. Is there any way you can just take copies of everything for analysis at HQ?"

Ok, maybe I wasn't quite at the point of showing actual common sense yet. Kayla was right, there was no point us doing any of this on-site.

"Uh... y-yes, good idea. I've got the bits with me to make copies, it just needs setting up."

"Then that's what we'll do. Todd, can you let Colin down to the basement?"

Todd led me down to a windowless room with a few server racks, a couple of file cabinets and an alarmingly rusty-looking sewage pipe. I started the process of cloning everything onto a hard drive. My hands were shaking so much I kept making typos, so it took me far longer than it should have. Once it was up and running making copies of everything we went up to reception and I repeated the process to Mo's reception computer with a different hard drive. Todd flitted back into the bowels of the building, and a little while later Kayla reappeared, so I filled her in.

"It's all running. Now we just need to let it finish. There's maybe an hour left."

"Perfect. Now, you're going home. There's a cab about to arrive outside for you. I'm going to finish up here and I'll unplug the drives when they're done. You're going to go freshen up, catch an hour or so of sleep if you can, then pick things up in the Bunker at eight with the rest of the team. I'll meet you there with the SSD cards."

I felt a huge surge of gratefulness towards Kayla, and even for a second had a *very* uncharacteristic urge to hug her.

"Thank you. I... thank you."

"Not a problem. We need you as sharp as possible tomorrow. Thank you for coming out in the middle of the night."

"No... no problem. Uh..."

"Yeah?"

"Am I going to be fired?" I blurted out.

"Of course not!" said Kayla, looking genuinely shocked. "These things just happen sometimes. Go on, get out of here. I'll see you in a few hours."

I slunk out of reception, noting that the car park was still pretty full. It seemed that none of the MDG team had left the building yet. Maybe Todd was still hoping he could get Kayla to take statements from them all. A Prius was idling by the exit, and it flashed its lights as I looked over. I opened the back door, slumped inside, and let the driver glide me back into the night.

6

At 8am I was back in the Bunker with the rest of the team. Kayla had rung round and got everyone to come in an hour early. All eyes were on Anil, our CEO. It was the first time any of us could remember the big man himself making a personal visit to the Bunker. In the normal run of things he managed to keep himself away from direct interactions with the rank and file, preferring to delegate everything via his senior management team. But this was no longer the normal run of things.

He stood just inside the doorway, shadowed by Brad, his executive flunkey. For a short, balding man Anil had an impressive presence. The expensive suit helped, I'm sure, but I think it really came down to twenty years of taking it for granted that he was *in charge.*

"Well, we finally got breached. First time ever. You could say that we'd had a good run of it until now, and that it was bound to happen eventually. Personally I don't see it that way, but that's neither here nor there. What we have to do now is deal with the situation, deal with it fast, and deal with it effectively. Being blunt, the reputation of the company is at stake, and with it, our future."

There was something a little too polished about the way Anil spoke when he was addressing a room. At first I'd thought he pre-prepared his speeches, but then I noticed he spoke exactly the same way when he was giving off-the-cuff responses. I was deeply intimidated by Anil.

"What matters at this point is the narrative," he continued. "If the narrative is that due to our incompetence thieves managed to make off with millions of pounds of a client's money, then frankly we're finished. We'll be out of business within the year. But, if the narrative is that, due to our investigative efforts, millions of pounds of a client's money is retrieved and a gang of cyber-criminals is brought to justice, then we'll be fine.

"As of right now, this is the number one priority for the board, the executive group, and the company as a whole. There are three teams working exclusively on this issue. The first is PR, who are monitoring the situation and drafting a playbook for every scenario. Like I say, what matters above everything is the narrative. The second is Scimitar, who are running recon to establish everything they can about the group calling themselves Pony Club and try to trace the parties involved. The third is, as of right now, Foil. I need you to work out everything about the hack: what the vulnerability was, how it was exploited, and what clues have been left behind. You built it. You're best placed to find the hole in it. I want you to know that you'll have any and all support you need. Anything else we can do to help, ask Kayla, Kayla will ask Brad, Brad will ask me, and we'll make it happen. Any questions?"

Debi put her hand up.

"I'm assuming anyone with pre-booked time off coming up needs to cancel their plans?"

"That's an operational detail, so I'll leave it to Kayla and Brad to work out between them."

"If we're going to be crunching system logs can we have some more powerful machines?" put in Rémy. "We can get more done if –"

Anil silenced him with a raised hand.

"Again, that's an operational detail. Resourcing is for Kayla and Brad. Anything else? Ok. Make me proud."

With that he turned abruptly and strode out, Brad scampering after him.

"So..." said Rémy in the silence that ensued. "Does that mean we get better computers?"

"I'll see what I can do," replied Kayla. "Alright, so does everyone know broadly what happened? Ok, so – "

"Uh, not really," said Bled.

"Did you read the email briefing I sent?"

Bled shrugged.

"Eh..."

I could see Kayla clench her jaw slightly.

"Ok, well, Colin, do you want to give a potted summary?"

I cleared my throat, and fighting against the embarrassment and self-consciousness that conspired to squeeze my throat shut, forced out an explanation:

"Uh… MDG got hacked. They had seven million pounds or so in Burncoin in Labyrinth, and someone social engineered the receptionist into running some, uh, well they put in some commands on the reception computer, and that… somehow they got the, uh… private key. We think. "

"Wait, what?" said Rémy, incredulously. "How is that possible? Wasn't the whole point that we'd make something like that impossible?"

I turned an awkward shade of crimson. It was the thought in everyone's heads, but Rémy was the first to give voice to it: *Colin dropped the ball.*

"Uh… it's…"

"There's a lot we don't know yet," interjected Kayla. "But we've got our marching orders. Rémy and Bled, you're going to be looking at the reception computer to see if you can extract any clues about what it was they got Moritz to do on it. Debi you're going to look at the Labyrinth servers to try to work out what happened from that end. And Colin, you're going to do an analysis of the source code, see if you can figure out from first principles what the vulnerability could have been."

"Is that wise?" asked Debi. "I mean, Colin designed the whole thing and wrote the bulk of it. He might be too close to it to spot the problem."

That stung. It was a reasonable point, but... had Debi already lost faith in me so completely?

"That's true," I said, trying to keep my tone of voice neutral.

"Well," replied Kayla. "And he doesn't spot anything, or if anyone else gets stuck, we'll rotate roles so that someone else takes a turn. Meanwhile I'll be liaising with the other teams and getting whatever additional information we need from MDG. If there's anything you need to know from them just tell me and I'll get answers. Alright? How's everyone feeling about this?"

Rémy shrugged. Bled stared, glassily.

"It is what it is," said Debi.

"Then let's get to it. This'll be fine, guys."

Kayla's tone was encouraging, although her expression was anything but.

*

Mum was always an expert at that: saying one thing out loud, and then using pointed looks to express the complete opposite. She started doing it round about the time she started therapy, post Little Sis's departure. Apparently Terry, her 'facilitator' (who later became her partner and whisked her off to start a bohemian retirement life in Cyprus), was helping her build up an 'emotional-behavioural toolkit' to stop herself being overwhelmed by her own negative thoughts. I was never clear whether passive-aggressive eye contact was explicitly one of the tools Terry taught her in their sessions, or whether it was merely a side effect of some other approach.

Either way Mum never *said* that she blamed me for the Incident. But whenever the subject came up, or anything else was mentioned that was tangentially related, her eyes would twitch over to me. Just long enough to make contact. Just enough to let me know what she was really thinking.

And likewise, whenever she watched me fail in the years that followed, when I got too tongue-tied by self-consciousness to make myself understood to the train conductor, when I couldn't open the strawberry jam and had to pass the jar to Big Sis, when each successive pair of trousers stopped fitting, she never *said* anything at all. But the resigned disappointment in her eyes... In time that expression even became a regular fixture in my dreams.

*

We had all been working quietly for a couple of hours when the silence was broken by a *sotto voce* 'Oh' from Kayla.

"Hm?" said Debi.

"Nothing. Well, uh... ok, so Todd just emailed. Moritz Ortlauf – Mo, the receptionist – is in the hospital. Todd says he was found unconscious by his flatmates this morning.

"What happened?"

"Uh... I don't know. Todd just says, 'I thought you should know. Stay safe'. What does that even mean? Does that mean he was... assaulted?"

"Shit," murmured Bled.

"Whoa," said Rémy. "What do you think? The hackers are covering their tracks? Sending a hit squad after everyone involved? I think we need bodyguards!"

"No," said Kayla. "Don't be ridiculous."

"It's not ridiculous. He's actually in the hospital, isn't he? It's not a, whatever, a fucking April fool?"

"No, but there's endless ways he could have ended up there. It could have been an accident, or a medical condition, or anything."

"Then why did Todd tell us to stay safe? I'm telling you, we need bodyguards. This is some serious shit."

Kayla glanced down at her phone, then sighed. "Ok Rémy, I will raise the issue with Brad. Happy?"

Rémy smiled. "Fuck yes."

Kayla rolled her eyes and turned back to my computer. Debi caught my eye, wheeled her chair over to me and under her arm showed me her phone screen. On it was a message sent a minute earlier from her to Kayla, saying simply: "Jst agree w him 2 shut him up & we cn all get back 2 work".

I nodded. It was a good call: deprived of an opportunity to feel like he was being shot down or ganged up on, Rémy would probably have forgotten about the whole thing by lunchtime.

But shutting down Rémy's histrionics wasn't the only thing on my mind. For all that he couldn't help himself from taking the idea to an extreme... was he right? It was strange: for all that my entire career had been spent, fundamentally, trying to thwart crime, I'd never really thought much about the criminals who were my adversaries. Were they the sorts of people who had the resolve and the means to commit murder to get what they wanted?

I didn't have much of an opportunity to process this, because my thoughts were interrupted by a sharp intake of breath from Debi.

"Guys? It just went public."

"What did?"

"The whole thing. These guys 'Pony Club' have been all over Twitter showing off about hacking MDG... And it's got picked up by TechCrunch."

"Already?" asked Kayla, aghast.

"Holy shit," breathed Rémy. "Are we famous yet?"

"No, Paladin hasn't been named. But they already seem to know pretty much everything else. The headline is '£10m reportedly stolen from art seller in digital heist'. They go on to name Maison de Gauguin, Pony Club, and even.... Oh wow. They know who the buyer was. Apparently it's someone called Lena Mueller who's a partner in a venture capital firm in Berlin. How the hell did they find that out?"

"Did MDG make a statement?" asked Bled.

"Er... no, it sounds like they haven't officially commented. Hmm..."

Kayla reached over and pointed at Debi's screen. "There: 'According to someone with knowledge of the company, this is the first time in Maison de Gauguin's history that it has been victim of this sort of crime'. So someone from MDG leaked it?"

"Knowing that lot, a journalist just rang up and asked them some questions and it didn't occur to them not to answer," said Debi.

"So it's just a matter of time before they find out about us, right? We're going to be running away from journalists now?" asked Rémy.

"Don't say anything," said Kayla urgently. "Seriously, if ever you find yourself talking to a journalist, don't say *anything*."

"Jesus fucking christ Kayla, I get it, ok? I'm not stupid. Maybe you need to go home and get some sleep because you're being a real dickhead right now."

Rémy slouched back down into his chair, pulled his headphones on and turned his attention back to his screen.

"I just–", started Kayla, then gave up when she saw he wasn't listening. "Ugh. I need some caffeine."

She took a breath, then stalked out of the Bunker.

"Alright people, fun's over. Back to the grindstone," said Debi. Everyone turned back to their screens. But I noted that I wasn't the only one who immediately looked up the story online rather than doing any actual work. It seemed that this Lena Mueller had a relatively low profile compared to some of MDG's other members. She ran a venture capital firm called Strawberry Capital. They had been one of the early investors in a fantastically successful telecomms startup called Quarc, the darlings of Silicon Valley a few years previously. They were eventually bought by a massive financial systems conglomerate called Finisys, for an undisclosed sum rumoured to be around $650m, presumably netting a huge windfall for Strawberry Capital in the process. That must have been how Mueller had come up with £7.4m to spend on contemporary art.

Lena Mueller. So that was the name of the person whose money I'd lost. I hoped she was insured.

7

How do you always manage to get everything so wrong, Colin?

I suppose that another person, having experienced an incident like the Incident, might devote themselves to self-improvement. They might reflect upon a sister fighting for her life in a foreign hospital, observe the pitiful state she ended up in and the life she was condemned to, recollect her blood quite literally on their hands, and think to themselves, "I must do better."

Not me.

I believe in being pragmatic. I believe in discovering and acknowledging one's limitations, and then living within them. If it had been one failure, or even just one category of ineptitude, that would be different. But what was demonstrated that awful morning in Thessaloniki was that my deficiencies were so manifold, so diverse, and capable of wreaking so much pain, that to pretend that they could each be isolated from my core self, and individually fixed or upgraded like defective components of a computer, would be sheer fantasy.

So instead I chose to design a world that existed within a strict set of parameters to ensure that, despite my faults, I could achieve a tolerable quality of life while minimising the distress I caused to other people. I have defined a set of rules for myself, and I live my life according to them. Quiet stability, that's the name of the game.

*

I was in a whirl, completely befuddled and utterly unable to concentrate. Having the comforting fiction of my own competence so abruptly swept away left me with a huge jumble of mixed-up thoughts and feelings, and the inner voice telling me just how stupid and awful I was drowned out any attempts at rational thinking. I couldn't make any kind of start on the task assigned to me.

So I ended up spending the morning idly fixing punctuation marks in our system documentation. Several years ago, Bled had built himself a custom mechanical keyboard with all the keys in unusual places, because he'd watched some YouTube video telling him it would make typing more efficient. Only he'd never quite configured it properly, and it meant that certain characters always came out wrong. In particular, every time he typed a hyphen ("-") it came out as an en dash ("–"). It didn't have a practical impact on his work, so it took me a long time to notice, but when I did it drove me nuts. Finding and fixing his mistakes was in no way productive, but at least it made me feel slightly less miserable, for a time.

I took a brief break for lunch upstairs in McDonald's. I tried to focus on my audiobook, but I kept seeing images of Mo unconscious, beaten to a bloody pulp by unknown assailants. Unbidden, the Gabardine Suit Game started to play itself in my head. The man sat opposite me was hunched over something he had on his lap. Was it a knife? Could I defend myself with this laminate tray? The kid with the laptop in the corner – timewasting undergraduate or Pony Club capo?

I was unsettled, and my stomach ached because of it. I ate an additional Big Mac meal to try to soothe myself, but it didn't help. Somehow, despite all my efforts to protect the world from my destructive incompetence, it was all happening again. I didn't know what sort of state Moritz was in, or what the prognosis was. Was he in a critical condition? Would he make a full recovery, or would his life end up like... I felt myself wincing. I didn't actually know what Little Sis's life was like now. Being honest with myself, it was because I didn't want to know. She may have been the one to sever ties in the first place, but in the years that followed she had occasionally got in touch, and I'd always been the one to let things slide. I told myself it was because I was sure she was just being polite, and didn't actually want to see me, but really it was because *I* didn't want to see the wretched life she'd been reduced to. I'd already learnt my lesson, already felt enough shame. Judge me if you want, but there's only so much guilt a person can take.

*

I spent the rest of that day, and all of the following one, continuing to get absolutely nowhere. And I wasn't the only one who was stymied. At 6 o'clock on Friday, when Kayla called a meeting to hear our progress, she was met with a series of dejected shrugs. No one had found anything helpful.

Only Debi had anything to share:

"It's not much, but I do have something. So: we keep records of literally any time anything happens on Labyrinth – when someone signs in, when money moves in or out, everything. And the weird thing is that none of these records indicate any money being moved around on Wednesday. *But* we're also missing some other stuff. Like, on the Monday, I can see that someone logged out in the afternoon, but there's no record of them logging in at any point before that. But they must have logged in, otherwise how else could they have logged out?"

"That's interesting," said Kayla. "So do you think someone has tampered with the logs?"

"Maybe," said Debi, "But there's something about the things that are absent from the logs. I can't quite put my finger on it, but it feels like there's a pattern."

"It *feels* like it?" parroted Rémy scornfully. "The fuck does that mean? I didn't know we were fucking *feeling* our way through this."

"Rémy, come on," said Debi wearily. "I've been staring at the data for two days, and my brain's telling me there's something there, I just haven't worked out what it is yet."

"Women's intuition, huh?" muttered Rémy with a smirk.

Debi exploded.

"Ok listen here you patronising misogynistic shithead, I will bury this *fucking* keyboard so far up your–"

"Guys, GUYS!" Kayla snapped. "We're all stressed, we're all tired, let's keep it civil, ok? Now, Rémy, you don't get to say things like that, ok? If you don't get it, then when this is all over I will happily, and at length, explain to you why. For now just take my word for it. And Debi, now's not the time to have this fight."

Rémy briefly looked like he wanted to argue back, but Debi fixed him with a glare of such intensity, while, I noted, holding her rather large and heavy mechanical keyboard in her hand, that he remained silent.

"Ok... ok," said Kayla. "Look, sounds like there's maybe something worth pursuing there. I was going to rotate people around, but do you want to keep going with it?"

"No," said Debi, after a pause. "I could use a break, to think about something else for a bit. Maybe someone else with fresh eyes could take a look."

"Sure. Then how about Rémy, you look at the source code, Debi you take a look at Moritz's computer, and maybe Bled and Colin you guys can have a crack at these logs. Let's put in a few more hours tonight, and then... I mean, I hate to ask, but –"

"– but we're coming in tomorrow, aren't we?" finished Debi. "That's fine, I think we all expected it."

There were half-hearted nods all round.

"Thanks guys," said Kayla. "Ok, I'd better brief Anil. Wish me luck."

When Kayla stepped out, I got started trying to analyse the server logs. I didn't get very far before messages started appearing from Debi on YakYak, our team's instant messaging tool.

@D: Do you see what I mean about the gaps?
@C: Still just poking around for now

A few minutes later:

@D: I'll forward you the list of times when I think there should be a log entry but there isn't one.

@D: It's hard to be sure, because there aren't many situations where we can say for certain that an event happened at a precise time that we can cross-reference with the logs

@D: But it definitely feels regular somehow, even if it's not at the same time each day.

"Hey Colin."

I looked up. Debi gestured at me.

"Check YakYak."

"I'm still getting set up."

"I know, but... just think about it, yeah? I think it's worth exploring."

"Ok. I'll take a look after I've checked a couple of other things."

Debi gave me a withering look.

"After you do the same basic checks that I've already done, you mean?"

"I just... need to get my bearings, then I'll get on it."

Debi rolled her eyes and went back to her screen.

*

Mum announced our holiday on the Friday afternoon at the very start of the autumn half term. In typical Mum fashion she had booked our flights at lunchtime, on a whim, for the following morning. Big Sis couldn't come, of course, as she was getting stuck into her first term at drama school, but that didn't seem to bother Mum. She practically glowed with glee as she chivvied us up to our rooms to start packing.

To be honest, I was relieved. Family life had been getting pretty ropey without Big Sis around to keep the peace between Mum and Little Sis, and stay on top of pesky little things like ensuring there was food in the fridge. I had been rather dreading a week of being at home without her. The resort Mum had booked looked rather run-down even in the brochure, and because it was the end of the season apparently most of the local attractions would be closed, but nevertheless, there would be activities to keep Little Sis busy, and a buffet restaurant in the resort that meant none of us would have to try to cook. All in all, I thought it would be A Good Thing, and Little Sis agreed.

"We need to be careful, though," I said solemnly, before we went to bed that night. "Greece is a very dangerous place, and if anything goes wrong we'll be a long way from home."

I had no real reason to believe that Greece was dangerous. In fact the brochure specifically assured us that Thessaloniki was one of the safest spots in the Mediterranean. It was just the sort of caution Big Sis would give us whenever we were about to set off on an outing, and I considered myself to be *in loco sororis magnae.*

Little Sis rolled her eyes at me and went back to her packing. I never could get her to take me seriously.

8

"I told you! I told you! Naa-naa I told you!"

As I walked into the Bunker on Saturday morning Debi greeted me with a dance and a stuck-out tongue.

"Huh?"

She held out her phone. On screen was a YakYak message from Bled from just before 4am:

@B: Couldn't sleep. Figured it out. Explain later.

"I messaged Bled about the log timing thing too, and unlike *some people* he didn't ignore me. He had a look at it last night, and he's cracked it. So I believe, Mr Clayford, you – ah, Rémy! I've just been explaining to Colin how you and he can get down on your shiny little knees, open those sad mouths and SUCK MY BALLS."

She was buzzing with excitement. Rémy, who had just walked in, gave me a quizzical glance. I didn't respond. I was busy processing the intricacies of being invited to perform what was technically an act of oral sex on Debi. Despite the obvious anatomical impossibility of the offer, I couldn't help but get rather flustered by the idea. I realised I was in imminent danger of getting an erection. I sat abruptly down at my desk to hide my embarrassment and crotch.

Debi didn't notice. She was too busy doing a one-woman conga around the office blowing raspberries and singing a little song to herself.

"Stu-pid men don't lis-ten, when De-bi's got the an-swer, fuck you all ex-cept Bled, hap-py times for De-bi..."

By a little after nine everyone was present, and Kayla called for a catch-up.

"So Bled, Debi tells me you've made a breakthrough?"

Bled gave a shrug.

"Yeah, I guess."

There was a pause.

"So...?" prompted Kayla.

"So, you know how every night at 4am we automatically take the whole system offline and sweep the log files for signs of tampering? Well, we misconfigured the timing of the sweeping bit. It doesn't happen every twenty-four hours. It happens every two point four hours. And every time, for a couple of minutes while the log files are being swept, we're not able to *write* log files. So every couple of hours there's a couple of minutes when anything you do won't get logged. I guess Pony Club waited until a sweep was happening, then logged in, swiped the money, cleared all transaction records for the day and logged out again in the space of a few seconds so they wouldn't leave a trace. Pretty clever I guess."

He shrugged again, half-heartedly. I looked round at Debi, who was sat dejectedly in her chair.

"Tamper sweep. I can't believe I didn't think of that. Bugger. Bugger bugger bugger."

"Don't be down," said Kayla. "We just had a big win, and it was your research that made it happen!"

"Yeah but if I'd just thought more about what could have caused the gaps we might have had it days ago."

"And you could have taken the credit, huh?" said Rémy, sympathetically.

"Sod off," snarled Debi, and I suspected Rémy's remark had hit home: Debi had put in a lot of legwork but Bled was the one who'd made the breakthrough, and that must be galling for her.

"The point is," said Kayla, "this is really great news. Now we know how they hacked us."

"Well, no, we know how they covered their tracks," said Bled.

"Oh sure, but I mean, this is a big piece of the puzzle, right?"

"Meh," said Bled. "It doesn't really help us with the hack itself."

"You know sometimes I wish you guys would be a bit more positive," said Kayla, a note of frustration entering her voice.

Rémy rolled his eyes at her. Then, with a gleam of mischief in his eyes, turned to the room.

"Ok, so which of you guys fucked up the tamper sweep, huh?"

"Wasn't me," said Bled. "Maybe it was you."

"Me? Fuck that man, I had nothing to do with it. I'm not getting fired for this."

"No one's getting fired for this," said Kayla forcefully.

"Bullshit. Anil needs someone to take the fall otherwise no one will work with us anymore. And who's going to be the one to go: the one who *didn't* write the code that fucked up, or...?"

"Come on, it was a tiny mistake. So the tamper sweep runs more often than it should. Someone probably just left off a zero somewhere, that's not something you get sacked over, that's a typo. The only person who messed up was..."

Debi suddenly trailed off.

"Me," I said quietly. "I was responsible for rolling everything out. I should have checked the setup more thoroughly."

"Maybe, but you're not getting *fired* for it," said Debi.

Rémy shrugged dramatically. Everyone else stayed quiet, and their silence spoke volumes.

"Alright, if you say so," said Rémy eventually.

*

There were no further breakthroughs that day. We'd hit a wall. At best we had an explanation for the *absence* of some evidence. Pony Club had covered their tracks so convincingly that if it wasn't for the small matter of £7,369,129 that had gone walkabout I'd have dismissed the whole thing as some sort of misunderstanding.

According to the updates they were sending through, Scimitar, the team who were attempting to investigate the hackers themselves, were making no more progress than we were. Up until this point no one had heard of Pony Club outside the hacker community. They didn't have much of a public presence, and few people had ever claimed to be members. Someone who went by the handle Divvi claimed to be the 'Equestrian in Chief' on a couple of forums, and someone else called Draconix had a Reddit account where they described themselves as 'Pony Club's Club Secretary'. In the aftermath of the hack there had been a couple more tweets from Pony Club-controlled Twitter accounts referencing the theft and generally insulting MDG, but no official statement. They appeared to be nobodies, with no connections and nothing to say for themselves. They were also now multi-millionaires.

At 9pm Kayla sent us home and instructed us not to come back the next day.

"I've squared it with Brad. Everyone's exhausted, and grunt work isn't getting us there. We need insights and fresh ideas, and for that we need a bit of a break. So take tomorrow off, do something completely unrelated, and let's come back and hit it hard on Monday."

"Anyone wanna review this week's riddles before we go?" asked Bled.

No one did. Everyone just wanted to escape the office. We agreed we'd roll over the weekly competition to next Friday.

I went home planning to spend the next day mostly sleeping (and possibly pouring out my troubles to Big Sis in the hope of eliciting a sympathetic response), but at eleven I got a call from Debi, who had other plans.

"It's on."

"What is?"

"Games afternoon. Tomorrow. Chez nous. The whole gang's going to be there. You have to come."

"I don't really –"

"Like Kayla said, it's a chance to do something completely unrelated. Come on, you love board games."

I knew Debi liked board games, but I had no idea why she thought I did. I'd never played any with her, and never expressed a desire to. I supposed I just seemed like the type.

"I can't. I've got –"

"Bollocks. You never do anything on a Sunday apart from play video games. I'm not going to discuss it with you, you're just going to turn up at ours tomorrow. One o'clock."

"I really –"

"Okseeyoutomorrowbyeeeeee."

"But…. I don't know where you live…"

Debi had already ended the call. But when I checked my phone screen I saw I already had a message from her with her address. She must have sent it while she was talking to me. Goodness but she was thorough.

I couldn't think of anything I wanted to do less than go play games with everyone I'd just spent all week locked in a room with at work.

And yet, Debi had invited me to her home. That was… worthy of consideration. I decided to take a view in the morning.

9

The following day started with delivery of my weekly food order. It's a big operation. Aside from sorting and storing the food itself, there's the tricky issue of the handover: I don't like that I have to interact with a delivery man who's seen the ridiculous quantity of stuff that I've ordered, and the whole affair is rendered more embarrassing by the fact that he has to lug it all up a flight of stairs, meaning my gluttony is not just risible to him, it's also inconvenient. I therefore, as I'm sure you'll understand, get a bit anxious in the run-up to his arrival, so from about twenty minutes before the start of my delivery window I start hovering awkwardly in my hall, listening out for a van and fidgeting on my phone, unable to concentrate on anything else.

This week my driver was actually running a bit late, so I wasted more time worrying than usual, but at least it was someone new, who seemed no keener on meeting my eye than I on meeting his, so we conducted the hand-off with a minimum of bother. I could then relax, check use-bys and put everything away at my leisure.

That done, and somewhat to my surprise, I completed my pre-flight checks a little after midday, heaved myself out of my flat, and set off for Debi's. Apparently I didn't dare defy her summons. I knew that the day would be a bit awful, but the thrill of being in Debi's house, of seeing the parts of herself that she normally kept private, was beguiling. And, I thought to myself, if the afternoon's activity was board games, just sitting quietly and playing the game might be considered an acceptable level of participation, and that way I could be seen to be doing my bit socially without having to do anything awful like make conversation.

Plus, it would get Big Sis off my back for *weeks*.

The journey was predictably horrible. I don't like taking routes I'm not familiar with at the best of times, and Citymapper told me I had to change at Stratford, which is one of my least favourite places in London. While waiting on the platform there I managed to get surrounded by a group of loud teenage girls. They kept making silent eye contact with each other and then bursting out laughing. I couldn't work out what it was they found so funny, so I had to assume it was me.

I turned up at my destination just as Jason, Debi's husband, was leaving with the kids. I had met him at previous years' office Christmas drinks (at which attendance was, to my horror, mandatory). The first time he had made several polite attempts at engaging me in conversation and I, mute with shyness, had tried to hold up my end purely by nodding and smiling. After a couple of minutes he asked me if I was alright, and I realised that, through continually bobbing my head up and down with a grotesque rictus plastered on my face, I must be doing a passable impression of an epileptic having a seizure. He seemed genuinely concerned. Too flustered even to *consider* talking, I gave him a shaky thumbs up and fled, spending the rest of the evening hiding in the passage leading to the fire exit.

In subsequent years he restricted himself to a brief greeting and a single pleasantry when he saw me, much to the benefit of us both.

Today Jason gave me a friendly nod and waved me in, then went back to threatening, cajoling and pleading with his daughters to get them out of the door complete *with* coats and scooters but *without* the pet hamster that one of them seemed intent on smuggling with her. Once they were safely gone I made my way further into the house.

I don't know exactly what I had been expecting, but Debi's home was less... *gothy* than she was. A 3-bed terraced house in Leyton, it had dark wood floorboards, a cast iron bannister on the stair, lots of pot plants and a small garden. No satanic altars, no pythons in tanks, no death metal music blasting from black-spiked speakers, just good taste in a minimalist sort of way. For a family home with two small children it was surprisingly tidy.

Eventually I reached the kitchen, where I found Debi, Bled and a stranger setting out vegetable-based snacks around the large kitchen table. Bled saw me and nodded. Debi beamed.

"Colin! Perfect timing. I need you to whisk this."

Before I had time to react to the presence of someone I didn't know, she thrust a bowl into my hands containing something white and mushy with green flecks in it. It also held a device, part aluminium and part faded bakelite, that I eventually realised was a mechanical whisk. It had a little handle that you turned to make the spinny bits spin. I put the bowl down on the counter and gave it an experimental twist. Green-flecked white blobs burst merrily out of the bowl onto my face, clothes and surroundings. Debi shrieked with laughter.

"On second thought, give me that back. Can I get you to chop some tomatoes? Actually no, never mind. Let's not risk any more accidents. Here."

She tossed me some kitchen roll and I dabbed at my t-shirt.

"Now, Colin, this is Holly."

My instinctive reaction to unexpected social introductions to women is to keep my eyes firmly on the floor and, if I'm feeling particularly brave, utter a strangled 'Hng'. Long experience, however, has taught me that it is important to override my instincts, so I made myself look up, carefully directing my gaze at the centre of the stranger's forehead. That way I could give the rough impression of making eye contact without subjecting myself to the trauma of actually doing so.

"Hullo!" said the woman, cheerfully. With my eyes fixed just below her hairline, and social anxiety giving me a quick dose of tunnel vision, I couldn't make out much of her appearance immediately. She seemed to be around thirty-ish, give or take a decade, fairly overweight (compared to a normal

person, that is – compared to me she was a stick), with very
blonde ringlets and a round face. Her accent was northern, although I've never had a good enough ear to be able to place
anything above Birmingham with any confidence. I had a moment of panic when she started moving round the table and
I thought she might be planning a cheek-kiss greeting, but it
turned out she was just heading to the sink to fill up her water
bottle.

"H-hi," I forced myself to say, and was proud of myself that
it came out at a more or less audible volume.

I couldn't think of a follow-up. There was a moment's silence. I turned to Debi.

"Is, uh, anyone else from the office...?"

"Nah, couldn't convince them. But that's fine, four's
enough."

Oh. A third of the people in the room were strangers. This
was already not what I'd signed up for. I realised I was starting
to sweat.

"Now," continued Debi, "I've got a couple of heavy-weight
options for what we can play later, and we can have a fun time
arguing over which we choose, but I thought we could break
the ice with something lighter. So: Charades, Pictionary, or
Taboo? Or a mix?"

An immediate roaring started up in my ears, and I felt my
chest tighten alarmingly. Those weren't board games. Those
were party games. I Do Not Play party games. I Do Not Play
party games *ever*. If you took the sum total of everything I find
difficult about social interactions and distilled it down into a

single activity, that activity would be Charades. I looked over at Debi to see if she was teasing me, but she just looked enthusiastic and sincere.

This was a disaster. I had to shut this down immediately.

"...Uh–" I started.

"Ooh, I always love a good charade!" cut in Holly.

"Charades? Sound good to everyone?" asked Debi, looking to Bled and me.

Bled shrugged. "Sure."

"I... uh..." I managed.

"Charades it is then!" Debi announced.

I felt my legs go wobbly, and put a steadying hand on the table.

"Are you alright, Colin?" Debi asked.

"...ngh..." I mumbled, sitting down heavily in a chair.

Debi eyed me thoughtfully.

"You do know," she said gently, "that you don't *have* to play. If you don't want to. Right?"

I could feel my cheeks burning. Not being able to cope with games like Charades and being forced to play them anyway is one thing. But not being able to cope with playing games like Charades and being forced to own up to that in front of colleagues and strangers is *so* much worse.

This seemed like a good time to action the Big Sis Contingency Plan: We'd long ago agreed a system whereby if I sent her a message comprising a single hand-wave emoji, she'd immediately ring me and tell me there was a family emergency. We'd devised it for exactly this sort of situation. The problem was that Bled was standing right next to me, and I didn't think there was any way of sending the message without him noticing. If I then got an immediate phone call he'd be sure to put two and two together, and that would be *mortifying*.

I briefly wondered whether I could get away with faking a heart attack. No, I was far too self-conscious to pull off something like that convincingly.

There was only one thing for it.

"…'s fine," I practically whispered, every syllable an effort. "It'll be fun."

*

I gave it a go. Ok? I did the best I could, and it was exactly as horrible as I thought it would be, but I got through it. I stayed almost entirely silent while other people were acting stuff out, and mostly got away with it because Holly made enough noise for all of us.

The first time I was up, I got lucky with my prompt, and with eyes firmly glued to the floor, made one gesture to indicate a book, and another to indicate a squiggle on my forehead, and Holly immediately gushed out the titles of all seven Harry Potter stories until she hit the one I'd been given, at which point I could nod and immediately sit back down.

My second turn, though, was a disaster. My prompt was something called 'Hot in Herre' which was by a performer who styled themselves as 'Nelly', and which I could only guess was a song. I didn't know how to indicate that I was describing a piece of music, so I pointed at my ear, and Bled kept bleating "Sounds like...? Sounds like...?" no matter how many times I shook my head. Eventually Debi twigged that we were talking about a song, and then we got stuck again because in indicating that it was three words long my fingers must have shaken too much, and Debi took that to mean that I was not indicating a three word title but rather that I was about to describe the third word *of* the title. No amount of re-gesturing with my fingers would dissuade her of this, and I was left trying to work out how the fuck to *mime* the made-up word 'Herre'. I just kind of goggled at that point until the timer ran out and I could shamefacedly hand my prompt card to Debi for inspection and sit back down, humiliated.

After several lifetimes in this wretched Gehenna, Debi announced that we had had a sufficient quantity of fun, and it was time to move on. By that point I had worked my way through all of the healthy and delightless snacks on my side of the table, and had lost a good portion of my bodyweight through sweat. We settled down to a proper board game, with dice and rules and counters, the sort of thing I could potentially have actually enjoyed, but I was now too flustered to really listen as Debi was explaining how to play it, and I didn't dare raise my eyes very high in case I made eye contact with anyone round the table, so I kept missing what other people were doing on their turns, and it was only about half an hour in that I started to get into the swing of things. I did finally achieve some small measure of calm, and had finally worked myself up to trying something a bit inventive on my turn, when -

"Oh bloody hell, Issy."

A small child had appeared in the doorway to the kitchen, its face a mess of mud, blood and snot. Underneath it all a lower lip protruded and wobbled. Moments later we heard a clatter in the hall and Jason appeared, holding another small child in a bundle at his waist. He was looking harassed.

"Well honey, the good news is that we still have two children. That fucking scooter –"

"Language!" Debi snapped.

"That *fudging* scooter, then, I swear –"

He got no further, because at that moment the child with the messy face started wailing at a volume quite out of proportion with its size. Debi got up and began the process of calming and cleaning, and it was generally agreed that the afternoon's activities had drawn to a close.

10

On my way home I took an executive decision and stopped in at the supermarket. Homemade tzatziki and carrot sticks do not a luncheon make. Running a mental inventory of the contents of my kitchen, I realised nothing therein was going to satisfy my current cravings for comestible comfort. I grabbed a bottle of coke and scanned the shelves until I saw some of those steak and kidney pies that come in tins and my stomach gave a little lurch to signify its approval. Perfect. I picked up three. It being a Sunday, the shop was winding down towards early closing, and the self-service tills all seemed to be switched off. There was a young, Asian, glamorous and bored-looking girl manning the till at the tobacco kiosk. I felt suddenly self-conscious buying ready meals and fizzy drinks in front of her, so, flustered, I doubled back towards the aisles looking for something healthy. But faced with endless options, none of which I actually wanted, indecision paralysis set in, and I got increasingly agitated hovering back and forth amongst vegetables and supplements. In the end I made myself grab a whole cauliflower and a pack of multivitamins.

It was only when I got to the tills that I saw the vitamins were for men trying to conceive, and apparently improved the quantity and motility of one's sperm. At that point it was too late to turn back, so I kept my eyes firmly to the floor throughout the entire checkout process, and could feel my face glowing red and sweat cascading down around my ears. I was so embarrassed I felt sick. I could hardly hear her ask if I had a reward card over the roaring in my ears.

I finally got away from the shop, feeling nauseous and stupid. I threw the semen-boosting vitamins in the first bin I came to. Then, after a moment's pause to collect myself, I threw the cauliflower in too.

Once I was safely home in my flat I put a couple of the pies in the oven, poured myself a pint of coke, and took a moment to breathe and reassess. I was ok, I told myself. It had been a horrible day to cap off a horrible week, and the shopping disaster had been the icing on the cake, but now all of that was over. I didn't need to hide under the duvet. I didn't need an emergency call with Big Sis.

That was the deal. When it all got too much, Big Sis talked me down. That was the arrangement we'd had in place since the Incident. In fact, it wasn't much more than an extension of the way we'd always operated. Mum had never really got the hang of parenting, so instead she delegated. Big Sis was responsible for us all, except to the minor extent to which she occasionally sub-delegated responsibility for Little Sis to me. We hadn't chosen those roles, but we accepted them and did the best we could.

Except that, when it came to it, I'd failed to uphold my obligations.

But tonight, I assured myself, things were under control.

I checked my phone. It was approaching 5pm. I should go to bed by midnight at the latest. That meant overall I had seven hours, seven blissful hours, of complete control. I surveyed my options. Play the new Total War game I'd not got around to trying yet? Oh God no. After this afternoon I wanted nothing more to do with games of any sort for a while. Netflix movie marathon? That sounded more promising. But after fifteen minutes of scrolling I couldn't find a single thing I wanted to watch.

I wanted comfort. I wanted to feel less like an alien freak. I wanted a sense of connection with another human being. I wanted... well, Big Sis be damned, I wanted Harlequin-Cyanide.

I logged into AltMatch, and saw with a jolt of delight that I had an unread message waiting from her. The delight swiftly turned to guilt when I realised that while I had never got round to telling her that I was quitting AltMatch, I had instead simply ghosted her. Feeling like a heel, I read what she'd sent:

> *Hey, just checking... You didn't respond to my last message. Is that because you don't want to chat any more? No problem if that's what it is, it's just I'm not very good at reading emotions and things – guess I'm a classic aspie AltMatcher lol – so I thought maybe I should just ask directly.*

Sorry, I'm probably coming across like a crazy. Seriously, no problem if you don't want to chat. X

I immediately started to compose a reply... then stopped. The green dot was showing for HarlequinCyanide. This indicated that she was online right now, and available for Instant chat. This was a slightly clunky feature of AltMatch, but one that was very much appreciated by its members: there were two 'modes' of chat. The first was called Correspondence, and functioned much like email. You were encouraged to write longer messages, but there was no pressure to reply to them instantly. The second, Instant, was more like modern messaging apps, a continuous conversation where you could see if the other person had read your most recent message. Normally I preferred Correspondence mode – it was less intrusive and came with fewer expectations of a quick response, which suited me fine. But every once in a while...

I popped up the Instant view.

THX1137: *Hey*

(THX1137 is my username on AltMatch. It's a sort of pun, referencing... you know what, never mind.)

...

<HarlequinCyanide *is typing>*

...

HarlequinCyanide: *Hey yourself!*

HarlequinCyanide: Good to see you on Instant. How's your day going?

THX1137: Awful. I got tricked into playing Charades.

HarlequinCyanide: Uh-oh... How was it?

THX1137: Ugh, as terrible as you'd expect.

HarlequinCyanide: Aww hun. Still, they say it's good to talk to people in the meatspace from time to time.

THX1137: I know. Hey, I'm sorry I didn't reply to your message sooner.

THX1137: It's been a hell of a week

HarlequinCyanide: No problem!

HarlequinCyanide: I'm sorry I sent you a crazy stalker-sounding message yesterday.

HarlequinCyanide: I re-read it this morning and I was so embarrassed lol

HarlequinCyanide: But tell me about your crazy week.

THX1137: It's just work stuff

HarlequinCyanide: What do you actually do?

THX1137: I work with computers...

HarlequinCyanide: Lolwut, you'll have to be more specific than that!

THX1137: Well, if you really want to know, I'm a cyber security consultant. I try to keep businesses safe from hackers.

HarlequinCyanide: No way!!!

HarlequinCyanide: Well then you're totally going to hate me, because I'm a bad-ass hacker.

THX1137: Oh yeah?

HarlequinCyanide: Oh hellz yeah. Like, today I hacked into the Pentagon, just for kicks.

HarlequinCyanide: And yesterday I hacked Mark Zuckerberg, found out when he plans to fix the shitty Android update for Instagram.

HarlequinCyanide: Tomorrow I'm going for the big one. I'm going to hack... the moon.

THX1137: Hahaha

HarlequinCyanide: So I guess you're going to have to, like, call the cyber-cops on me, huh?

...

HarlequinCyanide: Hey, you there?

...

THX1137: Sorry!

THX1137: I had some food in the oven. I nearly burnt it. But it's all ok.

HarlequinCyanide: Haha phew

THX1137: And yes, I am already deploying nanobots across the internet to track your location via a trojan horse backdoor exploit.

HarlequinCyanide: Haha sounds kinda kinky

HarlequinCyanide: By the way, you type REALLY fast, don't you?

And so it went on. We ended up spending most of the evening chatting on and off. Over the course of our back-and-forth, HarlequinCyanide told me a little bit about her life. She had been training to be a pastry chef but "some health stuff" had meant she had to give that up. Now she made money working from home as a freelance customer support agent, which seemed to mostly involve replying politely to angry emails and occasionally processing refunds for various different companies. She sounded like she was a bit reclusive like me. She seemed more confident than I was, though: certainly I'd never have dared make a single one of the relentless stream of raunchy innuendos that she punctuated her messages with.

It also goes without saying that as we talked I did a pretty thorough background check on her, to make sure she was who she said she was. Don't get me wrong, I didn't care in the slightest if she made up the pastry chef bit, or lied about any other particular detail about herself. Everyone lies on dating sites, especially AltMatch. It's a place for you to project who you want to be, not who you are. All I wanted to do was verify that she was fundamentally a real person, not a persona invented by a scammer. Lonely people are vulnerable and attract predators, and AltMatch had a persistent problem with fraudsters. In the past few months I'd come across a couple. Normally you could tell from their profiles – they used photos that were just slightly too good-looking, and played too much into traditional nerdy male fantasies. (*"Hi! I'm a 23-year-old ex-model, I'm new in town and lonely, and I'm just looking for someone to play video games with. Do you like Star Wars?"*) HarlequinCyanide didn't *seem* like that, but you could never be too careful.

I took her profile picture and ran it through a reverse image search, until I found an old YouTube channel with no videos but the same avatar. The username on *that* matched a DeviantArt account that was mostly sketches of designs for cakes, and the owner of that account called themselves Mary and had a Twitter account, and so on...

By the time I was done I was pretty sure she was real. I knew her name, I knew she lived in Chiswick, I knew the names of all the companies she worked for, and I knew that she could draw really well. I even found a couple of pictures of her from several years ago, although she was tagged in the background of some group shots, so they didn't give me much of a sense of what she really looked like. Either she was just very unlucky when it came to photographs, or she made a conscious effort to hide behind her hair whenever there was a camera around. All I could tell was that she had at one point been a brunette, she was quite large, very pale, and seemed to wear a lot of eye makeup. Not that any of that mattered, of course, but it did help assure me that she was real.

I decided that I would keep talking to her. Just for a little while. Just as a comfort thing while the whole MDG shit-show was in full fling. If it was only temporary then Big Sis didn't need to know. I went to bed feeling happier than I had done in a few days, which was good, because things fell apart pretty quickly after that.

11

It was mid-morning on Monday, and we'd all been back at it for a few hours. Kayla was off giving an update to Anil, and the rest of us had our heads down. The mood was better than it had been on Saturday. That is to say, everyone was pretty much ignoring each other and plugging away in silence, which was better than the bickering and sniping of the previous week.

Then Kayla returned and waved to catch my eye, her expression grim.

"Hey, um, Anil wants to see you ASAP," she said. "In Camelot."

"Is this... about the logs?"

"Um, I think it's best if you just go see him," she replied cagily.

As I got up I heard Rémy dramatically sucking in a breath. Debi kicked his chair.

I started to walk, and realised how weak my legs felt. If Anil wanted to meet me in the Camelot conference room rather than his office, that meant other people would be there. This was no cosy chat. Maybe the other people would be from HR. Maybe I really was getting fired.

I reached Camelot, and noted that it was one of the few meeting rooms not to have glass walls. It was for private conversations. The door was ajar, so I knocked and entered, and saw Anil alongside Brad as usual, plus Roisin, the birdlike head of PR.

PR. Not HR. That was unexpected.

"Colin. Come in, sit down," said Anil, unemotionally. "Kayla tells me your team made some headway on the forensics over the weekend."

"Uh… yes, uh, Debi and Bled worked out how they could have avoided leaving a trail."

"Mm. Bled's been impressing us for a while now," said Anil. "We'll keep an eye on him in future. But you still don't know how they accessed the system in the first place?"

"No. Um… no."

"Well so be it. I –"

"It was my fault," I blurted out.

Anil regarded me quizzically as I blustered on.

"The log problem… I didn't check that our security measures were running on the right schedule, so…. it's my fault."

I saw Roisin jot something down in the notebook in front of her. Anil thought for a second and then grunted.

"Ok. We'll have to think about what impact that has. I take it you haven't seen MDG's statement yet?"

"Uh…"

"They sent it to us first thing this morning. But we'll get to that. Roisin, do you want to explain what's happened since last night?"

Roisin nodded.

"Hullo Colin. So. Last night a tech news site called Humanalog – you know Humanalog? – they sent both us and MDG an email asking us for comments on an article they're ready to publish. They'd done a lot of digging, and they knew an impressive amount. They knew we had built the system that was hacked. They knew that at least part of the attack was through social engineering. They knew that it was an employee called Moritz Ortlauf who had been targeted, and that he's now in hospital. And the also knew something we didn't: That Moritz is there because he attempted suicide."

She gave me a second to let that sink in. I certainly felt like I was sinking, but, while I felt a wash of sympathy for Moritz, I didn't get what was significant about this revelation. So I just put on what I hoped was an appropriately serious face and nodded slowly.

"Apparently Moritz's mother confirmed it," Roisin continued, "He was very upset after he left MDG that night, sending lots of messages saying how ashamed he was to his family, and refusing to let his housemates into his room. Humanalog suggested he had a history of depression – although I don't know where they got that from – and that there were various unspecified other things going on in his life. Anyway, it seems that Moritz really believed he was responsible for the theft, and after a sleepless night ended up using a combination of pills and a razor blade to try to end it all. Thankfully unsuccessfully, although apparently it was a close-run thing."

Poor Moritz. I wished that when I'd met him I'd found a way of making him understand that it really wasn't his fault, that no matter how gullible he'd been, *I* was the one who'd let everyone down.

"Anyway, somewhat problematically for everyone, Humanalog decided to pin the blame on Moritz too. The line they went with in the article they sent to MDG for comment was 'Hapless Employee Conned by Fraudsters.' And MDG –"

"– Did this," broke in Anil, spinning his laptop round to face me. On screen was an email from Todd to Anil and Roisin. It read:

Here's the statement we've sent to Humanalog and will be releasing online. I'm sure you understand, and hope this will not affect our ongoing projects.

- T

"Maison de Gauguin are distraught to learn of the hospitalisation of our loved and respected teammate Moritz. Moritz has not been with us for long, but in his time with us he has proved himself to be able, loyal, and determined to embody the values that makes MDG what it is today.

"It has been reported that Moritz attempted suicide, and that this is in some way related to his involvement in a recent theft, about which rumours have also been circulating. It has even been asserted,

entirely incorrectly, that Moritz was at fault in relation to this theft. While the incident in question is a private matter subject to an on-going investigation, we would like to lay out certain facts in order to set the record straight:

"Last week a group of hackers managed to compromise our payment system and make off with a large sum of money, in the form of a cryptocurrency, which we were holding in escrow as part of the sale of an artwork by Nua Nigel. The exact details of how the money was stolen are still being established; however part of the exploit involved contacting one of our employees on false pretences and using deception to manipulate them, a process commonly known as 'social engineering'.

"While the employee in question was Moritz Ortlauf, there is no question that he was in any way negligent in his duties, and none of his actions can be attributed to malice or incompetence. He received a phone call and, being wholeheartedly committed to the MDG ethos of Customer Joy®, attempted to help the caller. He had no access to our payment system, and therefore no reason to believe that through his actions our payment system could be compromised.

"While Moritz's actions were used to perpetrate the theft, he himself cannot be considered to be at fault. Maison de Gauguin must therefore defend the name of one of our own who has been unfairly accused, and attribute blame where it is due: with our security contractor, Paladin Technologies Ltd, who built and sold the defective software, and specifically with Colin Clayford, the architect of

the system that was compromised. We are in consultation with our
lawyers and insurers, and, pending the outcome of the investigation
into the theft, will be taking appropriate next steps..."

There were a few more lines, but I couldn't read them any
more. My head started swimming and I thought I might fall
off my chair.

Seeing my expression, Anil correctly surmised that I had
reached the juicy part.

"Shit creek, eh? Personally, I love the bit where he says
he hopes this won't affect our ongoing projects. I prepared a
charming reply to him, using lots of very short words, but
Roisin won't let me send it."

I realised I hadn't breathed in about a minute, so I gasped
in a lungful of air.

"Uh... are they... will they... prosecute?"

"Hm? Oh, you mean sue? Lord no. I checked with the
lawyers, and our contract is absolutely watertight. Total *caveat*
emptor, and they must know it. They're just trying to do some
PR damage control. But they've done it by throwing us under
the bus."

"And you specifically," added Roisin. "That was low. Utterly unprofessional and completely unexpected. Obviously
we've wargamed what to do if a system we built is breached,
publicity-wise, but we never thought we'd have to deal with
an individual employee being singled out like this. It puts us in
a bit of a spot because now, reputationally, it's not just about
Paladin. It's about, well–"

"What Roisin is trying to say is that for the next couple of weeks every bored tech journo in Europe is going to be trying to find some reason to paint you as incompetent, and whatever they find hurts us as much as it hurts you," said Anil. "Which means we need to do some quite serious damage limitation."

"Am I fired?" I asked in alarm.

"Oh God no. No, there are very few scenarios where that reflects well on us. And of course you're a part of our team, and we don't treat our team like that," said Anil, almost successfully making it sound like that last sentence wasn't an afterthought.

"We just need you to help us keep this under control," said Roisin. "Don't speak to any journalists, I can't stress that enough. And by that what I really mean is, don't speak to *anyone*."

"I... ok. Uh... when will they release the statement?"

Roisin gave me a sympathetic look. "It went out at nine this morning. It's already trending on Twitter."

*

By the time I got back to the Bunker the rest of the team had evidently seen the statement. No one said anything about it, not even Rémy. There was just an awkward silence when I walked in. I sat down at my desk, put my headphones on, and tried to ignore the mutterings and exchanged looks happening around me. Occasionally I stole a couple of glances at the others, and tried to read their expressions. Disgust? Embarrassment? Pity?

While Roisin had strongly advised me not to obsess over the online reaction, I desperately wanted to see what was happening. But I didn't want to do it where the rest of the team could be looking over my shoulder. So I just sat there, and felt sorry for myself.

The day passed in a haze. I think I spent most of it staring at a blank screen, because at some point I realised my computer had powered itself down from lack of use. At 5:30 I gave up pretending I was doing anything useful, and quietly packed up my things and left. No one seemed to notice.

The area around my bus stop was nearly empty, except for a balding man leaning on a lamppost eating a burger. The Gabardine Suit Game took on an unpleasant new twist: I had considered muggers, murderers, fraudsters, thieves and more, but I'd never worried about journalists before. Was this man hiding a dictaphone in his food carton?

I started to murmur 'No comment, no comment, no comment' under my breath to practice getting the words out smoothly, then felt self-conscious and stopped. The man clearly wasn't a journalist, and wasn't remotely interested in my opinions. I hoped he hadn't seen me muttering to myself. Thankfully he didn't seem to be paying me any attention.

When I had made it safely home, and locked all the locks on my door, I slumped in front of my computer, promising myself I wouldn't look at what was happening online, wouldn't look for myself in the news. I decided instead to watch some TV, something calming, maybe some *Star Trek: The Next Generation.* I lasted all of two minutes before I finding myself searching "Colin Clayford" on Twitter, Reddit and Google.

It was bad.

It turns out the developer community, which touts itself as being welcoming and inclusive, really loves to put the boot in when someone is on the way down. There were already a few blog posts popping up pointing out that for a company to take the unusual step of naming and shaming a specific software developer I must have *really* screwed up.

Fuck.

I went to the cupboard in my kitchen, pulled out the big bag of marshmallow pieces and started chewing. It wasn't at all what I wanted, it was just to give my mouth something to do while I worked out a bigger meal. What I really yearned for, I realised, was a roast chicken with a tray of spuds, a couple of yorkshires and a bucket of instant gravy. That, by the way, was the dinner Big Sis had made every Sunday night after we visited Little Sis in the clinic. I hadn't had a craving like that for *years,* and and I didn't keep contingency chickens in my fridge. Raw chicken gives me the heebie-jeebies. So I ordered the closest substitute I could find: a few boxes of wings and fries from a local artisan kebab shop in Hoxton.

While I waited I set about trying to delete all my old social media accounts, before they inevitably started to attract trolls and hangers-on. I was slowed down because my fingers were shaking and I kept making typos.

The doorbell announced the arrival of the delivery man downstairs. I buzzed him in, and waited for him on the landing. He handed me my order with a condescending smile. Was he laughing at me because he knew who I was and how I was being humiliated online? No, get it together, why would a fast food courier know or care about the tech world? He was probably laughing at me because he'd realised that the fat man living by himself had ordered enough food to feed a family of eight. Just the normal sort of derision, then. Nothing special. I carried the greasy paper bag back into my flat and closed the door with a grunt.

I had just settled down in front of my screen with the food on my lap when there was a knock at my door. The delivery man must have forgotten part of my order. Although it all seemed there. Maybe some sauces? I opened the door again.

A stranger stood in front of me.

"Colin?"

"Uh…" I blinked. "Yeah."

Wordlessly he pulled a camera up from his side and started clicking it in my face. I panicked. I lifted my hand to push the camera away, then worried that might count as assault, so I held my arm in mid-air, ineffectively trying to block his lense's field of view instead. We stood there for a few seconds, me standing with my hand in front of my face, him impassively taking pictures of me. Then it dawned on me how stupid I was being, and I closed my door.

"Be seeing you Colin," he called out from the other side.

It was then that I realised I recognised him. He was the balding man who had been lounging on the street as I left work.

12

There was a dilapidated low concrete wall curving round the mini water play area at the resort, at one end of which some of the material on top had crumbled away, leaving a sharp point of stone, which made a dry crunching sound as Little Sis's temple collided with it and buckled inwards.

It was our last morning in Thessaloniki. Mum was spending it in bed, feeling unwell, as she had every morning. She blamed the food on the plane on the flight out. She was particularly unlucky to have been hit hard enough that she was still feeling the effects a week later, but at least she tended to perk up each day from around lunchtime, so that she could enjoy at least some of the holiday.

Little Sis and I had, therefore, got used to amusing ourselves. The resort was fairly empty, and we were the youngest people we'd seen there, which meant we had the kids' areas pretty much entirely to ourselves. We splashed around in the pool, tramped over the little hills in fruitless searches for interesting lizards and insects, and played made-up card games under the shade of palm trees.

By the final day, though, Little Sis was bored. And when she got bored she started looking for ways to get a rise out of me, just for the sake of something to do. She'd spent all week mocking my dogged adherence to the strict rules signposted around the play areas: I didn't yell or make excessive noise. I didn't bring my cans of coke into the playground. I didn't run in the water play area.

I didn't run in the water play area. And I told her she shouldn't either.

So, of course, Little Sis started running in the water play area. Round and round, faster and faster, as I stood in the middle, increasingly agitated, trying to explain to her the sensible, rational, logical reasons why obeying the signs, both in general and in this particular case, was very important, otherwise...

Someone else would have found a way of stopping her. But that would have required levels of persuasiveness, or perhaps quick-wittedness, that were quite beyond me. And then, of course, the inevitable happened, and one dry crunch later she was unconscious on the ground with blood snaking out from under her over the wet concrete.

But that bit wasn't my big screw-up. That was only the start.

*

It was Humanalog. Of course it was. Apparently MDG's statement had caused them to change the focus of their story from Mo to me. The piece went live at six the next morning.

The headline, in Humanalog's signature tabloid-y style, was simply: 'D'oh!', in huge letters, accompanied by a picture of me, in my doorway, squashing a flabby palm into my face. It did look for all the world like they'd managed to capture the exact moment when I realised I'd screwed up. The angle of the photo and some unhelpful lighting glare also managed to partially obscure what little hair I have, lending me, I will concede, me a passing resemblance to Homer Simpson.

The lede kept up the assault:

He was paid £100k a year to build a simple crypto wallet, but instead Colin Clayford produced something so full of holes that all it took was one phone call to a receptionist for thieves to make off with over £7m. And now the receptionist is fighting for his life...

A couple more shots followed further down the article, these ones showing my full face, depicting a disgusting, fat slob, the sort of person who you could easily imagine being lazy, stupid and in some way corrupt.

Of course, the story itself was riddled with inaccuracies and fabrications. For starters, my salary was nothing like £100k (it was actually quite a bit more). And nothing about Labyrinth was 'simple' – Todd's arcane requirements had seen to that. But none of that mattered. What mattered was that as of this morning, I was public enemy #1 in the eyes of the tech community. The story made it to the top spot on Hacker News within minutes, and infosec 'thought leaders' were spewing out reaction posts on their blogs so quickly I was pretty sure they couldn't have had time to actually read the full article.

Everyone agreed: If the system was that easy to hack, there was something horribly wrong with how it was designed, so the blame fell squarely on the shoulders of the architect of that system. A couple of commentators helpfully pointed out that if I was to blame for the hack, I was *also* to blame for Moritz's suicide attempt, and were he not to recover I would have blood on my hands. One went so far as to suggest that, given how wide open I'd left the door of the vault, you couldn't even fault Pony Club for wandering in and making off with the treasure. I was painted as a bigger villain than the criminals themselves.

All in all this was not a good morning. It made my stomach ache, so I ate a bag of Haribo. Not one of the little bags. Then I ate another one. My stomach still ached.

At 8am Kayla rang me.

"Stay home today," she advised.

"B-but I don't have access to any of the files here."

"Don't worry about that. You just take some time off. Have a quiet day."

"Am I suspended?" I said, panic rising. "Am I being fired?"

"No! No, you're definitely not being fired."

"But... suspended?"

"Well... Not really. Not officially. Anil just wants you to be... not working at the moment. Um. But it's only temporary, and it's just until this whole thing blows over. Look, I'm going to put it down as a... as a sick day."

"But I'm not sick," I protested.

"Are you stressed?"

"Y-yes of course."

"Well then. Honestly, don't worry Colin, it's fine, we'll have you back at work in no time. I promise. Ok?"

"Ok."

"Ok great. I've got to check in with Brad, but I'll speak to you soon, ok?"

And that was it. I stood, lost, in my sitting room. Suddenly I had nothing to do with my day. Ordinarily I would have rejoiced: an excuse to stay hidden away in the safety of my flat, my kingdom. But I had been expecting to work. I was ready to work. I was *supposed* to work.

And the more I thought about it, the more this suspended-but-not-suspended situation unsettled me. The idea that my professional status was in jeopardy was horrible. It wasn't just the uncertainty, although Lord knows I hate uncertainty. It was that, really, I didn't feel that I necessarily had much of an identity beyond my professional identity. Take that away and I was... insubstantial.

I managed to avoid eating a KitKat while I pondered what to do next. Unable to come up with a plan, I had another shower to buy myself some more time. When that was done I still didn't know what to do, but I reckoned that whatever I ended up doing with my day, it would probably involve my computer, so I sat down and logged on as a first step.

I had several emails waiting for me. A few were from journalists, requesting statements or interviews. I deleted them immediately. Then there were some from members of the public, mostly in the tech community. A very small number of those offered commiserations and sympathy with my current situation, but the rest were variously berating me, mocking me, gloating over my misfortune or in one case telling me I was 'scum' who would be 'put down soon enough' for my failures.

There was also one intriguing email, sent from a throwaway account, claiming to be from a 'Sandspidr':

Colin Colin Colin,

So you're taking the fall, my man. We at Pony Club send our condolences. You don't deserve the blame. You're a good coder. You're just not as good as us lol. We pwned you with our superior intellects, but don't let it get to you. The ponies trample everyone in the end.

If you ever need a reference let us know!

Pony Club (comin at ya from the keyboard of Sandspidr)

I supposed I should be grateful that at least someone was sympathetic. But it wasn't genuine, it was just a form of self-adulation. They had outsmarted me, and fundamentally they didn't want to diminish the scale of their achievement by acknowledging I made it easy for them.

My stomach was twisting itself into knots. More than anything else, what I couldn't bear in all this was that after nearly a week of searching we still had no idea how they had beaten my system. And the fact that I wasn't allowed to keep working on it...

I realised that without even thinking about it my fingers had hit the reply button to Sandspidr's email. It was probably pointless – he'd probably never check the sending account again. But still, I watched my fingers as they typed:

You compromised my system, and we don't know how. Because of that, the system will never be used again. So you don't get to use the same exploit twice. So you don't benefit from keeping how you did it a secret. So... please?

It was a silly message. I wasn't even sure what I was saying made logical sense. I knew I was offering no incentive to them to spill the beans. But not knowing how they hacked me was killing me.

My finger clicked 'Send'.

*

It wasn't enough. Just sitting there, waiting to see if 'Sandspidr' would respond, waiting to know if one of the Bunker Buddies would figure out something I'd missed, waiting for another journalist to find my flat and start hounding me... it wasn't enough. I couldn't, as Kayla had suggested, 'have a quiet day'. I needed to do something, *anything* more.

So I continued trawling infosec forums. At first it was just a grim fascination at how many people would rush to condemn me. But then I started to find posts where security professionals, ones who had nothing whatever to do with Maison de

Gauguin or Paladin, posited theories about what might have happened. They were, of course, largely off the mark in their guesses about how Labyrinth actually worked, so their theories about how it might have *not* worked, as it were, were pretty hopeless. But each one contained at least the nugget of an idea. Some were things I'd thought of before, investigated and discarded. Some were genuinely new to me, and with each of those I carefully thought through its plausibility... before ultimately dismissing it as unfeasible.

There were a couple where I didn't understand what the author was saying, so I replied to them, asking for clarification (of course, I was very careful to set up a clean user account each time – the last thing I wanted was for it to get out that the man who'd screwed up had resorted to asking for help from strangers on the Internet.) In one case in particular, the author, who had given himself the username 'Boffinism', confidently announced that this was a classic 'buffer overflow attack'. I won't bore you with the details of what that means; suffice it to say that it is a hacking technique that seemed me to be completely irrelevant to a situation like the one that had occurred. So I replied asking what he led him to believe that buffer overflows were involved.

Boffinism replied almost instantly:

I don't blame you for not seeing it. Nothing Pony Club have said publicly gives it away. But I've got a little insider info... Let's just say I wasn't always one of the good guys.

This was huge. It seemed that Pony Club were already leaking details of how they did it to the broader hacker community. If I could get hold of that information before the general public did, I might be able to salvage part of my reputation. I pressed Boffinism for more information, but he quickly grew cagey. He seemed not to want to risk in any way implicating himself. He restricted himself to dropping tantalising hints, none of which was enough for me to even begin to connect the dots.

Eventually, after much back-and-forth, he said:

You know, I'd be much happier discussing this in person. I don't need to be so careful about what I say when there's no paper trail. You're based in London, right? There's an Infosecs In The City meetup near Silicon Roundabout this evening. Come find me there and I'll tell you all you want to know.

And just like that, I had a lead. An unusual one, to be sure, but at last here was something that looked like it might help me get out from underneath this whole thing.

I asked Boffinism how I'd recognise him, but got no reply. I supposed that was something I'd need to work out for myself. So I started doing my research. Thankfully 'Boffinism' was a pretty unique nickname, and he hadn't gone to much trouble to disassociate it from his true identity. Quite quickly I found his blog, and from there saw that he'd given a couple of talks at tech events, and cross-referencing online archives of those event listings showed that his real name was Thomas Charles, and once I had that it wasn't hard to find a photo of him. He looked awkwardly skinny, one of those people who's all knees and elbows and acute angles. (I don't mean that as a criticism. I'd have traded my figure for his any day of the week.)

I now had everything that I needed, but I'm nothing if not thorough. I devoted the rest of the day to finding out as much as possible about him and the event he was going to be at this evening. I wanted to make sure there were no surprises. By mid-afternoon I was so engrossed in my investigations that I'd forgotten all about Paladin and the goings-on in the Bunker.

Then at 3pm Kayla rang. She sounded stressed.

"Hey, I'm so sorry to do this, but are you free to hop on a conference call real quick?"

"Uh, yeah... What's, uh-?"

"It's with Anil... and the police. They called in for an update, and they've got a couple of tech questions apparently.."

"No problem. When is it?"

"Right now. Can I ping you the details?"

"O-ok."

"Cool, speak to you in a second."

She hung up, and a second later sent the dial-in link through on YakYak. I dug out my headset and clicked through to join.

"– a serious allegation," came Anil's voice immediately.

"I am not alleging anything," replied another voice that I recognised as DI Otembi's. "I am investigating. That is my job, and it is what you have repeatedly been asking me –"

"*New caller...* 'Colin'*... has joined the conversation,*" chimed in the robo-announcer.

"Hey Colin," said Kayla.

"Well he's here now," said Anil, "and you can ask whatever you need to. I would simply ask you to weigh your words carefully."

"I always do, Mr Qazi," came the terse reply.

"Colin, I have Detective Inspector Otembi on the line, and her colleague, ah, Tom–"

"It's Ben," cut in Otembi flatly. "Ben is my lead analyst."

"Hullo!" came a chipper voice that was in stark contrast to the aggressive tones of Anil and Otembi.

"*Ben* and Ms Otembi have some questions about Labyrinth which I believe you're best qualified to answer, if you're happy to."

"S-sure."

"Great. Then he's all yours."

"Perfect. Good morning, Mr Clayford," said Otembi. "Ben tells me you've been subjected to a bit of a drubbing in the tech press recently."

"Uh...yes, I... yes."

"Well, I'm sorry. People always want a scapegoat, and journalists are often too impatient to wait for the facts. But I'm sure we can clear it all up soon enough. I'd like you to tell Ben how Labyrinth was built."

"Uh..." I started, unsure how to approach such a big topic.

"So what we mean is: it's a proprietary system, is it? A one-off?" interjected Ben.

"Yes."

"And none of it reuses components you've built for other clients?"

"No. We've never done anything with Burncoin before."

"Ok… ok," said Ben, thoughtfully.

There was a brief pause before he continued.

"And is much of Labyrinth accessible to outsiders via the open Internet?"

"None of it – there's no way of interacting with it unless you're connected to MDG's internal network in their building."

"We are a security firm," put in Anil. "We take this stuff very seriously."

"I'm sure you do," replied Ben, earnestly. "I'm just trying to rule a few things out. I'm sure you see where I'm going with this."

"Do enlighten me," growled Anil.

"Well, you've built this unique system from scratch that you only ever installed in one place, and that place is pretty… *opaque* to the outside world. So it would be very hard for an outsider to learn enough about the system to be able to uncover any sort of problems or weaknesses that it had."

"But someone *did* uncover, and exploit, a weakness in the system," continued Otembi. "So if the hackers would struggle to find those weaknesses from the *outside*, would you agree, Colin, that the best explanation is that the attacker learned about the system some other way?"

"I'm… not sure what you –"

"I mean to say, isn't it more likely that the attacker learned about the problems in Labyrinth by accessing the source code, presumably by infiltrating Paladin's –"

"What a ridiculous suggestion," cut in Anil, "And I think more than anything else it's indicative of your failure to establish any solid leads, causing you to fall back on the most absurd forms of speculation. Our source code is rigorously protected by established best practices, and we have endless documentation, certification and accreditations to prove it. Since you are evidently struggling to make any progress on your own I would recommend that you sit tight, and *we will tell you* when we have established who hacked MDG and how. *Goodbye.*"

There was a click, and I guessed that Anil had used the web interface for the call to abruptly boot out Otembi and Ben.

Then there was a pause.

"Well... this is a cluster-fuck," said Anil eventually. "We could cope with the world believing we had one duff project – it'd take a couple of years to get past it fully, but we'd get there – but if it gets out that the police think that we ourselves have been infiltrated... that's a business killer. Fuck. *Fuck!*"

I had never heard Anil this agitated before. I had never heard Anil *at all* agitated before.

"How can we help?" asked Kayla, sounding as unnerved as I felt.

"Give me a narrative. Work out what happened, and give me a narrative I can give the PR team. And if we have to... oh, for God's sake."

There was another click. I realised Anil had kicked me off the call too.

*

Every child automatically casts themselves in the role of superhero when envisioning their future self. Brave, strong, quick to act. The real world can be crushingly disillusioning.

When Little Sis collapsed I froze. It was immediately obvious that something was seriously wrong, but my only response to the enormity of what had just happened was to wait, statue still, for the problem somehow to undo itself. For the blood to go *back* inside her, for her to *un*land, *un*fall, *un*slip. But, no matter how long I waited, time stubbornly refused to reverse direction.

Finally, a lifetime later, I started to accept that this video was not going to rewind, and that things could only be fixed by moving forwards. But what to do? I stumbled towards her a couple of steps, then skittered back again, afraid to touch her. I had no idea how to help, no idea what she needed. I tried calling out, but the sounds died in my throat. I was completely lost, utterly out of my depth. And the spidery lines of watery blood kept steadily growing.

Finally, with so much time already wasted, I resolved to pick her up. She was lying face down in a puddle of ever-redder water. I couldn't even see if her mouth and nostrils were submerged. I gingerly approached, bent down, put my arms around her, and heaved... only to discover that, even though

I had occasionally lifted her in the past, there's a difference between carrying an obliging sibling and lifting a sprawling 40kg of unresponsive meat. I heaved, and I hauled, and she just *flopped*, scraping her already damaged head along the ground as I tried to yank her up by her midriff.

I stopped. This was hopeless. I was hopeless. I wasn't strong enough. I needed help. I tried to lay her out flat. I couldn't remember what the recovery position was, even though I'd *specifically* taught myself about it a couple of years previously in case I ever had to face an emergency like this. My mind simply wasn't working properly.

In the end, as a best guess, I laid her on her back with her head tilted to the side. Her face was a mess, and I had to force myself to look at her, to check that her mouth was open and not blocked by anything. She *seemed* to be breathing, and when I put my hand on her chest I *thought* I could feel a heartbeat, but I didn't trust myself with any of this. She was still bleeding.

There was still no one else around. Time to get help. I started running in the direction of Mum's hotel room, then stopped. Would she be in any position to actually do anything? She was ill herself. I was being cowardly. I needed to speak to someone else, someone who spoke Greek and so could call for an ambulance. I changed direction and ran to reception.

*

The call with the police had left me shaken. The suggestion that it wasn't just Labyrinth that had been infiltrated but also

Paladin itself was disturbing. The most shameful part of me wanted it to be true, because if that was the case then it might be someone *else's* fault, and my own screw-ups might be less significant. But in my heart of hearts I knew it was extremely unlikely. Paladin is the best of the best. It simply doesn't let things like that happen.

What *did* seem to be the case, though, was that fear of this suggestion becoming more widely circulated was likely to force Anil's hand. He'd need to take decisive action soon, and the abrupt way in which he'd booted me off the call when he'd started talking about it made it pretty clear who'd be in the firing line when he did.

All in all, it made my discovery of Boffinism all the more timely. As 6:30 hove into view I started making preparations. I checked and double-checked the contents of my wallet, to ensure it contained a full complement of useful things: cash, credit cards, debit cards in case the credit cards were declined, driving licence (provisional of course) in case ID were required for entry, and a print-out of my blood type (A positive) and allergies (penicillin, mango). I packed a rucksack with everything else I might need, including laptop (batteries checked to be at 100%), notepad and several pens, one portable charger for my phone and one mains charger (although my phone itself was also at full battery currently), bottled water, emergency snacks, tissues, toilet paper, hand sanitizer, plasters, and two sets of headphones.

I rooted through my clothes cupboard until I found a hat and sunglasses. The hat was a woolly beanie, far too thick for this time of year, and the sunglasses would look weird at night-time, but I'd sooner look like a weirdo than be recognised by anyone, especially since I was venturing into the heart of the tech scene, and a *lot* of people in tech read Humanalog.

Satisfied that I was ready as I could be, and after two precautionary trips to the bathroom, I went through my pre-flight checks, and then walked to the hall, took a deep breath, and put my hand on the inner surface of my door. It was time to work up the courage to leave the flat.

*

The woman who ran the resort had terrified me from our first day. She was short and squat, with an almost spherical torso from which protruded two thin, bandy legs. Her brows were thick, her bun stern, her blouse limp and sweaty. As Mum checked in, Little Sis started rifling messily through the activity leaflets in the rack in the corner of reception, until the woman, glowering, yelled at her, and then yelled at me too for good measure. It was hard to make out the specific words, thanks to her thick Greek accent, but her enmity was clearly conveyed nonetheless. Little Sis didn't seem to mind – things like that always slid off her – but I hated being yelled at. I hated being in trouble.

That whole week the woman at reception made me feel like I was in trouble, every time she fixed her bulging eyes on me.

"She's part frog!" exclaimed Little Sis to me, not nearly quietly enough, after she passed us on the path to the restaurant. "I've read about these, it was a flu vaccine they gave to some Greek children made using frog DNA thirty years ago, and when *they* had children they were all born part frog. I saw her gills sticking out from her armpits just now."

I tried to explain just how wide of the mark the chronology, anatomy, biochemistry and virology in that assertion all were, but Little Sis ignored me. The woman was a frog-woman, and would henceforth ever be known as such.

Frog-woman was at the desk when I ran from the water play area into reception.

"T-there's been a–", I started to say, but stopped as frog-woman directed a ferociously angry, silent stare in my direction. She gesticulated angrily with her left hand, and, as she did so, I saw that she had a phone clamped to her ear with her right. She was outraged at being so rudely interrupted from her call.

And that was when it happened. For all that I should have found a way to make Little Sis slow down, for all that I shouldn't have frozen when she hit her head, for all that I should have been able to carry her to safety, none of that even compares to what I did next.

I've always been scared of other people. Fundamentally, my driving emotion, through all of my life, when interacting with others, has been fear. Fear of humiliating myself, fear of upsetting them, fear of being told off. That fear has been a constant, right back to my earliest memories. I was afraid of the other children in nursery. I was afraid of my teachers in primary school. I was afraid of frog-woman. And, faced with a glimpse of her undisguised loathing of me, and mindful of how she might respond if I were to interrupt her further, I did the worst, most shameful, most unforgiveable thing imaginable: I waited.

As my little sister lay unconscious a few hundred feet away, as the haemorrhage swelled inside her skull, I stood silently, cowed by the sour-faced, dumpy hotelier. I *knew* that Little Sis was dying, that I, through inaction, was killing her, but *even so* I dared not, *could* not bring myself to interrupt. In those agonising minutes, as I waited quietly and frog-woman, ignoring me, carried on her phone chat, I came to understand, clearly and for the first time, exactly what sort of person I am.

*

I stood, with my hand on the inside surface of the door, waiting to work up the courage to leave the flat.

I stood silent. I stood still.

I stood there until my phone told me the event had already started. Then I stood there until my phone told me the event had ended.

Then I went back to the kitchen and cooked a carton of fish fingers and a tray of chips. Then I ate them. Then I went to the bathroom and took my contact lenses out, being careful not to meet my own eye in the mirror, and brushed my teeth, and applied my spot cream. Then I went to bed and tried not to think about the fact that in my heart of hearts I'd always known there was no chance I was ever going to make it outside.

A few hours later I fell asleep.

13

I sat at home, miserably gorging myself and playing computer games the next morning, and did the same all afternoon. I wanted to keep it up in the evening too, but it was Wednesday, and that meant it was time for my weekly phone call with Big Sis.

"How are you doing?" she asked me, gently. She'd seen the Humanalog piece, of course.

"Um... I've been better."

"Oh Boy," she said ruefully. "I've been spending my entire life trying to get famous and it sounds like you've beaten me to it."

"I... I don't like this."

"Are you coping? Are you getting any sleep?"

"Yep."

"Are you eating?"

"Yep."

"No, I mean, are you *eating*?"

"Oh... I mean, maybe a bit more than –"

"Boy! It's not healthy. I don't mean physically, I mean... that's not going to solve anything. You need to let yourself *feel* this stuff, you can't just bottle it up or you'll end up exploding one day."

"You're starting to sound like Terry."

"And Terry knows his stuff. Say what you like about him, he helped Mum be less unhappy."

"That wasn't the therapy. That was the se–"

"It was, though. He helped her *forgive* herself about Greece, which is exactly–"

"Stop making comparisons," I snapped. "T-the difference you seem to have missed is that it wasn't her fault in the first place. It was, once again, *mine*."

"It's more complicated than that, though, isn't it?" said Big Sis, sounding pained. "She knows she should never have put you in a situation like that. It was too much responsibility for you."

We'd had this conversation too many times in the past. I found it endlessly frustrating that every time we went over it, Big Sis didn't dispute any of the facts of what happened, but still somehow tried to deny the inevitable conclusions. I couldn't face going over the same ground yet again, so I changed topic.

"Look, I just... I really thought I was good at this stuff," I said.

"But you *are* good at this stuff. You've been a tech super-nerd for years."

"Well, yeah, I thought so. But, uh... have you heard of the Dunning-Kruger effect?"

"It sounds like one of Terry's prog-rock bands."

"It... it basically says that incompetent people tend to over-estimate their abilities. It's when you know so little that you don't even know how much you don't know. The point is, in tech everyone talks about Dunning-Kruger. It's the label you stick on the idiots around you to make you feel better about the fact that they're making your life harder. A-and this week I discovered that Dunning-Kruger is about me."

"Bollocks," snapped Big Sis abruptly. "Now you're just being maudlin. Sometimes you fuck up, and sometimes it's in public. But honestly, you just have to ride it out. One event does not define you."

I considered arguing, but decided against it. Big Sis had switched from sympathy mode to chivvying mode, and past experience had taught me that my window for pity had closed. Better to change the subject entirely

"How's it going with Ruby?"

Big Sis immediately let out a sigh.

"Well you know what, she really pissed me off this week..." she began.

*

Big Sis's latest emotional dramas were at least a distraction from my own woes, and by the time I hung up I wasn't in quite such a pitiful state as I'd been in at the start of the day. I did another successful inventory of my supplies (and this time I was careful to add two whole cook-in-the-bag chickens to my next grocery list – apparently *those* cravings were back, and I didn't want to be caught unawares by them again, given how disastrously wrong it had gone last time), and treated myself to a rewatch of the *City of Death* Doctor Who story arc. Four expertly crafted episodes, their quirky plot-line and dialogue betraying the pseudonymous involvement of Douglas Adams, were enough to get me back on an even keel. So long as I avoided thinking at all about the past, present, or future, I could convince myself I was in reasonable spirits.

The next day, though, I was back in a slump. My attempts to re-initiate communication with Thomas 'Boffinism' Charles were met with stony silence. Worse, the more digging I did on him, the more I began to suspect he had been bluffing about his privileged knowledge. Looking through his comment history on various tech forums, this wasn't the first time he'd confidently announced insider information on big events in the tech world, and I didn't come across any evidence to support any of his claims. I felt increasingly foolish for naively believing him, and tying myself in knots just because he'd dangled the possibility of telling me what I needed to know. That's the kind of gullibility that just goes to prove how much I'm not cut out for the real world.

Self-recrimination aside, where did that leave me? Stuck. Bored. Even, and this one was a bit of a shock, *lonely*. I'd never considered myself to enjoy, in any meaningful sense of the term, the company of my workmates (with the exception of

Debi, with respect to whom my feelings were rather complicated). When I thought about the Bunker Buddies, mostly what I thought about was how stressful I found it to navigate them: how I felt responsible for team cohesion, but was totally unequipped to defuse the tensions that arose between, say, Rémy and literally everyone else. Or how I felt complicit in the endemic gender biases that held back Debi as my subordinate even though in terms of raw skill she left some of the other Enterprise Architects in the company in the dust. I thought about how much I hated waiting at the bus stop with Bled because I felt obliged, but of course unable, to make conversation. How I so, so wanted to tell Kayla how impressed I was by how hard she was working, and how despite the gaps in her subject matter knowledge she still made immeasurable positive contributions to the team, but in three years had never even *started* to find a way of phrasing it.

Every thought I had about the Bunker Buddies wormed its way back to my own inadequacies, and I realised I was always too busy obsessing over those to notice that, despite everything, I liked being around them. Even when things were going wrong. Even when I had nothing to say.

It was a shame that such a revelation only came now, when, given how things were going, the chances were I'd never get to hang out with them again. Not unless by some miracle I could salvage something from the Maison de Gauguin disaster.

And then, as if on cue, Sandspidr emailed back.

You'll kick yourself...

That was all. Three words, but what a lot you could read into them. On the one hand, they were telling me that it was something obvious when you saw it. Not some previously un-heard-of vulnerability, not some extremely subtle edge case, but something that was staring us in the face all the time. Plus, the repetition of 'you'... did that confirm it was something I had done myself, rather than anyone else on the team?

I tried to take a step back. Take everything we knew about the hack, and work it through from first principles. Start from the simple premise that there was evidently a flaw in Labyrinth that needed to be found, work in everything we knew about how the attackers had acted and what weaknesses we'd discovered so far, and fill in the blanks from there.

I worked through every possibility. I spent all day on it. I got nowhere. I spent the evening sulking and eating pizza.

On Friday I picked myself up again and tried a new approach. The significance of Sandspidr's message wasn't the message, it was Sandspidr himself. (Or potentially *her*self, but statistically that was unlikely.) I went hunting for anything I could find online about him. Unfortunately there wasn't much I could turn up. He didn't post on any of the tech forums I knew about, either the respectable or the shady ones. Or at least if he did, he did it using a different username, and I had no way of joining the dots.

After lunch I started getting notifications from the YakYak app on my phone. It seemed like the Bunker Buddies were taking a break from work to finally get round to the riddle competition we'd missed last week, and people were taking time to get their answers in before the final scores were tallied. I was in the lead so far, having already solved Kayla and Rémy's submissions. No one had cracked Debi's. That left Bled's, which he'd only just submitted (it was one of those 'move one matchstick to make this sum work' things, which was, frankly, trivial and disappointing even by his standards), and my own entry, a sudoku-inspired puzzle that used Roman numerals and symmetry-based rules to make it more interesting. It was absolutely solvable through pure logic alone, but I seriously doubted anyone on the team would get it. This was the one competition I had been planning on allowing myself to win this month, after all.

I watched on my phone as Kayla asked for a couple of clarifications on Debi's puzzle (not particularly revealing ones, as all they did was to establish that the normal rules of physics applied), and Rémy swiftly solved Bled's matchstick problem. Bled then offered a wrong-but-not-entirely-without-merit response to my Roman clock sudoku, which left me in a quandary: for the competition to work, the setter of each puzzle needed to adjudicate all responses to their submission. Until I said whether or not Bled had got it right or not, they wouldn't know whether to assign points to me or him. But I wasn't sure that I was supposed to be active on YakYak, given that I wasn't really working for Paladin at the moment. Plus I wasn't entirely certain that the team would want me to be online, even if I was allowed to. I was disgraced, after all, and my failures had surely dragged them down by association. I was pretty sure that if I was them, I'd want nothing to do with me.

In the end I sent Kayla a private message offering to share with her the solution to my puzzle if she wanted to take over adjudicating it. She replied immediately:

@K: Hey! It's so great to hear from you! How are you doing?

@C: I'm fine. I'm so sorry about everything.

@K: ??

@C: Have you guys made any progress?

@K: Not really. Looks like Moritz had some sort of dodgy antivirus installed on his computer, and we think it deleted something from his hard drive on the night of the hack, but we don't know what it was and we don't know if it's relevant.

@K: We really miss you, you know that, right?

I felt a brief but powerful urge to reply that I missed them too, that I really wished I could be there with them. But I don't say things like that to people. Sentiments like that introduce a level of volatility to interpersonal relationships that I'm not comfortable with. And besides, I assured myself, Kayla was obliged to say something like that, but she probably didn't mean it. And even if she did, at best she was speaking for herself, and what she really meant was that she disliked having more responsibility to shoulder now that I was gone.

@C: I'm really sorry, I've got to go. Good luck with the riddles. If someone gives a right answer to mine I'll tell you.

No one else tried to solve my sudoku. The points I got for that, and for my solutions the previous week, made me the clear winner. Debi came second, thanks to no one solving her submission. I couldn't remember the details of it now. A locked box, and a thief who got the treasure out without opening it, was that it? There was an uncomfortable parallel with Labyrinth there, I realised. No wonder no one had solved it.

14

It was a tiresome weekend. I spent Saturday ignoring self-serving messages from Mum asking me to ring her because she'd heard that work wasn't going well from Big Sis and she was *oh so worried* about me. I played some ludicrously complicated real-time military strategy games to try to take my mind off everything, and ate fairly constantly to make myself feel better.

I also spent a fair amount of time on AltMatch for similar reasons.

HarlequinCyanide: Fuck me I had to deal with a lot of morons yesterday.

THX1137: ?

HarlequinCyanide: (work rant coming up)

HarlequinCyanide: Some guy who ordered a t shirt in the wrong size wanted us to send him a replacement for free.

HarlequinCyanide: But he wasn't prepared to send back the original. And he wanted a refund for it.

HarlequinCyanide: So instead of getting 1 shirt for £20, he expected 2 for nothing. Even though HE was the one who ordered the wrong one in the first place

THX1137: You can't blame him for trying

HarlequinCyanide: That's the sad thing. He wasn't just trying his luck. He literally thought that's what our "refund and replacement" policy meant. He wasn't angry or anything, he was just... confused.

HarlequinCyanide: And don't get me started on the ones ringing to cancel their gym membership who didn't realise they signed a 12-month contract. I swear my job is 90% talking to stupid people. I think my IQ is being drained out of me – not that I had much to begin with!

THX1137: Sometimes I worry that that's what people at work think when they talk to me.

HarlequinCyanide: Naw, you're an elite cyber-whatsit, right? I bet you're scary intelligent.

THX1137: Trust me, you can be intelligent on paper and still be a total fuckwit.

HarlequinCyanide: Nah, I don't believe you. You're no fuckwit.

THX1137: Don't be so sure. I screwed up massively recently.

HarlequinCyanide: I'm sure it wasn't so bad.

THX1137: I mean, we lost literally millions of pounds...

HarlequinCyanide: Fuuuuuck

HarlequinCyanide: What did you do?

THX1137: That's the worst part. I have no idea. I thought I'd done everything perfectly, and then... boom.

HarlequinCyanide: That sucks. I'm really sorry.

HarlequinCyanide: So, like, is that how much it'll cost to repair it?

HarlequinCyanide: Or, wait, do you mean you literally lost the money?

I started to type a reply, then pulled my fingers up sharply, Roisin's warning about not talking to anyone about the hack suddenly ringing in my ears.

THX1137: I'm so sorry

THX1137: I'm *really* not supposed to talk about it

THX1137: Sorry

THX1137: It's playing on my mind so much I'm not thinking straight.

THX1137: Forget I said anything?

HarlequinCyanide: Of course!

HarlequinCyanide: And don't forget, I'm such a high-powered hacker myself that I already know everything there is to know about you, so you weren't telling me anything new.

HarlequinCyanide: But your secret is safe with me.

*

At just after 4 o'clock on Sunday my doorbell rang, jolting me into an immediate state of panic. I wasn't expecting any deliveries. Could this be another photographer? A journalist? A Pony Club assassin?

I froze, of course, but could nearly convince myself that it was a deliberate choice, and that ignoring the doorbell was the most sensible course of action. But then it rang again, and again, and I began to worry that the person outside *knew* I was in and my refusal to acknowledge them was only making them angrier, which, given their likely motive for turning up in the first place, might not end well for me.

Eventually I picked up the entryphone and, in faltering tones, said, "Uh... h-hello?"

"Colin! Hi! Can I come up?"

I blanked for a second. The voice was so out of place in this context that it took me a moment to recognise it as Debi's.

Debi. Had come to my flat.

"Uh..."

"Come on Colin, I really need a wee."

Debi wanted to do a wee. On my toilet.

I buzzed her up.

Look. *No one* comes into my flat. I don't have friends over, and not just because I don't have friends. I don't want other people in here. I don't even let Big Sis in – I make her meet me in the café round the corner. The last time someone who wasn't me came into my flat was about three years ago, when my dishwasher broke. I basically hid in the bathroom the entire time the repairman was there.

And now Debi was heading up the stairs, and I was, to put it very mildly, flustered. I stood awkwardly in my hallway, and when she knocked I had to take a steadying breath before shakily opening up the door.

"Hey stranger," she said warmly.

"G'uh..." I breathed. "Uh... bathroom is, uh..."

"Oh, don't worry about that, I just said that to get you to let me in," she said breezily, brushing past me in a way that nearly caused me to topple over. "Lovely flat. A bit boyish, but I like it."

She grinned, and it was like I'd got a pat on the head from my favourite teacher (if I was physiologically and emotionally equipped to cope with forms of physical contact such as pats on the head, that is).

"H-how did you get my address?"

"Oh please," she replied dismissively, "I'm a security engineer and I've known you for more than a month. Of *course* I've got your home address. Also, your national insurance number starts with a J. Anyway, I just wanted to chat to you about some work stuff, if that's ok. Do you wanna put the kettle on?"

I did as she suggested, and then realised it was pointless because presumably Debi wanted tea, and I don't have tea in the flat. (The kettle is there mostly to make Pot Noodles.) I explained this apologetically to her, and she just rolled her eyes and fetched herself a cup of water instead. Then she marched into my sitting room, plonked herself down on the sofa, looked up at me and patted the seat next to her invitingly.

My sofa is small, and I am large, and I wanted to avoid touching her when I sat down even more than I wanted *not* to avoid touching her when I sat down. So I squeezed myself into the farthest corner as tightly as I could, awkwardly angling my knees off to one side. We sat there in silence for a second.

"So," began Debi, "When are you going to ask Holly out?"

"Uh, I don't... uh..." I stammered, completely blindsided. Who was Holly? Oh! The Charades woman. What on earth was Debi on about?

"Oh come on. *Surely* you realised why I invited you both over. She's single, and God knows I wasn't going to set her up with *Bled*. It's perfect, she's really nice, you guys have the same hobbies, and she's just your type."

"She's not my –"

I realised I didn't want to get drawn into a discussion about my 'type' with Debi. *That* conversation would get pretty awkward pretty quickly. So I changed tack.

"Uh... what hobbies?"

"Board games of course!"

"I... no. Thanks, but..."

"Well, don't say I don't do anything for you. Honestly, I've set this one up on a plate."

"Ok. Well, uh, thanks for explaining."

I started to stand up.

"Oh, no, that wasn't what I wanted to talk to you about," said Debi, shaking her head and gesturing me back down. "That was just a word to the wise. What I really want to talk to you about is Labyrinth."

"Yeah?"

This was, ironically, safer territory. I felt myself relax slightly.

"So I've been on source code duty for the past couple of days, while you've been out of the office, and... well, I think I've found something."

"S-seriously?" I squeaked, excitedly. "Something as in the vulnerability?"

"Well, look, I'm in the very early stages. I'm hoping to settle down with it this evening and make a start on it, but... I actually wanted to ask your advice."

"Uh... Ok..." I said cautiously. This conversation was a rollercoaster already, and I still didn't know what she had actually come to talk to me about.

Debi paused briefly, as if searching for the right words. That wasn't like her. She was normally completely self-assured.

"After... after the logs thing, I was quite upset. I put a lot of effort into understanding what was going on there, and then Rémy tried to shut me down, and let's be honest *you* tried to shut me down too, and then Bled took an interest and ended up swooping in to take all the glory. And look, goodness knows I'm not some ego-obsessive or anything, but I really felt like I deserved some of the credit."

She took a sip of water, and I realised that at the moment *she* was the one avoiding eye contact.

"And now I think I may be on to something, and I don't want the same thing to happen again. So I haven't told anyone about it. In fact, I got the basic idea earlier this week but I didn't even look at it until this morning so I could do it at home without anyone else being able to see my screen. Which is crazy, and paranoid, but... I really want this one. I know that's selfish. Because if I shared where I'd got to so far, maybe someone else would have got us the rest of the way already, maybe Rémy or Bled would have unravelled the whole thing by now. But still, I want to keep it to myself. I guess what I'm asking is... is that ok?"

I considered for a moment. I didn't think Debi had ever asked me for advice. She was showing a vulnerability I'd never seen before. God help me, I couldn't even begin to unpick the surge of emotions that provoked in me.

"I think you should keep it to yourself until you crack it." I said, after a pause. "If you've found something after the rest of us have all tried and failed, you deserve the credit. If that means doing it quietly by yourself, then that's fine by me. I... I think you're within your rights to do whatever you can to get the recognition you deserve. I know it can be an uphill battle at times being... a woman... uh, I mean, a woman engineer, so... yeah. Use this. Plus, knowing you, you'll have it all figured out faster than anyone else could anyway."

Debi smiled sheepishly.

"Aww... you're the best Colin. But the other thing is... well, Labyrinth is your baby. And I know it hurts when other people criticise the things you care about. If I find something, and it's an actual security hole... will you be upset with me?"

I shook my head.

"Honestly at this point I just want to know. If you can put me out of my misery you'll be doing me a favour."

Then Debi leant across and gave me a big hug. It was incredibly uncomfortable, because (a) there's my thing about physical contact in general and (b) I'm pretty sure no one can pull off a seated hug with aplomb. I just sat there awkwardly; I didn't hug back. But I didn't pull away either.

Eventually Debi straightened up.

"Also, speaking as a friend here, have you heard of Perspirica? It's, like, an industrial strength anti-perspirant. Jason's dad uses it. I'm just saying... maybe try it out?"

15

How do you always manage to get everything so wrong, Colin?

Those were the first coherent words out of Mum's mouth after I woke her up and explained to her what happened. She looked at me, her expression anguished and panicked, but the sentiment expressed by her intonation was, more than anything else, one of disappointment.

Then came the flurry of activity. We hurried down to reception, where frog-woman *again* chastised me for waiting for her phone call to end before telling her what had happened. She then explained to Mum, who was verging on hysterics, how the ambulance had already left with Little Sis in it, and why she couldn't *possibly* drive us to the hospital or lend us her car, but she'd be happy to call us a taxi.

The shrivelled little taxi driver who eventually came seemed confused as to where we were headed, and frog-woman had to spell it out several times for him. Apparently there were several hospitals in the region, and they hadn't taken Little Sis to the closest one. On the drive over, he several times tried to ask us something, but he knew no English and, despite his growing impatience, my grasp of Greek didn't magically improve over the course of the journey.

The hospital itself was a nightmare of confusion. No one knew who we were, or where Little Sis might be, or who we should ask, and Mum just repeated "English, English, English" whenever a new person approached. Finally, just as we began to worry that frog-woman had sent the taxi driver to the wrong hospital, a bilingual nurse took charge of us, walked us all the way from one end of the complex to the other, and introduced us to a surgeon holding some bits of paper with the name 'Daphne Clayford' on them. He explained, with her translating the complicated bits, that she was alive, but in a critical condition. We could not see her yet. They had just removed a section of her skull, which they were holding onto for future re-insertion. The danger at the moment, he said, was not from the damage from the original impact, but from the build-up of pressure on her brain from the internal bleeding that had followed in the subsequent minutes. Time was of the essence in situations like these, we were told, and as he said this my legs started wobbling and I ended up flat on my back in the hospital corridor, the nurse fussing over me and Mum not even trying to conceal her frustration.

The next day I flew back to England by myself. Mum stayed on, to be with Little Sis. She said she couldn't manage looking after me too. It was easier for everyone this way, she said. So Big Sis met me at Gatwick and took me back home. She had only heard a very mixed-up, garbled version of events from Mum, so she needed me to explain everything that happened. I tearfully told her everything, how I froze, how I was too weak, how I was too scared, how because of me part of Little Sis's skull was in a freezer in a hospital.

"Oh Boy," she said, and pulled me into a hug. "You weren't cut out for any of this. You just can't cope, can you? But it's ok. I'll look after you now, I promise."

LAMDA said Big Sis could re-start the course again the following year, and she moved back home to take care of me. Little Sis was eventually transferred back to England, where they reconstructed her skull, and came to the ghastly realisation that something had gone wrong with the wiring between her head and her body, and she was effectively paralysed down her entire left side. Her rehabilitation was drawn-out and not hugely effective. Mum was more or less by her side every day. I visited her too, at weekends, but I never knew what to say, and she never seemed keen to talk. She knew whose fault it was. I could see it in her eyes.

Finally, she was discharged. Her left leg meant she couldn't walk, and without the use of her left arm either, crutches didn't really work for her, so she was given a wheelchair. Mentally she was more or less back to normal, but something in her personality had changed. The doctors occasionally mentioned 'dysexecutive syndrome', but never really explained it. She had always been outspoken, but now she was more so. She was quicker to anger, quicker to criticise. She fought with Mum constantly. And she more or less ignored me.

It wasn't long before she announced that she'd been making inquiries, and had found a charity scholarship program for children with disabilities that would pay for her to attend a private boarding school. She'd already completed the application forms, she just needed Mum to sign them. A year before she'd been my closest and only friend. Now she was prepared to leave her entire family behind just to get away from me.

*

Anyway, speaking of awful moments in my life: Monday started with a message from Kayla:

Can you come in to the office? Anil wants to see us first thing.

By itself that first sentence would have been cause for celebration. I had been dreading another week of kicking around at home by myself. But the second sentence annihilated any the joy inspired by its predecessor. Anil was not the sort of person who asked to see you when things were going well.

It took me seventeen minutes to muster up the courage to make it out of my door. In the past week I hadn't once left home. As much as my flat had started to feel stuffy and claustrophobic, the outside world was now a much scarier place than it had been before. It was only fear of incurring Anil's wrath by not turning up on time that eventually propelled me out and down onto the street, and even then I had to stop myself turning tail when I reached my bus stop.

Kayla intercepted me at reception.

"It's so good to see you!" she exclaimed, and maybe it's just my ego talking but some of her enthusiasm sounded almost genuine to my ears.

"H-hi. Uh… do you know what this is about?"

She shook her head, and shepherded me towards Citadel, one of the meeting rooms. The door was open, so we went in. Anil was there, with Brad and, unexpectedly, Debi. But a Debi who looked so different to her usual self that for a moment I almost didn't recognise her. Gone was the goth attire, and in its place she was wearing a long navy skirt and a white blouse, with a high neckline and sleeves long enough to cover almost all of her tattoos. She was wearing a bare minimum of makeup, ditching her trademark black cherry lipstick entirely. She looked, to be honest, pretty much like a normal person, for the first time since I'd known her.

Kayla was clearly as nonplussed as me, but Anil impatiently gestured for us to sit down, denying us a chance to gawp.

"Thank you everyone for coming in," he began, "The reason we're here is that Debi contacted me last night, apparently having found the vulnerability in Labyrinth."

"Seriously?" exclaimed Kayla. "That's great!"

"Well, I still haven't got all of it worked out," said Debi. "I don't quite know how they exploited it, but I've definitely found a vulnerability."

Only yesterday afternoon she'd been in my flat telling me she had the beginnings of something. Clearly she had had a productive evening. Either that or she had under-played just how much she had already worked out.

"Uh, how… I mean, what did you find?" I asked.

"So I was wondering how they might have accessed the system, and I took a look at the account recovery mechanism. The PIN system is –"

"Maybe take the explanation offline," broke in Anil, and I saw the disappointment in Debi's face as her chance for a big reveal was denied. "We can pore over the technical details later, but right now we have a couple of urgent questions we have to answer. The first is this: based on your understanding of the flaw, Debi, how could the attackers have come to learn about it?"

Debi frowned.

"Oh. Gosh. I haven't really thought about… Well… it's such a specific sequence of events that I don't think trial and error would get them there, because it's pretty obscure."

"What if they had access to the source code?"

"I mean, that would help," she said, thoughtfully. "But… well, being honest with you… and I don't want to sound like I'm showing off… our entire team has been scouring the source code for two weeks and we didn't spot it. The only reason I worked it out was that I already knew there was an error somewhere, so I just kept searching. So for someone just hunting through the code on the off-chance they could find a weakness… I mean it's possible, but they'd have to be a serious genius."

"Very well," said Anil. "So the vulnerability was extremely well concealed while also being extremely potent. Then the second question is this: Would it therefore be reasonable to assert that the easiest way for someone to come to know that the vulnerability existed would be if they had been responsible for placing it there in the first place?"

"Um... what?" said Debi, blinking. She looked as confused as I felt. Was Anil suggesting...

"Being frank, I have been harbouring this suspicion for some time now. The chances of the flaw being created accidentally and discovered through sheer luck seem dwindlingly small. As there are no other credible explanations, Debi, do you agree that it would explain rather a lot if this vulnerability you have discovered was placed in Labyrinth deliberately?"

"Well... yes."

"Debi!" said Kayla, looking shocked. Anil ignored her.

"And who specifically wrote the code in question?"

Debi swallowed, and looked at me.

"I..." she hesitated. "I actually wrote a couple of functions in that module, but the bulk of it was... Colin."

"Now hold on," said Kayla. "It's way too early to start accusing –"

"No one is accusing anyone of anything, Kayla, not yet," cut in Anil. "We are trying to work together to establish –"

"How can we work on anything together if we don't even know what the issue is?"

"Fine," said Anil, slightly more testily than usual. I got the sense he wasn't accustomed to being interrupted by his subordinates. "Debi, for Kayla's sake can you give at least a high-level overview of what you've discovered?"

"Well," began Debi, with less enthusiasm than before, "I was thinking about how a user could bypass our usual security mechanisms, and I started to poke around in the rather complex system we have for resetting your password if you forget it. Anyway, a lot of it hinges on generating a unique temporary PIN code and texting it to you. I went looking for ways someone could find out what the code is without being the recipient of the message, through some sort of side channel, and –"

And then it clicked. Side channel. A memory of a thought process burst back into my mind. A little under a fortnight ago, half-awake, in the shower, I had thought of an issue. It was massively speculative, right on the boundary between the possible and the merely theoretical, but I had picked up on it.

"It's a timing attack," I said. "Oh good grief. The way we built it... uh, theoretically you could try to guess the PIN and could measure how long it took the server to respond to infer how many digits you'd got right. But if you tried that it would immediately show up in the logs unless..."

Another piece of the puzzle fell into place.

"Uh, unless you knew that there were a few minutes every couple of hours when the logs weren't working."

There was a silence. I looked over at Debi, who was nodding at me, her face carefully neutral.

"You... knew about this?" asked Kayla.

"Yes. No. I think I figured out part of it a while back but I didn't join the dot–"

"Colin," said Anil. "Discovering a vulnerability of this magnitude and not disclosing it immediately is a *huge* infraction."

"No, I... I forgot..."

The look in Anil's eyes told me that he was treating that excuse with *exactly* as much sympathy as it deserved.

"Being blunt here, you've just admitted that you knew about the vulnerability before it was exploited. I don't think you appreciate the pressure I've been under from the board to take some strong action in order to take back control of the public narrative. Particularly in light of the press storm you've managed to whip up around yourself personally..."

Anil kept talking but I stopped listening. My entire world was collapsing around me. In the space of 5 minutes I had gone from merely incompetent to *criminal*, all thanks to... thanks to Debi. Who had just handed Anil my head on a plate.

Debi who was dressed to impress today.

Debi, who had yesterday asked my blessing to try to use her discovery to strengthen her standing at Paladin, even if it meant landing me in trouble. And I had encouraged her. Only now was I learning what the consequences of that truly were.

I had to give her credit, though. The vulnerability she had found was incredibly obscure.

In fact, it was more than obscure. It was *impossible.*

"T-this isn't right," I said, only realising once the words were past my lips that I was speaking out loud. "We only give you three tries at getting the PIN right before we change it. There's no way you'd be able to guess it unless you could get it to reset to the same PIN every time, and–"

"Oh sure," said Debi, "There are lots of practical details that we haven't nailed down yet – I've only had the weekend. But... the principle is there.."

"But it's too obscure. They said it was something simple..." I tailed off.

"Who said it was something simple?" asked Anil, his voice heavy with suspicion. "Colin?"

I closed my eyes.

"Pony Club. They contacted me last week."

"You didn't mention this before."

"I... I didn't think..."

"Christ, Colin, of all the imbecilic... God, I doubt I really want to hear the answer to this, but I don't suppose you happened to inform anyone about this potentially *massively significant lead*?"

"N-no."

Beside me I could see in my peripheral vision Kayla covering her face with her hand. Debi caught my eye and gave a half-smiling, semi-sympathetic little shrug as if to say *I'm sorry for you, but you dug that hole you're sitting in yourself.* Which was fair enough really.

Anil looked across at Brad, who had sat silently through the whole exchange. Brad looked back at Anil, and gave a small but unmistakable shake of his head.

"Colin and Debi, could I ask for a couple of minutes to discuss this with Brad and Kayla? If you wouldn't mind, just wait outside."

The two of us rose and left the room, closing the door behind us. A long silence ensued, during which I did my level best to bore a hole in my shoes with the power of my gaze.

"Well that escalated quickly," said Debi eventually.

"Yeah."

"I didn't think you'd be landed in it quite so hard when I –"

"When you told Anil I'd probably done it deliberately?" I said bitterly.

"I didn't say that."

"No, but you didn't *f-fucking* well disagree!"

I was amazed by the words that were coming out of mouth. I don't *do* outward displays of emotion. I certainly don't shout at people. But just this once I didn't seem to be able to stop myself.

Debi's face hardened, and she shrugged.

"Anil asked for my honest answer, and all I said was I can't see how *else* they could have figured out about the timing attack." She spoke to me like she was chastising a small child. "You can be angry at me all you want, but I think when you've calmed down you should reflect on whether I'm really the enemy here."

Then the door opened and Kayla was motioning for me to come back in. Her expression told me very clearly what was waiting for me inside.

*

I was formally suspended, effective immediately, pending a full investigation into my involvement with the MDG heist. Paladin immediately released a short statement to that effect. They didn't go into any specifics, but their pointed use of the phrase 'deliberate or otherwise' made it pretty clear to anyone paying attention that the two possibilities under consideration were negligence or collusion.

There was no coming back from this one. Even if it was eventually established that I wasn't in fact a part of Pony Club, my professional reputation would be forever absolute garbage. It was one thing for an irate client to be making hostile allegations; it was quite another to be disavowed by my employer. No one in the industry would so much as touch me now.

With Kayla in tow, Brad escorted me straight down to reception as soon as Anil was done with me, where he made me hand over my ID badge and keys. I wasn't allowed to actually leave until Brad could confirm that my access to all internal systems had been revoked, so while he headed back into the building to run through the appropriate processes, I waited awkwardly with Kayla, continuing to stare at my shoes as much as possible. She had been almost entirely silent since Anil informed me of his decision, and it was only when I heard a strangled sniff that I looked up and realised she was crying.

"Oh, uh, hey..."

"Oh god I'm sorry. I shouldn't... It's just that it's so unfair! And I know it's only a temporary thing and I know, I *know* it'll all be sorted out, but I've just been working so FUCKING hard to keep everyone together, and, and I haven't even *slept* in about two days and now suddenly we're all just kicking you when you're down just for the sake of a fucking 'narrative', and all the team solidarity I've been trying to build over the last year counts for *nothing* when there's a sniff of a promotion, and I'm just... I'm just sick of it. I'm sorry."

"It's ok," I said awkwardly. Then: "H-hey, what promotion?"

Kayla looked at me.

"Who do you think takes over as tech lead in the Bunker now?"

"Debi? But... I mean, she didn't know I'd be getting suspended."

"No, but she sure as shit tried her hardest to make it happen, didn't she?"

"It's not like that. She just wanted her contribution to..."

I tailed off. I realised I had no reason to be defending Debi. It was just a knee-jerk reaction to take her side. Something I needed to work on, probably. Actually no, no it wasn't. I'd never get the chance to take Debi's side on anything ever again.

Brad returned.

"You're all sorted. So that's it. Um, take care of yourself. We'll... we'll be in touch, obviously. Well, us or the police. In the meantime, um, lay low, yeah? Try to stay away from the press, and it goes without saying, don't make any public statements, don't contact any other employees or clients. Maybe... take an online course or something?"

"Brad?" said Kayla, wiping her eyes. "Stop talking."

"No, I just mean that –"

"Oh my *God* Brad!"

He stopped himself and nodded. Kayla then turned to me and gave me an awkward hug. I did my best not to flinch and squirm.

"Take care of yourself. We won't abandon you. We'll figure out what happened, and we'll show it wasn't your fault. It'll be ok. I promise."

"Well..." interjected Brad, "You probably shouldn't say that until –"

"Brad I swear to fucking God if you don't walk away from here immediately I will resign here and now and I *will* tell HR about Riga."

"Ok... ok," said Brad, raising his hands and backed away.

Kayla and I shared a look. I had no idea what the significance of Riga was, but there was some satisfaction to be had from seeing Brad put in his place.

"I'll speak to you again soon, ok?" said Kayla.

"Ok. Uh... thank you. For everything."

I turned and walked out of the office.

16

I made my way home in a daze. The bus stop was crowded, but I didn't even bother with the Gabardine Suit Game. It didn't seem to matter. Nothing did.

A 149 arrived, and I heaved myself up to the top deck and found a space to sit. The bus drifted northward, and as it went, slowly my thoughts began to settle into something approaching coherence. The figure that kept appearing in my mind's eye was Debi. Alongside the expected surging sense of betrayal, and the old tide of complex emotions ranging from fear to lust, something new was emerging: suspicion.

The thing was, I agreed with Anil. If Labyrinth really was vulnerable to some massively obscure timing attack (which still didn't feel right to me, but I had to let that slide for now), and Pony Club had indeed used it, then the best explanation, surely, was that the vulnerability was put there deliberately by the person who wrote the code. I couldn't blame anyone for coming to that conclusion. However, *I* wrote the code. And I definitely didn't do it deliberately, and I definitely didn't tell Pony Club about it. In which case, the *second* best explanation for what happened was that the vulnerability had been introduced accidentally by me, and then someone malicious had found it. It would have to be someone who had spent a *long* time poring over the source code, with an excellent understanding of the system as a whole, a very sharp mind and a comprehensive understanding of cyber-security. I knew only one person who ticked all of those boxes, and that was Debi. Of course, it was no big revelation that Debi found the vulnerability; she had, after all, announced as much just now. But the question that started buzzing round my mind as I sat on that bus was, *when* did she find it?

Suppose she didn't spot it over the weekend. Suppose she spotted it several months ago. Suppose she was disillusioned with her role at Paladin, languishing in the Bunker, not taken seriously by her male colleagues, and feeling the financial pinch while trying to raise two children in London. Just *suppose* it occurred to her that what she had uncovered had significant value to a certain sort of person, and she decided to make the most of it. She could have got in touch with Pony Club and helped them plan an elaborate heist. There's an awful lot they would have needed to put in place, but that's ok; there was no rush. So long as they could track payments as they came and went, they could set things up at their leisure and then wait for a big enough transaction to come through to make it worth their while to strike – such as, for example, a £7.4m payment for a Nua Nigel original. Debi's only problem then would have been to make sure she was beyond suspicion after the event.

If that's what happened, then Debi had played her part brilliantly. Rather than cover her tracks entirely she had allowed the details of how the attack occurred to leak out piece by piece in such a way that the trail of blame led to my door, not hers. There was not a shred of suspicion associated with her. Fuck, she had even got a *promotion* out of it. And who knew what kind of a cut she might get from Pony Club?

My thoughts were interrupted by a plain-clothed inspector appearing on the upper deck and asking for tickets. She offered some minor pleasantry about it being a nice morning and as usual, I froze up, unable to think of a response, so I just sort of grunted and looked down at my hands. She waited a couple of seconds, until it became clear she wasn't going to get an answer and then moved on, and I felt my usual pang of social guilt.

When she was gone I tried to pick up my previous train of thought, but already my suspicions concerning Debi seemed a bit ridiculous. She was, in her own way, as hard as nails, but she wasn't that calculating, not that callous. Right?

But, however you looked at it, I was done. Regardless of the specifics of the vulnerability, regardless of how Pony Club had achieved what and who helped them, my career was over. Pony Club had compromised my security system, the world had found out, and the head that rolled was, rightly, mine. I could never go back to infosec, never have a presence online. The best case scenario was that I could adopt a pseudonym and perhaps scratch out a living doing bottom-of-the-pecking-order freelance web development gigs. Pony Club could keep their Burncoin; Debi could keep her promotion; Paladin and MDG could say whatever they liked about me. I was simply out of the picture. Worst case I'd get hauled in by DI Otembi and convicted of something ridiculous simply for lack of anyone else to pin the blame on. It just depended on how much more of a kicking the universe wanted to get in before it was done with me. On balance, it was no less than I deserved.

*

Home was the last place in the world I wanted to be. In the past week it had transformed from sanctuary to prison. I wanted to leave it again as soon as I walked in through the door. But that was a ridiculous impulse, and I dismissed it firmly. Where on earth else would I possibly go?

So I bumbled around my flat, distractedly hopping between the kitchen (even though I wasn't really hungry), the bathroom (even though I didn't need to do anything in it), and my chair (even though I couldn't settle in it). I had no idea what I was doing. I didn't have a very clear idea of who I was any more. I had been *Colin Clayford, Enterprise Security Architect at Paladin Technologies Ltd* for so long that if you took away the epithet I wasn't sure what remained to be claimed by *Colin Clayford, Unemployed.* Gods, maybe I should have invested in a hobby when I was younger, just for the sake of a little ontological continuity.

In the end, it wasn't boredom that brought me back to Pony Club. It wasn't curiosity. It was desperation. I needed to know how badly I had messed up. The only bit I had ever really liked about adult me was that I thought I was good at my job. I knew for certain now that I was never as good as I thought. But for the sake of preserving my basic sense of self I needed to believe that I wasn't quite as grossly incompetent as the world now thought me. And to justify that belief, I needed to know more about what actually happened.

I couldn't face having yet another go at dissecting the code I'd written. Increasingly that felt like the wrong place to look for answers. Realistically, the only people in the world who actually knew how Pony Club had hacked us were Pony Club themselves. If I was going to go after the truth, the most efficient thing would be to get it from them. Boffinism was a dead end, and my attempts to interrogate Sandspidr had been a total failure, but was there another way?

How would Pony Club have planned this? Surely there was more than one person involved. If so, how did they talk to one another? As an organisation I was prepared to believe they existed exclusively online. They were probably a group who'd found each other on the dark web and never met one another in person. So they must done all their communication over the internet. Often, distributed hacker collectives use a large and ever-changing network of chat apps, forums and more. Some are more accessible to outsiders than others, and the more accessible they are, the less of value that's said on them. But at the heart of it there's always a *place*, whether it's a website, a WhatsApp group or an email mailing list, where the core team talks openly. It's very hard to reach, this innermost layer of the onion, but that's where the real secrets are to be found. Groups like that pay an awful lot of attention to making sure their written communications stay secret. But everybody slips up eventually...

I would never normally have taken this approach. It was too vague, to untargeted, too tangential. But I had nothing else to be doing, and I was dimly aware that if I didn't do *something* I was liable to start crying, and I had a suspicion that if I began I'd find it very difficult to stop.

I used as my starting points the various forums and cha-trooms I knew of where wannabe hackers vied for kudos by bragging about their exploits. I found a few mentions of Pony Club on a few of these message boards, and let myself dive down a couple of rabbit holes, tracking the people who mentioned it across the Internet to see where else they cropped up. Before I knew it, a couple of hours had passed, and I had found my way to a semi-hidden forum that had been frequented by Pony Club's apparent leader, 'Divvi', in the past few months. It wasn't much – obviously these were publicly accessible sites and therefore no one would put anything sensitive on them – but I did find a lot of interactions between Divvi and some small-time hacker who went by the handle RattMan, mostly about obscure ways of hijacking the cameras in baby monitors. The final exchange ended with Divvi saying: 'Let's talk more in private – come find me on Stableyard.'

That was it, I was sure of it. That was where Pony Club talked, openly, to one another. A few more searches confirmed it: every so often, in the context of Pony Club, hackers would make discreet reference to something called Stableyard.

But even though I now knew what it was called, finding it wasn't straightforward. No one ever explained how to get to it. The access point was evidently a secret, and one that was guarded jealously from the uninitiated.

However, a secret like that doesn't last long on the Internet. There was always someone stupid or malicious enough to let it out. A few very precise searches of online archives of since-deleted forum discussions, and I had it: a link to a Tor site on the dark web. I loaded it up, and found there was just one publicly accessible page. At the top it said, simply:

'Welcome to the Stableyard, official home of the Pony Club. Tell us why we should let you in.'

Underneath was a text box and a submit button.

Time to get creative. I introduced myself as 'morlok'. I made up a respectable mid-level hacker resume, and dropped heavy hints that I had information to share. I set up a new email account set to forward everything to my Gmail, and included the address along with everything else, so they had a way to contact me. Once I'd read over my submission a few times over, with fingers trembling with excitement, I hit 'submit'…

And frustratingly, all that happened was that the form was replaced with a little message saying: 'Thanks. We'll get back to you.'

That was it then. Nothing to do now but wait and see. I checked the time, and was shocked to discover it was 1:40am.

Without realising it I'd been at work at my computer more or less continuously for well over 12 hours. I'd barely eaten in that time, and I hadn't felt tired at all. In fact, for the first time in a long time I had felt fully energised. But now, leaning back from my laptop screen, I did feel the pull of sleep, so I logged off, scoffed some biscuits, and crawled into bed.

17

The morning brought with it a pleasant surprise. The Stableyard admins had sent me a message: They had already reviewed and approved my submission. I was in. Offering a quiet prayer of thanks for the speedy efficiency of the hacker community, I clicked on the link they'd provided and logged on.

Stableyard wasn't much to look at: a very basic, old-fashioned forum with profile pages for each user and not much else. The forum was divided into 'channels', each devoted to particular topics. But the bulk of the channels were closed off by default, and accessible by invitation only. As a new user, I only had access to the 'General' channel. It turned out that even within Stableyard there were layers of access, and I was still on the outside.

I spent an hour sifting through General to see if there was anything there relating to Labyrinth or timing attacks, but everything in it was fairly nondescript chatter. There was a rudimentary search function, and I searched for references to anything to do with Maison de Gauguin, Paladin and Burncoin, but there was nothing I could dredge up beyond people posting inane things like 'Holy shit, congrats on the Guagin hack – ponies making BANK!!'.

Interestingly, Sandspidr didn't seem to have any presence in the General channel. This strengthened my suspicion that Sandspidr was just a throwaway handle being used by someone else in the organization. But Divvi and Draconix, the two names Scimitar had uncovered in relation to Pony Club, both cropped up from time to time. I was clearly in the right place.

I considered my options. I was fairly confident that somewhere in one of the private channels there would be some record of some people either planning or bragging about the MDG hack. I could see that there was a channel named 'Targets', which seemed like a good candidate. But to get access to that I'd have to worm my way into the trust of the admins, and that would take time.

I didn't feel like waiting, so I hacked Stableyard instead.

*

So here's the thing: while hacking stuff is in some ways fun, sexy, glamorous even, shoring up the defences *against* hackers is really rather boring. I should know, I made a living from it. Which means that *even hackers* won't necessarily bother to put in the work to keep themselves safe, because there are just so many other things they'd rather be doing.

You see where this is going, don't you? I turned everything I knew about security on its head and used it to start looking for illicit ways in. Thanks to a bit of luck and a lot of patience, eventually I found a way of smuggling a sort of digital parasite, a little bit of malicious code, onto the computer of anyone who visited my profile page on Stableyard. The parasite did a few things: First, it searched the Targets channel for references to the MDG attack. While I didn't have access to that channel myself, I reckoned that some of the people who viewed my profile would, so I could 'piggyback' off them to find what I was looking for. Second, it took note of the visitor's username, and sent me that. Third, it ran a series of checks to try to establish the identity of the visitor, sending me their physical location and the name of the WiFi network they were connected to, as well as the details of the computer they were working from.

Once my hack was up and running, I introduced myself on the forum, and mentioned that I'd put some links to my previous work on my profile. If anyone was interested, I hoped they'd at least open up my profile page to have a look, causing my evil little parasite to do its thing and send me the results..

It took me the whole of Tuesday and most of Wednesday to find the vulnerability and build an appropriate script. By the time I had everything up and running and had emerged from tunnel vision mode I was exhausted and very much wasn't excited by the prospect of interactions with another human being.

But it was Wednesday evening, and that meant it was time for my weekly phone call with Big Sis.

*

"What the hell do you mean, 'suspended'?"

"I'm sorry," I said, not entirely sure what I was apologising for. "Uh… they've got this theory about what happened, and I don't think it's right, but… well, they need to figure out the… PR side of things… so they have to blame someone, and I guess… I'm right there…"

"Oh bloody hell." She took a breath. "I think it's time to get out. What happens if you just resign? Give it all up as a bad job, and move on."

"I don't know," I replied. "But, I mean… I don't really want to resign."

"It's not just about what you want at this point. I can't… I can't protect you from all this stuff. I'm sure there's other sorts of work you could do. How about accountancy?" she suggested brightly.

"I don't want to be an accountant! Look, I'm trying something at the moment that –"

"What do you mean?" asked Big Sis, instantly suspicious. "What sort of thing?"

"Nothing, I'm just… doing a little bit of investigating on my own account."

"That sounds shady."

"It's fine. I know what I'm doing."

"No you *don't*, Boy," said Big Sis firmly. "Look, this is a crisis. You can't cope with crises. You know that. And I understand that you're flailing around grasping at straws, but this is exactly what I'm here for: to let you know when you're out of your depth. And it's now, Colin. You're out of your depth *now*. So I'm sorry, but I need you to stop doing whatever it is you're trying to do, and start doing what I tell you to."

Big Sis would have made me draft a resignation letter and sign up to an accounting course then and there if she could, but in the end was at least semi-satisfied with my assurances that I would think about it, that we would talk again on Sunday, and that I wouldn't do anything stupid in the meantime.

I was torn. On the one hand, I knew what she was saying made sense. This was the kind of situation that had me at my very worst, and my judgement was inevitably suspect. Honestly, at this point, the mere fact that I was trying some clandestine surveillance of Pony Club was in itself strong evidence that such a course of action was a terrible idea. Big Sis said it was time to give up and move on, and Big Sis knew what was best for me.

And yet...

*

I couldn't sleep that night. My Stableyard hack hadn't yielded any results yet, so I had to find something else to occupy my attention while I waited. For no reason I could discern I found my thoughts drifting back to Debi's riddle. A locked box in a room, and a thief without a key entering the room and leaving with the treasure's contents. Was it something about the order of events? Did the thief start off with the treasure and leave, then come back empty-handed later? I checked the wording of the riddle. It was fairly unambiguous. Damn Debi. Maybe I should just acknowledge she was, in the final reckoning, a bit brighter than me. She solved the Labyrinth mystery, and I couldn't solve her riddle.

I went to check again whether anything had come in from Stableyard, and, disappointed again, found myself logging on to AltMatch, just for the sake of something to do. I was gratified to see that HarlequinCyanide was online.

HarlequinCyanide: You're up late

THX1137: Yeah, got an itch I need to scratch

HarlequinCyanide: I bet you do lol. Late nite incognito mode session??

THX1137: No! Not like that

HarlequinCyanide: WHEN are they going to add emoji to this thing? I can't BELIEVE it won't let me send phallic eggplant / laughing crying. THERE HAS NEVER BEEN A BETTER TIME

THX1137: I'm so embarrassed

THX1137: I just meant there's something I'm working on and I can't sleep for thinking about it

HarlequinCyanide: Aw that's much less exciting

HarlequinCyanide: Alright, entertain me. What are you working on?

THX1137: It's nothing

I caught myself. What was the point of hiding all this? I really liked HarlequinCyanide, but what kind of a relationship was it if she didn't know anything about my life?

THX1137: Actually no

THX1137: It's something

THX1137: Did you see anything on the news recently about Maison de Gauguin and Pony Club?

HarlequinCyanide: Er, no?

HarlequinCyanide: Hang on, just Googling it

...

HarlequinCyanide: Oh shit, yes, I remember now. Hackers stole a bunch of money, right?

HarlequinCyanide: Holy SHIT, were you involved with that?

THX1137: Yeah. Not in a good way. Google 'Colin Clayford Humanalog'

THX1137: That's me.

That bit was painful. It wasn't telling her my name. It wasn't even letting her see how much the journalists blamed me for the screw-up. It was pointing her towards an article with a photo of me in it, let alone a photo as unflattering as *that* one. But sod it, if I was going to be open, I had to be open, and to hell with the consequences. If she stopped talking to me as soon as she found out what I looked like then, well, so be it.

She took a long time to respond.

...

<HarlequinCyanide is typing>

...

HarlequinCyanide: I'm so sorry. That's messed up.

HarlequinCyanide: Is it, like, true? The stuff they say?

THX1137: Sort of. I designed the system that was hacked. We don't know how they hacked it, but the signs point to it being my fault.

HarlequinCyanide: But if they don't know, then it's not fair to blame you, right?

THX1137: It turns out that fairness doesn't really come into it.

...

HarlequinCyanide: I'm Mary, by the way.

HarlequinCyanide: If I get to know your name it's only fair you get to know mine.

THX1137: Thank you. That actually means a lot to me.

HarlequinCyanide: So what is it you're doing this evening?

THX1137: Well, you know the hackers, Pony Club? I'm sort of trying to hack them back

HarlequinCyanide: WOW. That's seriously cool!

HarlequinCyanide: So... how? Is it about chasing them through cyberspace, or what?

HarlequinCyanide: Full disclosure, and sorry if this comes as a shock to you... I'm not *actually* a master hacker. I fooled you with my unrivalled powers of deception for the sake of comic effect.

THX1137: You don't say?! I'm dumbfounded

HarlequinCyanide: LOL

THX1137: Well, I found a place they hang out online. I guess I'm trying to infiltrate it.

HarlequinCyanide: Badass! Is it safe?

THX1137: I'm being careful. They'll figure out eventually that someone's running exploits against them, but they've not got a way of tracing it back to me.

THX1137: I think.

HarlequinCyanide: Well be careful, ok?

THX1137: To be honest, there's not very much they can do to me. That's the joy of having already hit rock bottom.

HarlequinCyanide: Aw hun...

THX1137: Sorry, I didn't mean to sound all self-pitying. I'm fine. Honestly.

HarlequinCyanide: Good.

HarlequinCyanide: Well, I'm going to bed. Have fun scratching your itch...

HarlequinCyanide: SLY FACE EGGPLANT FIREWORKS DAMMIT

She didn't go to bed. She didn't go to bed for a very long time. I only found this out when I woke up in the morning and saw that I had a long-form "Correspondence" message from her from 3:27am.

Hey,

I felt really weird seeing that article. Like, the whole point of this site is that you get to control your image to other people on here. It made me feel like things are uneven between us now, like I can see what's behind your profile but you can't see behind mine. And that bugged me, more than it should. I guess it's because I like you?

Anyway I wanted to even things out. This took me way longer than it should have, and it's probably stupid but... yeh. Thought it was only fair. Sending this before I chicken out again.

Mary XxX

The message had an attachment. It was a video.

Breath catching in my chest, I downloaded it straight away and opened it up. It was very short, just a few seconds. There was Mary, facing the camera, sitting at a cheap Ikea desk in a small room covered in posters and paintings and sketches. She was... cute. The photos I'd dug up of her when I was verifying she was real didn't do her justice. She was probably technically obese, and that red mark under her left eye (a birthmark? a burn scar maybe?) was quite prominent, but she was a hell of a lot better looking than me, that was for sure. Her hair was mostly short and mouse-coloured, and she had green bangs at the front. She had dimples. She was smiling bravely, but mostly she just looked uncomfortable. Her voice, when she spoke, was quiet and reedy.

"Hi Colin. Um, I just... I just wanted to show you something from me that was a bit more, I dunno, real. Sorry. It's silly. I just… yeah. Anyway, I'll speak to you again soon. If you still want to. Ok bye."

That was it. It was, to my memory, the nicest gesture anyone had ever made on my behalf, and it put me in a blissfully good mood for the day.

Until, that is, I found the error I'd made in my Stableyard hack late in the afternoon. A tiny typo, nothing more, but it meant that if anyone had visited my profile page, even though my parasite would have wormed its way onto their computer and collected all the information I wanted, it wouldn't have managed to send any of it back to me. No wonder I hadn't received anything.

It was hugely frustrating, because probably by now half the users on the site *had* seen my message and looked at my profile, and wouldn't ever bother to look back again, meaning I'd squandered my one opportunity to learn about them.

I fixed the typo, and then had a think about what else I could say in the General channel of the forum to get people's attention again. Nothing sprang to mind, so I scrolled up through recent posts to get some inspiration. I found yet more insipid, unhelpful mundanities.

Divvi: (April 27 17:40) Guys, I'm telling you, Detroit-style pizza is the answer. I don't care what the question is, it is the ANSWER

Borange: (April 27 17:40) That the square one? Gonna be a while before that makes it to Riga lol

Divvi: (April 27 17:40) There's a place near me that just opened up. Honestly, it's all I ask out of life.

Borange: (April 27 17:41) I thought you were Pittsburgh, not Detroit? You Americans have such weird place names.

Divvi: (April 27 17:41) I am Pittsburgh! That's why it's called a Detroit-style pizza. If I was in Detroit they'd just call it pizza.

Borange: (April 27 17:42) Touche

lowkey: (April 27 17:48) Guys you're making me hungry for pizza. (And I second what Borange says about American place names, btw.)

Divvi: (April 27 17:48) Sorry to do that to you dude, guessing what you call pizza in Cambridge tastes like ass.

lowkey: (April 27 17:50) That's where you're wrong, old chap! There's a place right by the station, open all night, serves it to go by the slice, so good it'd make you weep. Weep!

Divvi: (April 27 17:54) I'll believe it when I taste it.

Divvi: (April 27 17:54) And before you ask, no, I'm not flying all the way out there to try it. Divvi's Law of Academic Cuisine: If the clientele is mostly nerdy students, the food will suck. Always.

lowkey: (April 27 17:55) Your loss! Actually, fuck it, it's all I'm going to think about today. @Draconix, you want pizza again?

Draconix: (April 27 17:59) Always. Love that place. But it'll take me a little while to get to you. Meet you there in, say, 90 minutes?

lowkey: (April 27 18:01) Deal.

Hang on. It was a little after six now, so that last message had only just been sent. This was an *incredible* stroke of luck: Despite having members all over the world, I'd just discovered that two Pony Clubbers, Draconix and lowkey, were planning on meeting near Cambridge train station, in an hour and a half. I checked Citymapper. If I left right now I could just catch the 18:39 from Kings Cross and arrive at Cambridge station at just a little after half seven. I might actually be able to lay eyes on two members of Pony Club.

Maybe it was the residual elation caused by the video from Mary. Maybe it was a tiny act of rebellion against Big Sis's insistence the night before that I should give up. Maybe it was an increasing feeling that I had nothing left to lose. Wherever it came from, it inspired a weird, giddy energy that was enough to propel me out of my flat, without even bothering with my pre-flight checks, without even pausing at my door, armed only with my keys, wallet and phone. I didn't plan; I didn't think; I just went.

18

It went horribly wrong. Of course it did.

I just barely made the train from Kings Cross. I bought
tickets on my phone on the overground on the way there, then
had a bit of a palaver getting through the barriers. I hadn't
taken a national rail train in years, and wasn't quite sure how
to scan my digital ticket. By the time I boarded I was very out
of breath and flustered, and picked up several stares from the
other passengers. The only available seat in my carriage was
next to a grumpy-looking young man in a suit who was jug-
gling a laptop, a sandwich and a coffee. I briefly considered remaining standing, but then the train jolted into motion, nearly
toppling me over, so I thought better of it and started to sit
down. Unfortunately, as soon as I did so it became immediately clear that it would be impossible for me to arrange myself
on the seat without either pressing my thigh into the grumpy
man's or completely blocking the aisle. I opted for the latter,
as the lesser of two evils, but misjudged my positioning, and
almost immediately toppled off the chair, landing awkwardly
on the ground and bumping my head into the bare knee of the

lady on the other side of the aisle. Horrified, I scrambled up and, face burning with shame, fled.

Mercifully the far end of the train turned out to be far less crowded. All in all, though, I probably wasn't in the most balanced and stable state of mind when, twenty minutes in to the journey, I got a new email in my inbox. It was from Sandspidr. It read:

Nice try, Colin. But did you really think we wouldn't notice? Stop now, or there'll be consequences...

My stomach convulsed. I looked round the carriage in alarm. Were they tracking my location? Was I being followed? I scanned the faces of my fellow passengers. A teenager looked up, caught my eye, and scowled. A woman had her face largely hidden by a book. Was she peeking at me from behind it? I tried to huddle down into my seat, but only succeeded in giving myself a wedgie.

This whole journey had been a terrible mistake. I needed to get off the train. For a desperate moment I eyed the emergency stop lever above the doors at the end of the carriage. But, panicked though I was, even I could just about see that that wouldn't solve anything. I was stuck on here until the next station. And then I remembered that this was a direct train, so the next stop was Cambridge itself.

Given half an hour of huddling miserably in my chair, with nothing else to do, I might have calmed down. I might have started thinking clearly. I might have concluded that Sandspidr's comment was almost certainly a reference to them knowing in general about my Pony Club hack, rather than them somehow knowing that I was, right now, on a train to Cambridge to try to identify Draconix and lowkey. I might have convinced myself to be brave, or at least to *act* a little more bravely, and stick to my original plan.

We'll never know, though, because then the train stopped and the lights went out.

It was only a few seconds, but in that brief moment of darkness I convinced myself I could make out the outline of someone lurching towards me, an object – sharp, heavy, ballistic, I had no idea – in their outstretched hand. In the pitch darkness I was absolutely, positively certain I could *see* it. I screamed, and threw my arm up to protect myself.

Then the lights flickered back on, and of course I found myself shrinking away from empty air, while the passengers around me unanimously turned to stare.

After a few minutes the driver announced that he was sure we'd be moving shortly, and would update us very soon. A few minutes after that he told us that there had been a power failure, and he was awaiting information on how soon it would be fixed. Fifteen minutes after that he gave us his sincere apologies and told us to make ourselves comfortable.

*

We eventually crawled into Cambridge at a little after 9pm. The driver assured us several times over just how fervently the train company wanted to apologise to us for this delay in our journey. By that point my nerves were shredded and my only thoughts were of getting home, and even more pressingly, of eating as much as I could physically cram into myself before I was sick, and possibly a little more as well. As there weren't any trains leaving the station in any direction for at least the next half hour, I took the opportunity to research the local food options, all the while keeping an eye out for Pony Club spies and thugs. And that's when I discovered that there is no pizza restaurant anywhere near Cambridge station.

I was confused. Had they been talking in code? Did 'pizza' mean something other than pizza? Did 'Cambridge' mean somewhere other than Cambridge? Then I realised that of course it did: I had absolutely no reason to believe Draconix and lowkey were based in the UK. The chances were they were talking about the *other* Cambridge. The one in America.

How do you always manage to get everything so wrong, Colin?

I was a hundred miles from home, for no bloody reason whatsoever. What on earth had possessed me to make me think charging out into the world on the trail of crooks without a moment to stop and think was a good idea?

Worse, my phone battery had just fallen under 30%, and seemed to be losing a per cent every four or five minutes. There was a very strong possibility that by the end of the night I'd be phoneless.

The vending machine at the station accepted contactless payments. I could have got more and better food at the station café, but that would have involved talking to someone, and I was trying to conserve all my social energy for a forthcoming, dreaded interaction with the station assistant. When I finally worked up the courage to approach him, and after a couple of false starts managed to communicate that I needed to get to London, he shook his head sadly at me.

"No more trains to London tonight, mate," he said. "You could try getting across to Stowmarket and getting back via Colchester, but last I heard that wasn't running either. You're best off coming back tomorrow."

I gawped. He gave me a sad smile, then turned his attention to another would-be traveller. I resisted the urge to burst into tears.

Finding a bench to sit on, I surveyed my options. There was no way Big Sis could come and get me. She didn't have a car, and besides, she was working this evening. So I wasn't getting home tonight, which meant I needed a place to stay. But I didn't know anyone within a hundred miles of here.

Or rather, I realised, I knew *one* person within a hundred miles of here. Someone I'd tried to avoid thinking about for years. Was there any way I could just ring up and...? No. Of course not. I put the thought from my mind. I needed to find a hotel. I checked my phone, and gulped when I saw it was down to 22% battery. That's the closest to empty I've ever allowed it to get. I did some hasty Googling, and established that there were two hotels right on the station road. Surely one of them would have a vacancy. Putting my phone back in my pocket, I made my way back through the main entrance.

There was a man waiting outside the station. He was wearing motorcycle leathers, and a large helmet with the reflective visor pulled down, and was leaning up against a lamp-post. That in itself was odd: there was no bike in sight, and he looked like he could have been there a while, so he had no reason to keep his helmet on except to conceal his face. As I emerged he turned his head in my direction, and then kept it there. Even without being able to see his eyes, I knew he was fixing his gaze on me. I took a few experimental steps. I was pretty sure his head turned to keep me in the centre of his field of vision. I faltered and stopped.

We stayed there for a few seconds, frozen. Then he unfolded his arms and pushed himself up off the lamp-post, and I lost my nerve entirely and bolted back into the station.

The only train running was a slow service in the direction of Ipswich. The rational part of me knew that I was being ridiculous, that the lamppost-leaner was nothing to do with me, and no kind of threat, but by that point the rational part of me was being trampled roughshod by every negative emotion in my repertoire. I boarded the train.

I couldn't get home, and I couldn't stay in Cambridge. I had only one option left, ghastly though it was sure to be. I pulled out my phone, and, with very mixed feelings, pulled up the number of someone I hadn't spoken to in a very long time.

*

My battery gave up the ghost just as the train pulled in to Elmswell station, where I alighted.

I followed the instructions I had been given, crossing the footbridge and looking for a blue SUV. There it was, idling across two disabled parking bays. I shuffled over, and opened the passenger-side door.

"Fucking hell, you're enormous," said Little Sis as I started to manoeuvre myself in.

"I... uh, s-sorry," I stammered, and started to get out again.

"No, no, I'm sorry, sorry I didn't mean that," she said briskly, without a hint of contrition. "You just took me a bit by surprise is all. Anyway. Hi. You ok?"

"Uh... sort of," I said.

I felt a sharp stabbing pain in the back of my neck.

"Stop that Tish," said Little Sis, distractedly, as she pulled out of the parking bay.

"Hello Uncle Colin!" came a chirpy voice from behind me.

"Hello, uh..., hi." I said, craning to look round at the little boy I had not previously noticed in the child seat behind me, who was holding a large plastic sword.

"*This* little snot-bag wouldn't go to sleep, so rather than leave him to wreak havoc in the house I've brought him with me," said Little Sis. "He was very excited to hear he'd be meeting his long-lost uncle Colin. I've tried to explain to him that you don't have a present for him, but he refuses to believe me."

"No, I... sorry. I didn't..." I murmured uncomfortably.

"Don't worry, he needs to learn that there are at least some people in the world who won't bloody spoil him rotten. His other uncle, Ruaridh's brother, gives him a multipack – a *multipack*! – of chocolate buttons literally every time he comes to visit. It's a disgrace. We've had to stop inviting him."

"Uh... oh."

I didn't quite understand the significance of chocolate buttons, and wasn't sure if this was an elaborate way of chiding me for *not* bringing something for the little ones. Titian and... Cressida, wasn't it? Big Sis kept in touch with Little Sis, and occasionally fed me updates, but it was all superficial stuff. Against the odds she'd met someone – Ruaridh – and they'd got married. His income was apparently just enough that she didn't need to try to hold down a job. Somehow, and perhaps ill-advisedly, they'd managed to have two children. I didn't know how much help she needed looking after them.

I was surprised she'd come to meet me herself, and frankly astonished to see her behind the wheel. I glanced furtively across at her as she drove. To be honest, I'd been expecting something more elaborate, some complex mechanism to allow her to control a whole vehicle with half the normal amount of working limbs. But it was all rather unexciting: an automatic car, with a little knob attached to the steering wheel so that she could control it with her right hand alone while her left rested in her lap. A little pad next to the knob had buttons on it that must control... indicators, I supposed. Maybe windscreen wipers? I didn't know enough about cars even to make an educated guess. Either way, driving a car seemed to be no more challenging for Little Sis than for a norm-... a fully able-bodied person.

With her sitting down, driving her almost-normal car, the limitations imposed on her life by the Incident were less visible than I'd been expecting. I snuck a glance at her forehead, looking for...there it was. White, narrow, taut. With the exception of one or two big family functions that Big Sis hadn't let me wriggle out of, I'd barely seen Little Sis since she effectively moved out of home aged fourteen. Her face had, of course, changed over the years, to the extent that this evening I hadn't been fully confident I'd recognise her. But I knew what the scar looked like. I knew *exactly* what the scar looked like.

We soon pulled in to the driveway of a truly enormous old farmhouse. Thinking about it, Big Sis had said Ruaridh worked for a bank. I'd assumed that meant he was some sort of bank manager or mortgage advisor. Now I started to suspect it was something a bit more high-powered. I was glad of it: presumably having a lot of money made it easier to accommodate Little Sis's disability. Outbuildings were strewn everywhere, and in one side of the garage sat a Porsche. Little Sis drove into the other side and turned off the engine.

"Alright monster," she said to Titian. "Go do a wee, then run upstairs and get into bed. Don't you dare wake your sister. I'll be up to give you a cuddle in a little bit, but I will bite your face off and feed it to the werewolves if you're not in bed when I get there."

Titian, apparently unfazed by this bloodcurdling threat, scampered out of the car, and away through a doorway in the back of the garage. I clambered out myself, and awkwardly shuffled round the bonnet to help Little Sis, only to realise she was already out and settled into a wheelchair she had magicked up from somewhere.

"Right, I need to spend some time wrestling Tish back to sleep. Is it alright if I show you to the spare room and leave you to your own devices?"

She led me into the house. It was immaculate. And even larger on the inside. We went through a utility room, full of neatly folded clothes and bedding, a kids' arts and crafts room which, despite the messy-looking handprint-paintings and glue-sploshed collages tacked to the walls, was nevertheless suspiciously clean and tidy, and then a kitchen where a huge tureen of something sweet-smelling was bubbling away.

It was the kind of house that had low doorways and uneven floors everywhere. There were no ramps or anything like that. but Little Sis adroitly navigated her way around.

"Uh... you're very... adept," I said awkwardly.

She snorted.

"Well yes, quite astonishingly I am capable of traversing my own home. I'm not one of your bloody Daleks, you know."

We reached the bottom of a small staircase, and she looked round at me with a mischievous grin I recognised from decades past.

"Watch this," she said. Then she bent down, scooped up her left ankle with her right hand and pushed herself up to standing with her right leg. There must have been some sort of hook or strap built into her trousers somewhere, because suddenly she was standing with her right hand on the banister and her left leg neatly folded up behind her. Then, using her hand for support she hopped – *hopped* – up the stairs, to another chair that was waiting at the top. The steps on the stair were short and wide, but still. I was aware my jaw was hanging open. Once settled she stuck her tongue out at me.

"Bet you can't do that."

I began to realise that some of my assumptions about Little Sis's life may have been unfounded.

Once I had rather self-consciously heaved myself up the stairs after her, she showed me to a spare room. Well, it was more of a suite really, with its own sitting room, bathroom and even a kitchenette.

"It's where we'll put Ruaridh's mum when the time comes," she explained. "Can I get you anything?"

"No, I –"

I stopped myself. I hated making trouble for people, but there were times when you had to forget social convention.

"Do you have a phone charger I could borrow?"

19

I slept in late. At about 10 o'clock, Little Sis knocked on the door and woke me up.

"Morning, sleepyhead. Jesus, you look awful."

"Ungh?"

"Your eyes are all red."

"Oh. I... I think I slept with my contact lenses in."

"I've got saline solution. Now, if you don't need to get moving first thing, while you're here I could use some help in the garden. Ruaridh's coming back tonight and I want something to show off about."

"Uh –"

"Shower first. I'll have some breakfast ready for you in the kitchen. Then if you're not outside in 20 minutes I'm coming back here with Tish's water cannon."

She exaggeratedly tapped an imaginary watch on her wrist and left. The old Little Sis would have followed through on a threat like that. In fact, she'd probably have only had the patience to wait 10 minutes before the soaking began. She had changed, of course. She was a grown-up now. But...

I got up.

Ten minutes later, showered, dressed and with eyes refreshed, I came downstairs to find some toast in a rack on the breakfast bar in the kitchen, next to a butter dish and selection of home-made preserves. I ate the toast with plenty of jam, and then ate some more of the delicious jam by itself, washing it all down with a couple of strong coffees from the blessedly straightforward machine on the counter. As I ate, I looked round the kitchen. Despite being utterly vast and stocked with terrifyingly professional-looking and enormous stainless steel appliances, pans and utensils, it nevertheless managed to have an air of idyllic rural charm. There were jars filled with jams and jellies on several shelves. In the cold light of day I could still see no obvious concessions to her disability. How on earth you conduct an industrial-scale preserve-making operation in a kitchen like this if you've only got the use of one arm, I wondered?

I also noted that what I *wasn't* wondering about, for the first time in weeks, was Labyrinth, or Pony Club, or Sandspidr. Having been bounced into this entirely unexpected environment, I was forced (and also a little bit grateful) to let *those* thoughts take a back seat for a bit. Not to worry. I was sure they would still be there when I got home.

Little Sis was waiting for me on the gravel outside. She was sitting in a battered-looking wheelchair with chunky tyres and mud spatters on the frame.

"Time to earn your keep," she said brightly.

She led me to the back garden and had me follow her around with a wheelbarrow while she yanked out what were apparently weeds from various flower beds, in order to make more room for what were apparently not weeds. Once my barrow was full of weed corpses (which, collectively, are heavier than you might imagine), she pointed me in the direction of the compost mound. I dutifully wheeled my way over to it and emptied it out, before rejoining Little Sis at the next bed, where we started the process again.

I lasted about half an hour before I had to sit down on a bench. Once sat, I found it extremely difficult to get up again. I felt woozy, my legs were wobbly, and I seemed to be thinking at about a quarter of my normal speed. After what must have been somewhere between thirty seconds and two hours, Little Sis appeared at my side with a banana and some orange juice. I received them gratefully, and within a few minutes my head felt a little bit clearer.

"God, you really are a mess," said Little Sis, once it was clear I was no longer in danger of actually fainting.

"Sorry… it's just quite hot out here."

"It's seventeen degrees."

"Oh."

She hoisted herself out of the wheelchair and sat next to me on the bench.

"I don't get it. You used to be… well, you weren't skinny, but you were normal, at least. And you could at least stand up for an hour without going hypoglycaemic."

"I… I eat too much."

"Well, yes. That's something of an understatement. *Why* though?"

"It's just what I do to, uh, to feel good. Instead of, you know, normal human stuff."

"What do you mean, 'normal human stuff?'"

"You know, interactions with people. Hugs. Hanging out. I don't know."

Christ, this was uncomfortable. But while I didn't trust my legs to support me, Little Sis had me trapped. And yes, I was aware of the irony therein.

"And why don't you do interactions with people?"

"Because I can't," I mumbled. "It doesn't work. I always get it wrong, and I end up hurting people."

"How do you hurt them?" she persisted.

So that was it. Little Sis was finally ready to talk about the Incident. I wasn't sure what she wanted to hear, but an apology seemed like a good place to start.

"I... I'm really sorry. I should never have... you should never have been left alone with me."

She frowned.

"What are you on about?"

"At... at the resort. Thessaloniki."

She stared at me for a couple of seconds, then threw her arms into the air.

"Oh for... are you still sulking about that? Look, I was being a dickhead, I tripped and fell, and I'm sorry if you found that upsetting, but are you really trying to blame me for your self-esteem issues? It was just an unlucky fall."

It was my turn to frown.

"I'm not blaming you for anything, I- I'm trying to say... sorry. I never said it, not properly."

Little Sis cocked her head to one side.

"Boy, you said sorry literally every time you saw me for 6 straight months. It drove me completely loopy. All I wanted to do was move on with my life, and every time you walked into the room you went all hangdog and wouldn't meet my eye, and you wouldn't say *anything* at all except sorry. Honestly, the last thing I would want from you is *another* apology."

"I... oh," I said. "I didn't... Sor-... I mean. Ok."

A new thought struck me.

"Uh... so was that why you... left?"

"Oh for God's sake. No. I got myself into Lord's Manor because I couldn't bear Mum any more. *That* had been brewing since long before we went to Thessaloniki. Come on, you must remember my relationship with her had been falling apart for ages. After the accident she became completely impossible. She wanted to wrap me up in cotton wool, and it got to the point where she was genuinely psychotic about it. I couldn't *move* without her telling me off. I thought I was going to explode. I had to get out of there."

"But," I said, falteringly, "you left... me... too."

She gave me a sideways look.

"For someone who's not blaming me for anything you're pretty good at laying on the guilt. Look, I'm sorry, I didn't handle things at all well. It's just that... well, I was your only friend, and that sort of meant that you had to be my only friend.

You didn't leave much room for other people. Which was fine when we were little kids. But at a certain point there was, well, *girl* stuff that I wanted to do, that I couldn't do with you. Then when I got out of hospital you stopped being any use at all, right at the time I needed an ally against Mum the most, and when I went off to Lord's Manor you weren't exactly quick to pick up the phone, and I suddenly made a bunch of new friends, and so... I suppose it was just easier to let things drift.

"And I am sorry, I really am. I know that you were going through your own thing, and you didn't have anyone to go through it with you, and I'm sorry that we never really reconnected, and that is on me, I know. But look, we were children. We've all moved on since then. Right?"

"Uh..."

"Oh! That's it isn't it?" she exclaimed, suddenly animated again. "You haven't moved on! You're still a sulky adolescent trapped in the body of a, a..."

She showed me the small mercy of not finishing that sentence. I felt that the word 'manatee' was hanging in the air between us in the brief silence that followed, but perhaps that was just me.

"You know what, it's not even your fault, is it? Does Big Sis still buy your underwear?"

"She helps me out," I replied, reddening, "With some things."

"Bloody hell, she's been treating you like a child for 20 years. *That's* why you keep acting like one!"

"That's not f-fair," I said. I'd forgotten how direct Little Sis had become after the Incident (thanks, frontal lobe damage), and I didn't like it. Nor did I like how she was so keen to trivialise the Incident, as though it hadn't completed changed the course of her life, as though it wasn't justifiable for it to have affected mine.

I took a breath, and realised I maybe I was the one being unfair. I was angry because I was agitated, and I was agitated because she kept alternating between telling me things I dearly wanted to hear (such as that she didn't still blame me for the Incident) and telling me things I very definitely didn't (such as that the reason she stopped talking to me was that she just didn't *like* me very much). If her way of dealing with the Incident was to trivialise it, then so be it.

But equally... the life she had since created for herself didn't seem *quite* so constrained by her physical limitations as I'd expected.

We lapsed into silence. After a pause Little Sis shifted herself back into her chair.

"Thanks for helping me with the gardening. I need to pick up Tish from nursery, then I'll make some lunch. The trains are running again today, so let me know when you want to go back to London and I'll run you to the train station."

*

Lunch was a chaotic affair. Little Sis tried to get me to explain how I'd come to be stranded in Cambridge, but Titian had the attention span of... well, probably the attention span of a typical four-year-old. I don't really know how children work. In any case, he kept interrupting so as to tell me about his favourite characters, I think from a TV show or maybe a book (he wasn't great at supplying context), and whenever Little Sis tried to steer the conversation back on track he would wait no more than ten seconds before interrupting again. She cheerfully called him a variety of names and uttered increasingly severe threats, and none of this deterred him in the slightest.

"Never have children," she eventually said to me. "Now that I understand what Mum was up against I have a lot more sympathy for her. There are days I long to be back in an office, staring vacantly at a spreadsheet."

"I, uh, I'm sorry you couldn't have had more of a career," I said, trying to sound sympathetic. "I think you could have gone a long way."

"Couldn't?" said Little Sis, frowning. Then she rolled her eyes. "Oh fuck off, prowess in the *advertising* industry is not correlated with number of functional limbs. I didn't give it up because I didn't have prospects. I'm a hot female in a wheelchair, I was an HR department wet dream. There are entire teams whose sole justification for existence is to facilitate jobs for people like me. (Tish, shut up or I will boil you into jam.) I quit because, if you will permit me a moment of self-awareness, I was still pissed off with how shit Mum was at parenting, and given the opportunity I wanted to prove that I could do a better job than her. Well, joke's on me, turns out it's really fucking hard, but I'm committed to the little bastards now, aren't I?"

She stuck her tongue out at Titian and he gleefully reciprocated, slopping juice out of his mouth in the process. I tried to remember what Little Sis had used to say she wanted to be when she grew up. All I could remember was her occasionally announcing she would be a pirate. Jokes about peglegs aside, I probably couldn't blame the Incident for her not pursuing that career aspiration.

"So anyway, back to yesterday: your company has suspended you, you're pissing about at home, and *who* is it you think you're going to find in Cambridge? Oh never mind, you can tell me later... *Tish!*"

*

After lunch Little Sis shooed me and Titian away so she could tidy up before taking me to the station. He scampered outside in the direction of the largest treehouse I have ever seen, and I took myself up to my room for a brief rest. I was still feeling weary from the morning's exertions, so I lay down on the bed and permitted myself a forty minute doze.

When I woke up it was dark outside, and a girl, older than Titian, was poking me in the calf. Cressida. I groaned and looked at her. I must have had quite a scowl, because I saw the tail end of a mischievous grin disappear from her face, to be replaced by solemn shyness.

"'S dinner," she mumbled, before scrambling away.

I sluiced more saline solution into my once again bleary eyes, then headed downstairs.

"Colin," called a deep, deadpan voice as I reached the hall. It sounded like a rather disappointed statement of fact, but I assumed it was meant as a greeting. There, in the entrance to the dining room, was Ruaridh, opening a bottle of wine. He had a shiny face, a high forehead, and dark, expressionless eyes. I had met him once before, at a family wedding several years ago, and he had given the impression of being thoroughly bored by my presence. But to be fair he gave that impression when interacting with everyone else there, too.

"H-hello," I replied.

"So you're staying with us?"

"Uh, I mean, I didn't mean–"

"Fine. Trains have got my schedule all skewiff. I nearly didn't come back tonight. So it goes. Drink?" he asked, pointing the neck of the wine bottle at me.

I shook my head to decline. I've never liked the taste of wine. Ruaridh gave a minute eye roll, and poured three large glasses. He took a swig from one, wordlessly pushed the second into my hands, and carried the third through to the kitchen.

"Daff! Merlot."

After a few seconds of standing by myself in the dining room feeling foolish, I followed him through. I immediately wished I hadn't. He and Little Sis were standing, pressed against each other, his arms encircling and supporting her, she tipping her head up, he craning his down, and they were muttering sweet nothings amidst noisy kisses. Embarrassed to have intruded, I winced and left again, but not before I'd awkwardly made eye contact with Ruaridh.

I sat down on a chair in the dining room and took a couple of sips of wine. I still didn't like the taste.

Eventually everyone else converged around the table, and food appeared as well. There were two dishes on offer: toad-in-the-hole for the little ones, and some exotic fish thing for the grownups. Somehow Little Sis had whipped up the whole spread while I slept, and still found time to pick up Cressida from school. I gazed sadly at the children's batter-smothered sausages. There wasn't enough for me to have a helping too, which meant I was stuck with the pretentious fish.

I mostly tuned out of the dinner conversation. Ruaridh updated Little Sis about things to do with his work, none of which made any sense to me. And he tried to interrogate the kids about their achievements during the week, but they were more interested in a game between the two of them that mostly involved them shouting 'You're a bumbag' at progressively higher volumes, and laughing raucously.

Eventually Ruaridh decided to drag me into the conversation.

"So have they arrested anyone in your Bitcoin thing?"

Oh. *That.* I realised I'd managed to avoid thinking about it more or less all day.

"Uh, no. A-and it's actually not Bitcoin, it's –"

"Burncoin, right. Crypto's not my thing, professionally," he drawled, "but it's always good for a laugh when the price tanks.

What I don't get, though, with this whole thing, is who really loses out, if it's all only virtual currencies moving around anyway?"

"Presumably that woman, Mueller," suggested Little Sis. "After all, she bought a bunch of Burncoin with some very real money, handed it over to Maison whatsisname, and didn't get a picture in return. Or will she get it? I mean, she's paid for it."

I supposed Little Sis had found time to research the whole thing while I was sleeping, alongside everything else.

"Well that rather depends on the terms of the contract. Maison De Gauguin aren't the sellers, are they? They're an escrow service." Ruaridh's voice became fractionally less monotonous than normal. I guessed he was now in his element, talking about financial deals.

"So now that she's parted with the money, either she's owed a painting, or she's owed her money back. Frankly if I was Mueller I'd take the money back over the painting in a heartbeat. The people who fund her VC, Highgate Holdings, are about to take a pounding from the City for their failed bet on American Steel. If I were them, the first thing I'd ditch is a little boutique venture capital firm. I heard Strawberry made a packet from selling that startup to Finisys, but spending the windfall on art is frankly pretty fucking shortsighted."

Titian, who hitherto had given no indication that he was listening, now started chanting "You're pretty fucking shortsighted!" at Cressida until she reached over and pinched him on the arm hard enough to make him cry.

Little Sis and Ruaridh exchanged glances of increasing severity until Ruaridh sighed and hauled both children off to the kitchen, where I could hear him half-heartedly dressing them down.

"Thus endeth the repast," said Little Sis, resignedly. "Come on. If I take you to the station now you can still be home by bedtime."

*

We didn't speak much on the drive to the station. I'm a terrible conversationalist at the best of times, and the past 24 hours had been enough of a whirlwind that I was in no state to make chit-chat. Ruaridh's mention of Burncoin had brought the stresses of Sandspidr's threats and my abortive attempt to hunt down Pony Club in Cambridge back to the forefront of my attention, and my first night away from home in goodness knows how many years had me feeling generally unsettled.

But the thing that hit me hardest of all was the growing realisation that I had been, for a very long time, completely wrong about Little Sis. Wrong about the life she led now, wrong about what had happened in the aftermath of the In-cident, wrong even about what our relationship had been before then. It was all very... destabilising. But not *necessarily* in an entirely bad way.

"Are you going to be ok?" asked Little Sis as I got out of the car.

"Uh... I think so," I replied.

I started to close my door, and then stopped.

"A-are you happy? I mean… with how everything turned out? For you?"

"Of course," said Little Sis, without hesitating. "I have a hot tub, two longbows and Sky Cinema. I'm living the dream. And the kids are alright too I suppose. What about you? Are you happy?"

"Uh… I don't know. Um. Bye Little Sis."

"Bye The Boy. Ring me sometimes."

"O…Ok."

*

The journey home was blessedly uneventful. The train was almost entirely empty, and the two little old ladies sitting in my carriage were so unthreatening-looking I couldn't even commit to the Gabardine Suit Game.

I felt myself relaxing a smidgen. I was still away from home, still out of my element. But for reasons that I couldn't exactly articulate (although perhaps the glass of expensive, tangy wine I'd ended up drinking was helping) I felt fractionally calmer than I otherwise would have. There was a lot about my interactions with Little Sis that I needed to process, and I promised myself to devote some serious thought to it in the fullness of time. But in the meantime, I was happy just to sit.

When I got home, my first action was to log onto my computer and disable the parasite code I'd uploaded to Stableyard.

It was very much closing the stable door after the horse had bolted, but I hoped Sandspidr would be appeased.

Despite myself, I couldn't resist checking to see whether I'd managed to collect anything useful before I was busted. I skimmed through the information my parasite had dug up. It turned out that a fair few people had viewed my profile. They were spread fairly evenly round the world: there were visitors from eastern Europe, South Korea and North America. Nothing in the UK at all.

Most interesting were the searches my parasite code had conducted of the private Targets channel. It turned out there was indeed a thread on Maison de Gauguin. I only had access to the search result summary, which meant I could only see the messages that specifically used the terms 'MDG' and 'Maison de Gauguin', but it seemed like the conversation started with someone called ONEWORDALLCAPS (honestly, tech nerds should never be allowed to come up with their own usernames) asking who had been involved, a few days after the incident occurred. Ten minutes later, Draconix, the one who had the sudden hankering for pizza yesterday, had responded:

Raises hand sheepishly That was me. I guess it's 'official' then. We were the ones who hacked MDG.

Hugely fortuitously, Draconix had also been one of the people to check my profile. So I had a full file on them pre-populated.

Draconix was a 'platinum' user of Stableyard. That appeared to mean they were an admin, or at least a very longtime member. Clearly they were the real deal in the Pony Club hierarchy. According to the data I had scraped from their laptop they were based somewhere in Boston, Massachusetts. (Of course: Boston was just across the river from the *other* Cambridge, the one which presumably *did* have a pizza place near a public transit station.) In fact, I could do one better than that. They had connected via a public WiFi network named BaconTrayLovesYou. A quick Google on a hunch and... yes, there was a restaurant in Boston called Bacon Tray, on Commonwealth Avenue. I learned a few other titbits too, including the make and model of their computer: apparently an old Lenovo laptop.

So, in the past 24 hours an established hacker called Draconix, who had by his own admission participated in the MDG hack, had been sitting in a restaurant in Boston. On a Lenovo. Did that help me?

Forget the location for a second. The point was, Draconix knew how the hack was carried out. So how could I get that information from Draconix? My cover as morlok was blown, and I doubted I'd get a second chance to get into Stableyard on false pretences. I could try to dig up some other way of getting to Draconix online via some other site, but they'd be on the lookout for my approach now. So what else could I do? Go back to trying to sweet talk Sandspidr over email? Fat chance. Thinking about it, Sandspidr was almost certainly a Draconix alias: even unintentionally, people tend to follow patterns when inventing names, and the person in question probably took inspiration from dramatic-sounding animals, like dragons and spiders, when creating all of their monikers.

Maybe I should play it safe, and hand over what I had to the police. It wasn't hard evidence, but it might be enough to get them started. But no, I couldn't do that. First of all, the way in which I'd obtained this information about Draconix was pretty straightforwardly illegal. But also, based on what I'd seen so far I wasn't particularly confident in their ability or inclination to follow up properly on this lead. Otembi gave every impression of just wanting this whole thing to be over as quickly as possible. She didn't want wild goose chases, she wanted the shortest path to closing the case.

No, I couldn't offload this to someone else just yet. Somehow I needed to get some answers from Draconix.

I felt my stomach begin to curdle as I realised what I was going to do next.

20

HarlequinCyanide: Airport????

THX1137: Trying not to think about it too hard. I haven't been on a plane since I was a teenager.

HarlequinCyanide: Me neither. Everything about flying scares me.

HarlequinCyanide: Will you fit in the seat?

HarlequinCyanide: UNSEND. UNSEND.

HarlequinCyanide: I really didn't mean that. I don't know why I said that. I'm so so so so sorry.

THX1137: Honestly, it's a fair question. And basically the answer is no, I don't think I would fit in a normal seat, especially not on a 7 hour flight.

THX1137: That's why I'm flying business class.

HarlequinCyanide: JEALOUS EMOJI

HarlequinCyanide: But where are you going?

Sitting in the departures area at Heathrow I started typing a reply, and then stopped. Should I risk telling her?

I wasn't blind to the fact that Sandspidr had cottoned on to me hacking Stableyard the day after I'd told Mary about it. If 'Mary' was actually a profile being run by a Pony Club member, that would explain how they got wise to me so quickly. But I had checked and double-checked Mary's details, and she had such a comprehensive online footprint it seemed impossible that it could have been entirely faked. Especially since I now had a video of her. Unless Mary was living a comprehensive double life *and had been since she was 14*, I just couldn't believe she wasn't a real person. And besides, Pony Club were hackers. Was it really so surprising that they had systems in place to detect when their own forum was being hacked?

I decided it was a reasonable risk to take.

THX1137: Boston, USA.

HarlequinCyanide: Cool! Is this still to do with the hackers, though?

THX1137: Yep.

HarlequinCyanide: Is it safe?

THX1137: Well, Virgin Air has a pretty solid safety record.

HarlequinCyanide: No, I mean chasing these hackers around the globe. Is it a good idea?

THX1137: It's just a few days. Mostly I'm going to be camping out in an airport hotel. I just need to try something.

THX1137: Ok gotta go, we're boarding soon.

HarlequinCyanide: Well stay safe. I worry. Let me know when you've landed?

THX1137: Will do. TTFN

HarlequinCyanide: Buh-bye XxX

I was glad that *someone* knew where I was going. I hadn't told Big Sis. I knew if I did she'd try to convince me that I shouldn't – that I couldn't – do something as enormous and ridiculous and terrifying as this. And if she tried she'd probably succeed, because she was probably right. But I was trying not to think about that. In fact I was trying not to think too hard about any of what I was doing, and instead concentrating all my thoughts purely on how to get it done. That, I hoped, was the sweet spot, the middle-of-the-road approach that would save me both from the fear-induced paralysis that had prevented me chasing up the Boffinism lead and the chaotic spontaneity that led to the Cambridge disaster. I needed to be dispassionate, calm and detached if I was going to get through this. *Assess, respond, proceed.* That was my mantra.

It wasn't going very well so far. Not having flown since that miserable journey back from Thessaloniki, I got everything to do with air travel wrong. I'd had a hard enough time comprehending that checking in, which I had always thought meant confirming your physical presence at the airport, was actually now done online a day or so in advance of the flight itself. It was only through complete chance that I'd learned in time that I needed to apply for an ESTA to enter the United States. And of course I had humiliated myself going through security, trying to bring bottled water with me, leaving my phone in my pocket and my laptop in its case, and not waiting until called to go into the full body scanner thing. I'd ended up having a manual pat-down, which was excruciating (someone's *hand* was pressing into my *thigh…*), and being lectured on my responsibilities as a traveller. Through it all, I stared at the floor while I kept up a chant in my head: *Assess, respond, proceed.* Don't panic, don't scream, just *assess, respond, proceed.*

Now I was through all of that, and sitting in a departure lounge still trying not to think about the ridiculous stupidity of going to America to try to find Draconix.

Let's be clear. For other people that might be the very first thing they'd do in my position. For other people, hopping across the Atlantic to track down and confront the hacker who had cost them their job would make total sense.

But I wasn't other people. Talking to strangers gave me panic attacks. Fear of confrontation regularly stopped me sleeping at night. Even thinking about being in foreign countries gave me the heebie-jeebies.

In a way, though, all of that was precisely why I had to do this. When it came to tech Pony Club were, simply put, better than me. They had been running rings around me from the outset. Continuing the interaction in the digital arena would only ever end badly for me. The only way I was going to make any headway would be if I did something completely unexpected. And I strongly doubted Draconix would be expecting me to show up on his doorstep.

*

The flight turned out to be surprisingly comfortable. The business class seats were more or less wide enough for me to sit in, and the flight attendants largely left me alone other than to provide a steady supply of food, which was all I could ask of them. I was a bundle of nerves throughout (a combination of mild anxiety about flying and a very intense anxiety about what would happen when the flight *ended*), so to calm myself I ate, watched a couple of films, ate more, and pootled around a bit on my laptop once I realised that was allowed.

My one truly awful experience was trying to use the toilet. First of all I barely fit through the door, and once in I wrongly convinced myself that I had worked out how to lock it behind me, with the result that a glamorous American lady very nearly got an eyeful of my midriff and genitals, and I ended up so flustered I was completely unable to complete what I had gone in there to achieve.

Lavatorial disasters aside, the flight passed without incident. We landed slightly ahead of schedule in what was the early evening Eastern time, hitting the runway with a heavy thud that caused me to give an involuntary yelp.

I disembarked and joined the queue to get through passport control, ending up in the right-most lane for non-Americans, meaning I was next to the left-most lane for US citizens. I noted how at the front of my lane the officials were stern, terse and suspicious, while next to me they were all smiles and 'Welcome home's, and occasionally even indulged in a high five. I also noticed that, despite the stereotypes, the average bodily girth in the queue to my right was no bigger than my own queue's. My heart sank. I had entertained a gentle fantasy that America would truly turn out to be the land of the large, and that I would fit right in. In reality I was comically oversized whichever side of the Atlantic I was on.

The surly guard at the passport desk reduced me to a gibbering wreck with a single glare. He barked a couple of questions at me, and seemed unimpressed with my stuttered, single-word answers. He spent a long time staring at his computer screen, then eventually got out his stamp and aggressively thumped it onto my passport. As he shoved it back at me, he muttered something in a threatening tone that I couldn't initially parse. It was only after I'd shuffled meekly away that I realised his exact words were 'Welcome to America'.

Assess, respond, proceed. At least they'd let me through.

Another few glares from the customs people and I was allowed out through the one-way gates into a huge, grey atrium with a bewildering array of signs pointing away in all directions. The next item on my agenda was cash. I found a bureau de change where, after a few false, stammering starts, I managed to convey to the friendly middle-aged lady behind the counter that I wanted to buy some dollars. She, completely uninvited, passed time while her computer processed the details by asking me endless questions about my flight and then, out of nowhere, told me she loved my accent. To the best of my recollection no one had ever complimented anything about my voice before, and the wash of self-consciousness it precip-itated was enough to render me almost entirely mute, which made completing the rest of the transaction even more com-plicated.

Eventually I staggered away from the desk clutching a handful of notes and a comically long receipt. My first inter-actions with Americans had left me frazzled, and needing to soothe my nerves. Time for a comestible detour. I saw a Mc-Donald's kiosk in the distance, and sidled up cagily. I suddenly dearly wanted a Big Mac or seven, but the idea of another exchange with a stranger was temporarily beyond me. Then I saw – bliss! – that it had a touch-screen ordering station. *Assess, respond, proceed.* I instantly forgave America for all its other faults, bought a very large meal, and ate it fast, chewing with focus and vigour.

Feeling much restored, I decided I was ready to embark on the final stage of my journey. Apparently the hotel I had booked had its own airport shuttle service, but I couldn't see any signs, and wasn't sure who would be appropriate to ask. The taxi rank, on the other hand, had lots of cabs in it and few queuing passengers. With a wad of dollars in my wallet I was happy to splurge for the sake of reducing the number of obstacles I needed to overcome. My driver's grasp of English seemed limited, but when I stuttered out the name 'Western Inn' he nodded, and, to my relief, didn't attempt any further conversation.

The Western Inn had an unprepossessing exterior. Situ-ated just beyond the airport itself, it sat in an urban hinterland of grey concrete buildings, security fences and the pervasive smell of burnt rubber and petrol. By this point it was early evening, Boston time, and the firm breeze in the darkening air had a cold edge to it. I was grateful to get out of it, into the warmth and cheerful lighting of the cheaply-carpeted and somewhat run-down reception.

A couple of miscommunications with a receptionist later and I was in my hotel room with the door safely locked behind me. Before anything else, I took a soothing shower, then connected each of my devices up to the hotel Wi-Fi and worked my way through the last of the snacks I had bought at Heathrow.

Now, *assess, respo...* and at that point my brain told me it couldn't cope with any more stimuli today thank you very much, so I lay down in the agreeably large hotel bed and slept.

*

I woke up in the morning at about 6am local time feeling surprisingly refreshed and ready for the day. Apparently what my body clock had thought was a very late night had been balanced out by what my body clock evidently thought was a very long lie-in. Even more pleasing was the realisation that, despite the early hour, breakfast was already being served. I headed to the ground floor and followed a couple of other guests towards the breakfast area. Having heard encouraging things about American portion sizes and attitudes towards carbohydrates, I was initially disappointed by the rather sparse buffet, until I discovered the breakfast burrito station. A re-assuringly taciturn and non-judgemental attendant was making mounds of these delightful savoury bundles, and over the course of the next fifteen minutes I had four, all washed down with filter coffee that was weak enough that I felt justified in drinking several mugs' worth.

After breakfast I went back up to my room, where I was ambushed by a powerful urge to climb back into bed and stay there until lunchtime. That I should have come to a whole other continent, said a familiar and very reasonable voice in my head, was unfathomable and unmanageable, and the best thing I could do was hide away in my hotel room for a few days until I could gather up the courage to fly home again.

I knew I mustn't listen. The longer I stayed inactive, the stronger the voice would become, so I forced myself to get moving immediately. I carefully packed a rucksack with some essentials: my laptop, phone, battery pack, water and snacks from the vending machine by the elevator, cash, spare clothes, toilet roll, and spare contact lenses and solution. Then I went down to reception and forced myself to ask them to explain how the shuttle bus worked.

It arrived soon after, and I hopped on, and it took me to the airport subway station. After a harrowing interaction with a bored-looking man behind a perspex screen near the barriers I managed to buy a little plastic travelcard that would apparently let me use the subway as much as I needed. I had considered taking taxis everywhere, but decided against it. The drawing-of-attention involved in flagging down cabs on the street upsets me at the best of times, whereas public transport would let me come and go as a I pleased without having to interact with other people.

I spent an hour navigating Boston's haphazard subway network. For a system with so few routes, it had no business being as confusing as it was, I thought. Furthermore it, like all of America so far, smelled wrong, in a way that I could neither articulate nor ignore. And I realised I couldn't read the social cues here. When people were noisy, I didn't know if they were being rambunctious, or aggressive, or whether they were simply loud talkers. A woman, who seemed to me smartly dressed, flashed me a smile that revealed a mouth largely devoid of teeth. Was she in fact homeless, and therefore potentially about to accost me to ask for money? Or was dental care simply unaffordable to the American middle classes? It was all deeply confusing. I hunkered down in corners and tried to avoid all eye contact.

I finally emerged back into cheerful daylight on Commonwealth Avenue, where I made two realisations. The first was that Boston streets were a *lot* longer than London ones, and merely being on the right road was no guarantee that you were anywhere near your destination. The second was that, intriguingly, large stretches of Commonwealth Avenue were dominated by some sort of college campus. Was Draconix a student, I wondered?

After a bit of trial and error riding additional stops on the subway – which was actually more like an above-ground tram in that part of town – I managed to locate the block on which

Bacon Tray sat, and in the process discovered that I was in the heart of something called Boston University. I remembered reading that Boston had a higher student population than any other town in America while researching the trip, but I had thought that that really meant that both Harvard *and* MIT were nearby. It turned out there were additional, less vaunted colleges in the city, like this one. Still, it seemed like a legitimate institution. The street that ran through it was wide and well-maintained, and the red-brick academic buildings that flanked the road on either side were large and clean.

I eventually found Bacon Tray itself: a small bar-restaurant wedged between a sporting goods store and a hair salon. The window recommended that passers-by "Try our 'world famous' pancake stacks", and, despite the superfluous quotation marks, that seemed like as good a next step as any, so I went in.

Inside there was a long counter on the right, lined with a dozen bar stools, while a row of small booths ran along the left-hand wall, and a handful of tables were arranged at the back. I appeared to be the only customer. There was a woman sitting in one of the booths, but she was so immersed in paperwork and a laptop that I guessed she was a manager here: no one else would bring that much stuff with them to a restaurant. Despite its website boasting a full breakfast menu, clearly mornings weren't Bacon Tray's busiest time of day.

A lanky man with arm tattoos and hair that was such a shiny black it had to be dyed loomed out at me from behind the bar.

"Morning."

"H-hi. Uh... could I, please, have... some f-food?"

He nodded.

"Up at the bar?"

I looked suspiciously at the tall and spindly-looking bar stools. The man seemed to pick up on my concerns, because he added, "Or take a booth. I'll be right out with a menu."

I smiled gratefully and sat down at a booth one in from the entrance. It was good to get off my feet. I was finding being out and about in a foreign city where I didn't know the rules more than a little bit stressful, and that, in combination with the warm Boston weather, had made the morning's travel exertions thoroughly draining. I felt I had thoroughly deserved a second breakfast.

The server handed me a dauntingly large menu, which I had hoped to be able to ignore, since I had already decided to have the pancakes. But it turned out pancakes were merely a category of foodstuff here, and the menu had an entire column dedicated to pancake-related options. And it wasn't just a case of choosing one of them; I had an entire series of decisions to make, from the type of pancake batter to the size of stack to the sauces, toppings and sides. It was intimidating, and that, I thought, was unfair. Pancakes were supposed to be a source of comfort, not fear.

In the end, with a little prompting from tattoo man, I ordered five sourdough blueberry pancakes with bacon, honey syrup, pineapple rings and cream. I also ordered a 'root beer' out of sheer curiosity. That ordeal completed, I pulled out my laptop. Sure enough, there was a public WiFi network called BaconTrayLovesYou. I connected, and was online in a couple of moments.

I drummed my fingers on my touchpad. Now what? I went back to my pilfered records. Draconix had been logged on at 9am on Friday. So really... Oh no. I needed to have a conversation, didn't I? I steeled myself, and waited until the server returned with my drink.

"Thanks. Uh... e-excuse me. Um, were you here on Friday morning?"

"Here every weekday. Why?"

"I, uh... there was someone here. Uh, I was wondering if you'd seen them?"

"What did they look like?"

Ah.

"Well... They had a laptop. A Lenovo."

That got me a funny look.

"Sorry. We, uh, we met online. I don't know anything about them."

A frown.

"Like a blind date?"

"S-sort of... They were here at about 9am?"

He gave me a shake of his head.

"Nah, we don't open until 9:30. Was it 9am Eastern? Or, like, 9am British time?"

I did a quick mental double-check.

"Uh... 9am local time, I think."

He shrugged.

"Wasn't here then."

"Uh, ok. Sorry," I said, unsure quite what I was apologising for.

"No problem. Your food will be right out."

I sat back, dispirited. Could I have got it all wrong *again*? I went back to my logs and double-checked. No, it was definitely 9am Eastern Daylight Time. Draconix had definitely been in Boston. *This* Boston. And no, there were no other branches of Bacon Tray. I took a slurp on my root beer, which turned out to taste like cough syrup, but in an oddly appealing way.

On a hunch, I stood up and looked around at the woman in the booth behind me, the one I presumed was the manager. She might have been in before opening on Monday, and she had a laptop... but no, it was an HP, not a Lenovo. My disappointment was mitigated by the sight of a stack of pancakes, each as wide as my head and about half an inch thick, wafting towards me. At least the morning wasn't a complete write-off.

*

Half way through my food the internet died. I wasn't doing anything in particular, just browsing around to kill time as I chewed through my delightful and gratuitously over-syruped pancakes. I pulled out my phone, which had plentiful (albeit expensive) roaming mobile data, and a still nearly-full battery.

Behind me I heard a sigh of frustration.

"Jake!"

"Yeah?"

"Reboot?"

I looked round, and accidentally caught the eye of Jake, my server. He gave a tiny eye roll for my benefit, before bending down behind the bar.

"We just gotta put a password on it," he suggested to the manager lady.

"No passwords! I hate passwords. We need a better internet connection."

"So get a better internet connection."

"We can't afford a better internet connection."

There was something sing-songy about this exchange that made me feel like it was an argument they'd had many times before. Jake resurfaced and called across to me: "Your internet should come back in a minute or so."

"Ok, uh, thanks."

"It's students in the apartments above us. Too many of them jump on the WiFi, and the whole thing wipes out."

I nearly sprayed my booth with root beer.

*

After I had paid (which involved me panicking about American tipping etiquette and eventually adding a gratuity that was almost as big as the original bill), I started to make my way back to the hotel. I had a notion of what to do next, but it was going to be, to put it mildly, an ordeal. As the day's exertions had already been exhausting, I decided it could wait until tomorrow. That meant devoting the rest of the day to being quiet in the hotel.

Or did it? It occurred to me that I was further from home than I had ever been before, in a vibrant city filled to the brim with tourist attractions. Would it really be that awful to do a little sightseeing? That was what normal people did, surely. Perhaps it was worth giving a try.

I pulled out my phone and did a quick search for things to see in Boston. First up was something called the 'Freedom Trail'. I got as far as the first sentence, which informed me that whatever it was it was three miles long. Nope. The next suggestion turned out to be a *baseball* stadium, which I dismissed just as quickly. A few more uninspiring results and I was on the verge of giving up. Ah, but here was something: the New England Aquarium. I remembered enjoying the one in London as a child. It would be indoors, air conditioned, and not involve art or sports. Good enough. In awe of my own adventurousness, I planned my route on the subway and got moving.

*

I spent an hour or so communing with serene jellyfish and morose turtles through thick glass panels, accompanied by ambient music and blue mood lighting. I wondered briefly whether life would be better as a sturgeon. Everything seemed simpler underwater. There was a hypnotic quality to it all that even managed to allay my irritation at having no phone signal for the entire time I was inside.

All in all it was time enjoyably spent. I emerged back out into the outside world feeling refreshed and proud of myself for being so bold in a foreign city. I made a mental note to give the London aquarium another go when I got back home, and maybe even think about other places in London I could visit that weren't my flat or my office.

Then my stomach got in touch to make me aware that it had been a few hours since the bacon pancakes, and it was now most definitely lunch time. So I pootled to the nearest restaurant and ordered an "authentic" bread bowl clam chowder, a burger, and another of those oddly addictive root beers. While I waited for my food I fiddled with my phone. At some point data roaming had switched itself off, seemingly the result of a minor identity crisis my handset was experiencing as it tried to navigate American cellular networks. I put it back on, and after a minute or so as my phone got its bearings, a small herd of notifications shuffled onto my screen.

My good mood evaporated as I saw I had a new email from Sandspidr.

Colin... Did you know that Boston boasts some of the best stables in America?

Look, no more dicking around: The Ponies will come for you, and we will fucking cut you. We know everything. We see everything. We are in your laptop, we are in your phone, we are in the cables running under your feet, we are in the electromagnetic sig-

nals all around you. Stop trying to save yourself. Stop angering us. Go hide in a hole if you want to live. This will be your last warning.

They already knew I was in Boston. They were watching me. My stomach started twisting itself like a balloon animal.

It was Mary. It must have been Mary. But now they were claiming they had compromised by laptop and my phone too. Was that... was that feasible? Christ almighty, and that line about seeing everything: did that mean they had access to the city CCTV network? Or were they following me? Either way, I suddenly felt very vulnerable, alone in public in a foreign country.

I rushed to the nearest station and on the ride home played the Gabardine Suit Game in earnest. The woman in the trendy yellow blazer sat opposite was definitely watching me, relaying my position to her partners. The emo teenager to my right taking selfies wasn't actually using the front camera. Instead she was surreptitiously taking pictures of me with the rear one. The heavyset, sharply-dressed men standing in the aisle: were those gun-shaped bulges I could see in their jackets?

In particular there was a man with a buzz cut and dark rings around his eyes who sat near me, doing nothing, just staring into space. He had a rearing Eagle on his t-shirt and chunky, dirty boots. He got off at the same stop as me. I could feel him walking too close behind me as I shambled towards the exit. I lost my nerve and started running – or doing the best approximation of a run that I can do. The hotel shuttle bus happened to be already mercifully close by, and I scrambled towards it. I hauled myself on, took a seat at the back and looked anxiously for him through the window. There he was!

And then a woman walked up to him and they shared a hug and a kiss, and he smiled a warm and genuine smile and they linked arms and walked away.

I cursed myself. I'd spent so long imagining all strangers as enemies that I now found it impossible to tell when someone was a genuine threat. How could I know what to be afraid of when I was afraid of *everything*?

21

I spent the rest of the day hiding in my hotel room. I was too upset to be productive, too agitated even to watch TV. So mostly I just ate, ordering a continual stream of dishes up to my room and cringing at the increasingly amused looks and comments from Raul, the overly friendly room service attendant. None of them was what my stomach wanted (which was those microwaveable mini deep dish pizzas, for what it's worth), and none of them made me feel remotely better. I was very aware of the absence of my kitchen supplies.

It wasn't just fear of Pony Club's reprisals (although don't get me wrong, that was playing *heavily* on my mind). It was also the inevitable reaction to how stupidly adventurous I'd been in the past couple of days. What the hell was I doing in a foreign hotel room half way across the world? Why the fuck had I just wasted a morning in an *aquarium* when I was being pursued by an international gang of criminals?

I gazed gloomily out of the window. There wasn't much of a view. A large, blocky, windowless concrete building was directly opposite, with a very small sign on the side telling me it was owned by a distributor of various forms of vehicle tyre, but they spelled it with an American 'i', which made it look, to my eyes, ever so slightly unsettling and wrong. There was an American flag mounted, quite gratuitously it seemed to me, on the roof. Behind it I could see the tips of a foreign skyline, with buildings that looked nothing like London's. Everything was alien here, everything was just slightly off. I missed my flat terribly. I missed my bus route. I *really* missed my freezer.

And it didn't help that 'Mary' kept on messaging me, telling me cute stories about her day. The idea that she was a fiction that Pony Club had used to dupe me made me miserable, but the alternative – that they had found out I had come to Boston through some *other* means that I couldn't even comprehend – was even worse.

It had to be Mary, I told myself. Maybe the video she sent me was a 'deepfake', or maybe the woman in it was actually one of the hackers, and she had stolen the identity of someone who just looked a bit like her in real life – the real Mary – in order to make her profile more believable. I needed to be honest with myself: the real reason I was loath to accept that the person I thought I had befriended didn't really exist was that I wanted to keep believing that someone like Mary could genuinely be interested in me. But put my pathetic desire for meaningful connection to one side and this was the only explanation that made sense.

And yet Sandspidr had said that Pony Club was 'watching' me. What if Mary was just one of *several* ways in which they were tracking my movements?

I didn't know what to do, so I did nothing, except eat and eventually put myself miserably to bed.

*

The morning brought with it a grim resolve. Even if Pony Club knew I was here looking for Draconix, that didn't necessarily mean I wouldn't be able to find him. And if I could, then for the first time in this whole mess I *might* have some sort of an edge. And yes, evidently Pony Club would try to stop me, and no, I had no idea what resources they had at their disposal. But I had to try. What else could I do, after all?

I had a solid breakfast of burritos to settle my stomach, and then walked to reception to ask about the next shuttle bus back to the subway. I was told it would be a few minutes, as it was currently picking up some new arrivals, so I loitered in the lobby. There was a family waiting there already: two children, reading guidebooks and asking an endless series of questions of an exasperated mum, while the dad sat facing away from them, a black baseball cap and sunglasses on his head, staring down at the phone in his hands. He seemed so intent on ignoring his family that I wondered briefly if he had fallen asleep behind his glasses. But as I sat down, he flashed me a smile, and I guessed he was just very good at blanking them all out.

The bus arrived and we all clambered on, the driver loading up all the family's bags. I assumed that they were heading to the airport itself, not just its subway stop. The dad smiled at me again, and I began to worry that he would try to strike up a conversation, but he remained mercifully silent for the duration of the ride. When we arrived, the family milled around while the driver unloaded the bags, and I headed to the subway, but not before the dad flashed me one last smile. I was starting to get sick of the friendliness of Americans.

It was only when I sat down on the train and saw the 'dad' board by himself that I realised how seriously I had misjudged the situation. He wasn't ignoring his children because he wanted some peace and quiet; he was ignoring them because they weren't his children. He had been waiting, by himself, down in the lobby until I had arrived. Then he had seen me, and now he had followed me onto the subway.

I froze as he flashed me another smile, then sat down almost directly opposite, keeping his gaze permanently on me. Now the significance of the cap and glasses hit me: he didn't want anyone to be able to pick him out of a line-up later. I could feel my heart pogoing in my chest, and immediately started having trouble breathing. My head felt like it was being crushed by opposing tidal waves, and I noticed with alarm that my vision was beginning to grey out at the edges. This was a panic attack, I realised, and there was a good chance it was going to end with me passing out. I couldn't let that happen. I had to keep my wits about me. I forced myself to breathe as steadily as I could, and squeezed the handrail next to me to try to release some of the tension I felt. Slowly the grey tide began to recede, but the pressure in my head remained. And all the while the man sat opposite me, quite still, just staring.

I tried to think: The man meant me harm, that much was obvious. But for the moment he was doing nothing. Was that because he didn't want to do anything in front of witnesses? Or was he simply trying to time it right? Would he wait until we stopped at a station, then calmly pull out a gun, shoot me in the head, and slip out of the doors just as they started to close? If so, how could I stop him? Should I shout for help? Should I try to grapple him preemptively? Should I try to engage him in conversation and keep him talking until I could escape?

Of course, I did none of those things. I sat there, miserably frozen. We pulled into the next stop, and a few people got on and got off, but the man opposite me just kept staring. Then the doors closed and we started to move again. We made another stop, and then another. At the fourth stop, just after the doors opened, he suddenly shifted his weight. That broke the spell, and I bolted, stumbling off the train and onto the platform. I ran as fast as I could – which, honestly, was barely faster than a brisk walk – through the crowd on the platform towards an escalator, and hauled myself up that, through a corridor, then up a set of stairs. I reached a row of turnstiles and risked a glance behind me, and almost immediately I saw a black baseball cap bobbing up behind some tourists who'd just emerged at the top of the stairs. I fumbled my way through the barrier and through a station exit which turned out to lead straight into the ground floor plaza of a busy multi-level shopping centre.

I was gasping so hard I was starting to feel light-headed, so I took a second to try to catch my breath, leaning against a wall, hoping I would be concealed by the throng of people around me. It briefly occurred to me through the haze of fear that there was an irony at work. Ordinarily I would avoid places like this at all costs, precisely because they were always so crowded, and I had always thought I was terrified of crowds. But faced with *real* terror such as this, suddenly I was genuinely keen to seek safety in numbers. Different rules applied in different situations, posited a small part of my brain that was watching events unfold with a sort of fatalistic detachment.

In a similar way, it occurred to me, right now I needed to start thinking of these other people not as threats but as assets. I looked around, and my eye fell upon an information kiosk. Taking a deep breath, I stumbled up to it. A short, stout, closely cropped and bespectacled man was perched on a stool behind a counter, and smiled pleasantly at me as I approached.

"Good morning sir! How –"

"Helloineedyourhelpamanistryingtokillme," I blurted.

The man blinked.

He said something in response but I didn't catch it. The roaring in my ears became deafening and I felt my legs giving way. My vision went blurry, my chest tightened...

... and when I came to I was lying flat on my back with the bespectacled man crouching over me nervously.

"Are you alright, sir?"

"Uh... yeh," I mumbled.

"Great, great. I, er, I was worried I'd have to give you mouth-to-mouth, ha."

"No, no um, no need."

"Can I get you anything?"

"No."

"Sir, are you in danger? Should I call 911?"

"Uh…"

I thought about it. Had the man… had he *definitely* been following me? Was the baseball cap I had seen after I got off the train even his? Or had I just let myself be overwhelmed by the Gabardine Suit Game *again*? A surge of humiliation washed over me as I realised how ridiculous I must look. What if it had all been my imagination running away with me?

But then again, what if it hadn't?

Big Sis was right. I was completely out of my depth. I didn't even know what the threats were. I should give up now. Give up, go home, accept that I'd lost.

But…

"N-no, thank you. Sorry. Uh… w-where can I get a taxi?"

*

I was dropped off a block away from Bacon Tray and walked the rest of the way, glancing anxiously around every few seconds. There was no sign of the man in the baseball cap, but I couldn't help looking for him in every direction.

I stopped just across the street from the diner, and took a breath. This was going to be awful.

I crossed the street, and walked up to the doorway that was next to Bacon Tray's frontage. There were three buzzers, for apartments A, B and C. Without letting myself think too much about it, I hit the first buzzer. No response. I tried again. Still nothing. It was a little after 8:30 in the morning. No student would be out of bed yet, would they? I didn't know. Maybe American undergraduates were more proactive than their British counterparts. I tried the second buzzer. Again, no response.

I tried the third buzzer.

Nothing again.

Well, that was that. I started to walk away, disappointed and relieved in equal measure. Should I come back later or–

"Yeah?" came a crackly voice through the intercom.

"Oh, uh, I'm here to–"

"What?"

"I, uh, I need to speak to–"

The door was buzzed and clicked. I pushed it open, and made my way up the stairs inside.

Apartment C was on the first floor, directly above the restaurant. That was good. I doubted anyone higher up would get a good enough signal to log on to the WiFi. Forcing myself not to dwell on what would happen next, I knocked on the door.

It was opened almost immediately by a young man who looked to me to be South Asian or maybe Middle Eastern. I wasn't sure. He was a little bit overweight, and wearing shorts, a baggy t-shirt, and flip-flops. I got the impression he had been in bed when I had buzzed.

"Can I help you?"

I cleared my throat.

"Uh, are... are you D-Draconix?"

It sounded stupid, saying it out loud. He looked at me blankly.

"Nah dude, I'm Hiral."

"Ok. Uh... who else lives here?"

"My housemates. No one called, uh, Dragon or anything."

This was going exactly as badly as I would have imagined it if I'd let myself think about it in advance. That was why I'd tried not to think about it. Knock on a stranger's door and take it from there, that was the plan. Well, now I was there, and I was lost. This man didn't seem to be Draconix. There'd not been a flicker of recognition on his face when I said the name. So next I supposed I needed to get into his apartment and talk to his housemates. But any second now he was going to lose patience. I needed to do something big.

I took a deep breath. *Here we go.*

"Uh, I'm... I'm a detective, a-and I'm working on... a c-crimin..."

I tailed off. Hiral looked rightly unconvinced. I cringed. What a loser I was. I had tried to bluff and I couldn't even get the words out.

"I'm sorry man, I can't help you."

He started to close the door.

"No, please, sorr-... I–" I burbled, putting my hand on the door and stepping forward.

I am not a strong man, but I am a heavy one, and once part of me was in the doorway there was very little he could do to dislodge me.

"Hey!"

I could just about make out some details of the room behind Hiral. It looked like a typical student pad, messy and dirty, with miscellaneous empty drinks containers stacked on most surfaces. There was a central communal room that was half lounge, half kitchen, and four doors leading off it, one of which was evidently a bathroom. Of the remaining three, one was open – that must be Hiral's room – and one of the remaining two was just opening, and another man, taller than Hiral and skinnier, but similarly dressed, was stumbling out of it, probably curious about the commotion. He was clutching a laptop. I craned my head around an increasingly agitated Hiral, and caught a glimpse of the logo: it was a Lenovo.

"Listen man, you'd better–" Hiral was saying, but I ignored him.

"Draconix?"

The other man's eyes widened.

"Oh fuck!"

He froze for a second, then darted back into his room, and slammed the door behind him.

"I know who you are! I know where you live!" I shouted.

"Ok dude it's time for you to step the *fuck* back or I'm calling the cops right now," said Hiral, placing both hands on my chest and shoving. I stumbled back a step and he took the opportunity to slam the apartment door in my face.

"Draconix! Draconix!" I yelled again and again, sliding close to hysteria. "I know who you are! I know who you are! I –"

The door opened again. This time it wasn't Hiral behind it. This time it was Draconix.

22

Most hackers don't hack alone. For one thing the world of tech is constantly shifting, which means that to stay on top you have to be constantly learning, and it's far easier to learn if you have a supportive network of peers. Even criminals need study buddies. For another thing, precisely *because* the actual execution of hacks is a solitary pursuit, often undertaken by one person alone with a laptop, it tends to get lonely after a while, and hackers, like most people, crave companionship. So they look for people to talk to. But because the subject matter of their shared passion is fairly consistently illegal, they need anonymity. Thus they create aliases, personas attached to usernames, and they use those to interact with others in the online cybercriminal community. The system only works because hackers create careful disconnects between their online selves (with which they might, for example, explicitly take credit for their crimes) and their real life selves (who very much don't want to be apprehended and prosecuted).

I had just removed that disconnect for Draconix. As soon as he knew that I knew where he lived, I had him in my power.

Through me it was possible to tie everything illegal Draconix had ever done and bragged about to the awkward-looking student who lived in an apartment above Bacon Tray in Boston and was now eyeing me uncertainly.

"So... come in I guess," he mumbled eventually, and led me through the living room to his bedroom. The most immediate thing I noticed was the smell of recently-sleeping human. It was a relatively bare room, with a few clothes poking out of a wardrobe, an unmade bed, and a generic desk which supported a few empty tumblers and a dirty plate, a couple of token textbooks, a large gaming PC and a laptop-shaped gap in the clutter next to it.

He sat down on the bed and motioned for me to sit in his chair, which I did. I had a chance to look at him more closely. He hadn't shaved in a while, but didn't quite have what you'd call a beard. He had dark rings under his eyes, which were wide open as he stared intently at me. Mostly he just looked scared.

"So... like... who are you? Are you, y'know, with the cops, or...?"

"Uh, no, I'm –"

"Oh shit," he interrupted, his eyes widening. "Oh shit you're *him.* You're that guy... uh, the Paladin guy. Clayton? Dude we've been watching you *closely.*"

That was an understatement.

"Listen, man," he continued, "You gotta know that it wasn't me. It wasn't any of us, ok? We didn't do anything. So just... yeah."

I hesitated.

"You mean... you, uh, didn't steal the money from Maison de Gauguin?"

"Exactly. Not me personally, and not Pony Club."

"You... publicly took the credit. On Twitter," I said, frowning.

He shook his head.

"It wasn't us. I created a bunch of accounts a few years ago, then basically threw the usernames and passwords out to anyone who wanted them, put them on some forums. Gives us deniability, in case –"

"In case this happens. You can claim someone else had control of the account."

"Yeah, but it's true. And, look, this was huge. It was great for our rep – we weren't about to start denying it. Dude, we've been trying to work out who did it ourselves."

He looked earnest. But he was saying things that directly contradicted the facts.

"You owned up to it on Stableyard. You and at least one other person."

He closed his eyes.

"Oh fuck. You know about Stableyard. But..." he said, opening his eyes and frowning, "No, I didn't own up to anything."

"Yes you did. In the Targets channel right after it happened. ONEWORDALLCAPS asked who had been involved and you said you had."

"Bullshit."

"I s-saw the chat."

"Bullshit! Look, dude, I'll show you."

He opened up his laptop and started typing. A few moments later he got up and set it down on the corner of his desk so that I could see his screen.

"Look, here's what we said in Targets."

I looked. He had logged into Stableyard, and was in the chat archive for the Targets channel.

ONEWORDALLCAPS: *(April 14 13:59) Alright, if no one else will ask, I will: which one of you pricks did it? Who took out Maison de Gauguin? And what the fuck do I have to do to get a cut?*

lowkey: *(April 14 14:01) Am I going to be the only one to admit I had literally no idea this was going to go down?*

Draconix: *(April 14 14:03) Me either. Guess either I'm not as close to the centre of this thing as I thought, or we have a rogue operative on our hands!*

Divvi: *(April 14 14:03) Can confirm – this was not centrally planned.*

lowkey: *(April 14 14:03) So it wasn't us then?*

Divvi: *(April 14 14:04) Not _us_ us, but as far as I'm concerned, if a hacker uses one of our Twitter handles to announce a hack, that makes them a Pony, officially. Who shared all our Twitter accounts anyway?*

Draconix: *(April 14 14:12) *Raises hand sheepishly* That was me. I guess it's 'official' then. We were the ones who hacked MDG.*

 270

This was unexpected. My parasite code had managed to unearth the first and last messages in that exchange, but not the ones in the middle. What I had thought was Draconix's confession was actually nothing of the sort. I sat and thought for a moment.

"S-so... do you know who Sandspidr is?"

"Who?"

"Sandspidr. All one word, missing an 'e' at the end. He's been messaging me, uh, claiming to be from Pony Club."

He shook his head.

"Never heard of him."

"Ok... and do you know about morlok?"

"No... oh, shit, yes! He joined Stableyard a few days ago. Look, I can show you his profile..."

"No, no it's ok. I mean... do you know that morlok is me?"

"You're... oh *shit*. No, I... I had no idea. I was chatting to Divvi, we were excited, we thought that morlok would make a good recruit for... uh, for a research project."

I couldn't help rolling my eyes.

"For real! Listen, um, I know all about the hack. I mean, I read about it. And I'm sorry. I don't think you deserved to be fired. But you've seen for yourself... it was nothing to do with me. And I'm not doing anything... I mean I've not done anything... *serious*. I'm just trying to level up my infosec and get through college so I can make a living when I graduate, y'know? So, like... are we cool?"

I suddenly felt extremely tired, and I very much wanted to get away from this whining man who didn't know anything that could help me. I stood up with a grunt.

"Uh, I'm not going to tell the police that you're Draconix."

He sagged with relief.

"Thanks, man, I really appreciate it."

"I need to go. I have to work out... everything."

"Sure, sure, listen, if you need any help..."

He showed me out of his room and through the sitting room, past where Hiral was now sitting, looking confused. As he opened the apartment door for me he said: "Listen, so... how did you find me?"

I looked at him for a second.

"I, uh... I suppose I just kept trying."

*

When I got back down onto the street I felt so weak I thought I was going to faint again. I was completely out of my depth. If Pony Club weren't behind all this, who the hell was Sandspidr really?

If Mary really was Sandspidr's invention, that would explain a lot. It would explain how they knew that I hacked Stableyard and that I went to Boston. But surely it was stretching credibility to assume that, *prior to the hack*, Sandspidr anticipated that they would want to track my movements in case I started doing some unauthorised digging by myself, and so found me on AltMatch, created a *perfectly* faked profile and got chatting to me just so that they would be able to keep tabs on me in the aftermath in case I went rogue. In some ways, that notion made Sandspidr seem even more terrifyingly capable than if they had managed to learn about Stableyard and Boston through other means.

Either way, it was clear that Sandspidr would *not* want me knowing that he/she wasn't really part of Pony Club. How long was it before they discovered I knew the truth? Perhaps, if I was being watched, they already knew. If so, who knew what steps they might take to stop that information from leaking out? I still had no idea whether the man on the subway from this morning really had been following me.

I reached a decision: it was time to get out of Boston and go to ground.

I used my phone to book myself onto the first flight back to London. I took the subway straight to the airport. I hadn't left anything of value in my hotel room, and didn't dare go back there, in case another heavy was waiting for me in the lobby. I would email them to check out and let them know they could dispose of my left-behind belongings. With each passing minute I felt my courage drain away, to be replaced with terror and paranoia.

Once at the airport I heaved myself straight to security, where I briefly convinced myself that Sandspidr was actually in the CIA, and this was the point where I'd be taken off into a windowless interrogation room and never seen again. But, to my relief, there was just a bored guard who glanced at my passport and another bored guard who waved me through the scanner. I marched through to my gate, where I had another nervous panic at the final passport scan before boarding, but was allowed on the plane without delay. A little while later I felt a soft bounce as the wheels left the tarmac, and I was on my way out of the US.

Once we were safely in the air – and to think that only a few days ago it would never have occurred to me to describe being airborne in a little metal tube as 'safe' – all the pent-up adrenaline from the day's events seemed to gush out of whatever tight place it had been hiding in, giving me an uncontrolled fit of the shakes, enough that the flight attendant bent down to ask me if I was alright. I muttered something about stress, and she smiled and returned a moment later with a packet of pretzels.

I realised I was still desperately tired. Even though it was only lunchtime it had already been a hell of a day, and I didn't understand any of it. I reclined my seat and settled back to try to sleep. But I couldn't. There was an annoying glare from the laptop of the woman sat across the aisle one row in front of me. It was stupid, really: it only bugged me because I knew it was there. If I closed my eyes I couldn't see it, but its presence made me want to keep opening my eyes to confirm that the source of my irritation hadn't gone away.

She was producing all that glare because she had Excel open, which meant that almost her whole screen was white. From this distance I couldn't tell what she was working on, but if I leant forwards a bit I'd probably be able to make it out. It was almost certainly work-related, and might well have been confidential information. Numbers in spreadsheets tended to be sensitive, after all. And this woman had them up on her laptop, without a screen protector, so that anyone could see. Terrible, sloppy, unprofessional, etc, but the truth was we all did it.

All of us...

Could that have been it? If somehow they'd been able to see my screen, they'd have watched me hacking into Stableyard. They'd have been able to see me book flights and a hotel. But I'd done all that from my flat. There had been no one standing over my shoulder. Unless somehow there'd been a camera involved. A spy cam sewn into my hoodie without me noticing, perhaps? A long-distance lens pointing through my window?

I could feel myself finally drifting towards sleep. My train of thought was slowly morphing into a stream of nonsense. Screens, cameras, hackers, Little Sis, Mary, Debi, DI Otembi, Maison de Gauguin, Moritz... Screens and hackers and cameras...

I sat bolt upright and let out a sort of gasping squeal.

23

"Mr Clayford, I'm not interested."

"B-but this is the only way we'll find out how they hacked us."

"At this point I don't *care* how they hacked you. The specific technical weaknesses in your system are not my problem. Even if we manage to catch these people, the particular mechanism behind the hack is of no use when it comes to prosecuting them, for the simple reason that the average juror is too stupid to understand it. It just confuses them. I told you this before: we're only interested in information that helps us *catch* Pony Club."

"They're not even... Look, I just –"

"And anyway, you're not supposed to be even working on this, are you? Aren't you still suspended?"

"..."

"Just take some time off, Colin. You sound stressed. Spend time with your family."

"I tried that –"

"Listen, I have to go. Thanks for your call, but... don't call again. We'll be in touch if we need you."

"But –"

"Bye now."

DI Otembi had not been impressed by my bright idea.

I was sitting in a quiet cafe in Brighton, armed with new clothes, a new phone with a new number, a new laptop, and a waist pack (fine, a bum bag – Titian would be delighted) full of cash for expenses. During Little Sis's extended stay at the clinic here we had come to visit enough that, more than any other place outside London, I vaguely knew my way around it. I hoped my connection to it was sufficiently obscure that Sandpidr wouldn't think to look for me here. Wandering round brought back memories of awkwardly killing time, after Little Sis shooed us away but before our train home departed, and Big Sis plonking us down in seafront café after seafront café. She would read books about acting theory and drink mint tea, and I would read books about databases and eat pastries.

I was staying at a very cheap hotel under a fake name, avoiding using my credit cards, only going online using my brand new laptop (which I had paid cash for), and not logging into any of my old accounts. I had disconnected entirely from my previous life. It hadn't actually been much of a wrench. There wasn't much left of my old life to get upset about disconnecting from.

I was taking Sandspidr's threat very seriously. Whoever they were, they knew an awful lot about me and wanted me to stop trying to learn more about them, and had threatened to kill me if I didn't. I had no idea if they were the sort of person, or organisation, who would actually carry out their threats, but it didn't seem that far-fetched.

Of course, none of it would matter if I was prepared to do what Sandspidr wanted and *not* stand in their way. They had instructed me to go hide in a hole, and I very much wanted to do exactly that. But while sitting on the plane I had realised that there was still one more avenue I had yet to explore. And for all that I was terrified of Sandspidr, I couldn't *quite* bring myself to leave it alone.

I needed moral support, though. So I found a payphone and, after much fumbling around trying to work out how to make calls on it – I hadn't used one of these things since I was a teenager – I rang Big Sis.

As soon as she realised it was me she exploded.

"Oh my God, what's going on? I thought you were dead! I've been ringing you every hour, I've emailed, I even went to your flat, then I called Paladin, and I called the police and literally everyone I knew, and then Little Sis told me you were at *hers* last week and I mean *what*?! I... WHERE ARE YOU?"

"I'm s-sorry, I'm so sorry. I've been in Boston –"
"BOSTON?!"

"– and I found the hackers, only it's not them, and, uh, I know what to look for next, but I'm not safe so I didn't–"

"What do you mean you're not safe? What's going on?"

This was difficult. Big Sis was agitated, and her agitation was flustering me.

"The hackers," I tried again. "They're not who they're pretending to be, and they're threatening me so I need to hide, but–"

"Look, stop. Stop," she said firmly. "This is too much for you, and you're cracking up. It's ok. Listen to me. It's ok. You're safe. No one is out to get you."

"No, you're not *listening*," I said. "They are, they literally are. This isn't the suit game, it's real. B-but it's ok, I'm handling it."

"You're not. You can't handle it. Colin, *you can't cope with this.* I need you to let me take care of you. Wherever you are, I'll come to you right now. Just, tell me where you are, and I'll come get you."

I took a breath. I wanted nothing more than to tell Big Sis, have her come collect me, let her deal with everything. I shut my eyes.

"I'll call you again when I can."

I hung up.

*

I got a taxi from the rank at London Victoria, and asked the driver to take me all the way to Wimbledon. I felt myself getting more nervous the closer we got, and by the time we pulled into the car park I was a sweaty mess.

In daytime, MDG HQ looked even more achingly trendy than it had last time I was there, the brick-meets-steel construction reeking of neo-retro cool. I asked the driver to wait for me in the car park. I'd already racked up a ludicrously large fare, but I didn't want to have to sit around waiting for another taxi to turn up once I'd done what I came for.

Now came crunch time. There was an easy way and a hard way of getting what I needed. I clambered out and shuffled towards the building, muttering under my breath a fervent prayer that I'd be able to take the easy way. I scanned the car park and the outside of the building, but didn't see what I was looking for. If it wasn't out here I'd have to go in to reception. They might recognise me. Even if they didn't, they'd ask questions. I'd have to start bluffing, and that hadn't gone well for me recently. And the longer it took, the higher the chance that someone like Todd, who definitely would recognise me, might appear.

But there was nothing for it. I braced myself, and walked up to the reception door. I reached for the handle...

And stopped. There, on a small etched steel plaque to the right of my hand, was exactly what I was after: An image of a security camera, and below it the words: *These premises are monitored by closed circuit television. Security provided by Logicurity.*

I looked up, and saw through the glass door a receptionist at the desk. Not Moritz, I noted. Was he recovered yet? Would he ever be? As I grappled with a momentary surge of guilt the new receptionist made eye contact, and she smiled at me. Panicked, I turned on my heel and walked as fast as I could back to the taxi.

*

"Hello Logicurity, Trish speaking."

"HithereI'dliketorequestcopiesofoursecurityfootage."

Not a great start. Sitting in the little B&B I'd booked myself into in Oval (which seemed as out-of-the-way as anywhere I could think of in London) I'd spent half an hour psyching myself up for this call, and much of that time had been devoted to practising my opening line. If I could strike the right tone at first, everything would be much smoother. But when it came to it I'd forgotten to breathe before speaking and now I'd fucked it all up already.

"I'm sorry?"

I cleared my throat.

"Uh, I'd... like to request copies of our security footage."

"All right sir, what company are you calling from?"

"M-Maison de Gauguin."

"Ok, and what date would you like footage for?"

"Wednesday the 12th of April."

"And would that be all feeds or just one particular camera?"

"Um... just the reception area."

"I'm sorry sir, we only catalogue by camera number. Do you have the numbers of the cameras in your reception? It should be on the yellow tag on the camera itself, or the bottom left of the display in your on-site monitor."

"Oh, uh... never mind, just send me all feeds."

"All right, not a problem. We'll courier a hard drive with the footage to you within 48 hours."

"Oh uh, great. That's great, thank you."

This was working. It was actually working!

"Not a problem sir, is there anything else I can help you with?"

Then I realised I'd forgotten about the most important part.

"Oh! Uh, can I tell you where to send it?"

"It's alright, we have your address on file."

"Uh, a-actually... I was hoping you could just email the files to me?"

"Oh. Um, well we don't normally... hang on, let me just check.... Can I pop you on hold, sir? It's just that we just set up a new procedure for releasing customer footage, and it's a bit strict on this sort of thing. Let me just see if someone from our operations team is around, is that ok?"

"Uh... sure."

"Ok won't be a minute."

Hold music started playing, then went quiet as my phone slithered out of my sweaty grasp and the speaker slipped away from my ear. I mopped my hands on my shirt and clamped my phone back to the side of my face. After a few minutes the hold music stopped and Trish came back on the line.

"Hello! Right, I checked and we can absolutely send you a download link to the footage. I just need to ask you a couple of security questions if that's ok, starting with your PIN."

I hung up the phone.

Fuck you, Trish, for doing your job properly.

I had really been hoping that if I just asked confidently enough they'd email over the footage. That was how social engineering was supposed to work. You just asked people for what you wanted in a way that made it hard to refuse. They weren't supposed to remember to follow procedure.

Part of me knew that if I'd been better at this I could probably have busked it, come up with some convincing reason why I didn't have access to the security PIN, come up with some excuse for urgency, applied a mixture of charm and manipulation and walked away with the goods.

But that wasn't me. I had strengths, and I had weaknesses, and oh boy was chatting to strangers on the phone a weakness.

Time to rethink.

Logicurity evidently had an extensive archive of footage from Maison de Gauguin's security cameras. MDG had several security cameras in their reception, which meant there was a significant possibility that there was a camera trained on Mo's computer screen at the time of the attack. My big insight while sitting on the plane back from Boston had been that there was therefore at least a slender possibility that the footage in Logicurity's archive would uncover what Moritz typed that gave the hackers the Burncoin private key.

Now, the two groups who could request that footage directly were Maison de Gauguin and the police. Indirectly, Paladin could probably get access to it by pressuring MDG. But I had no way of convincing any of those people of the importance of all this, because none of them really wanted to know what had happened. In their various ways they all wanted to sweep the event itself under the rug. So if I was to get the footage at all I'd need to get it myself.

Unfortunately, it turned out that simply asking for it didn't get me what I wanted.

I had to play to my strengths. I looked at Logicurity's website, which proudly detailed their systems. The cameras they used were digital, and sent their video feeds to a little black box on their clients' premises which periodically bundled it all up into one big file and sent it on to Logicurity's own server over the internet. It ran a piece of software apparently called Klaritee that actually stored all the files and allowed Logicurity employees to view them. So, thinking logically, my only chance of accessing that footage would be to get access to that server at the Logicurity office. And to work out how to do *that* would require a little more information.

*

Unnervingly, Logicurity's head office was located not all that far from my home in Dalston. Returning to my normal haunts made me feel terribly exposed. Not only was I more likely to bump into someone I knew, there was also the possibility that one of Sandspidr's minions was watching my flat. If so, I was putting myself nearer to them. The chances of either were pretty remote, but it was yet another fear to add to the growing pile.

As an initial reccy I simply walked up outside Logicurity's office – it was situated down a rather dingy back street behind a pub – and loitered just within range of the office wifi. The good news was that there was a guest network I could join for free. The bad news was that it was very effectively 'sandboxed' – I could get online, but I couldn't access any of their internal stuff.

I got my phone out and held it up to my ear, and started to do slow circuits on the pavement, occasionally nodding. Someone hanging out on a quiet street on the phone always looks less suspicious than someone just hanging out. My many years of analysing threat levels playing the Gabardine Suit Game had taught me that. I let my orbit bring me closer and closer to the glass window by Logicurity's main entrance, and allowed myself to glance briefly in every few circuits or so, still nodding, and occasionally muttering, 'OK' into my phone. I felt bloody stupid doing it, but I wouldn't have dared go near the door otherwise. After a few passes I could make out the basic layout of the room behind the window. It was a reception area, with a receptionist installed at a desk in the corner. Closer to the window was a coffee table with a few chairs dotted around it. Nothing particularly interesting, except... what was that cable running along the inside windowsill? It looked rather like ethernet to me. And that meant that, yes, there was a hole in the wall just to the left of the window, with some metal trunking leading off around the corner of the building and then down into the ground. Which probably meant that I was looking at the entry point of the broadband cable into the building. The main router would be just on the other side of the window. That's what I needed access to.

I went home to mull over the possibilities. If I came back at night with a hacksaw I could cut through the trunking and access the cable. I might be able to splice some sort of device into the cable, although this was *way* outside my area of expertise. But even if I could, that would still get me access *outside* their firewall, which wasn't very helpful. If I broke the window I might be able to reach the router and plug into that, but it would probably take a couple of days to figure out their network, and any tampering I did would be immediately signposted by the broken window, so would be shut down long before I got any use out of it.

No, I needed to get to that router without anyone suspecting something was amiss. A plan began to form in my head. A very, *very* illegal plan.

I didn't let myself dwell on how much trouble I'd get into. Instead I logged onto eBay and ordered some tech kit: I found a job lot of twenty little devices called Terrier Boards, which are basically credit-card sized computers with no screen or keyboard. I also bought a cardboard box, a battery pack, a couple of cables, a rucksack, a lanyard, and a cheap suit. I had it all delivered to my B&B. It cost a little over £500 of my swiftly dwindling savings, but if I pulled this off it'd be well worth it. And if I didn't, money would be the least of my worries.

*

A few days later, in the early hours of the morning, I dropped off the cardboard box behind the bins outside Logicurity's office. Inside, the battery pack powered nineteen of my Terriers. Each one was programmed to do just one thing:

connect to the Logicurity guest wifi and start aggressively up-loading and downloading hundreds of high-resolution video files. Together, they consumed enough bandwidth that I was confident they would bring the office internet connection to a standstill.

A little before 10 o'clock, feeling so nervous that I was struggling to breathe properly, I knocked on Logicurity's door. I was wearing my new suit, adorned with a lanyard, to which I'd attached a bit of paper with a printed photo of myself, a generic logo, and a made-up name.

The door was opened by a middle-aged woman who looked friendly but overworked.

"Yes?"

This, I realised, was the woman I'd spoken to on the phone, Trish. Would she recognise my voice? I froze for a second, gawping. I felt myself go crimson. But suddenly her face lit up.

"Have you come to fix the internet?"

I nodded enthusiastically.

"Come in, come in. I have to say, I'm very impressed with how quickly you came out. Normally it takes hours to get someone round."

I looked round at the room and saw the router, as expected, sitting on a low table directly beneath the window. I gestured at it, questioningly.

"Uh...?"

"That's it," said Trish. "It's been playing up all morning. Do you want a cup of tea? Coffee?"

I shook my head. I wanted to get away with saying as little as possible, to minimise the danger of her recognising my voice. Also, I was so nervous that if I opened my mouth I thought there was a danger I might just start screaming and never stop. I'd never in a million years imagined I'd ever end up trying to pull off the Posnett Gambit myself.

I eased my rucksack off my shoulder and sat myself down in front of the router, being careful to position myself so that my bulk obscured what I was working on from the room. With shaking hands I pulled out my laptop and connected it up to the router. I also pulled out my last Terrier and plugged that in as well, then carefully tucked it down the back of the table amidst a nest of other cables. It wasn't completely invisible, but hopefully it looked technical enough that no one would question it. Next I used my laptop to start monkeying around with the router to set up some instructions to allow me to talk to the Terrier from outside the office.

That done I pulled out my phone and opened up the app with which I controlled all of my outdoor Terriers, and instructed them to finish what they were doing and shut down. Within a few minutes they were all dormant. I ran a quick check with my laptop: with my devices no longer hogging the internet connection, download speeds were running at a healthy hundred megabits per second, as they should be.

"Trish, is the internet back?" came a male voice, very soon after.

"Let me check... ooh yes, it is. This gentleman has been working on it."

"Thank Christ. Great work Trish, thanks for sorting it so quickly. And sorry for getting so worked up earlier. You know how it is."

No wonder Trish had been so happy to let me in. Evidently her colleagues had been yelling at her about the internet all morning. I felt bad to have caused her that unpleasantness.

I put my laptop back in my rucksack and got up.

"Is that it then?"

I smiled and nodded.

"That's brilliant, thank you so much!"

I nodded again and she walked me to the door.

"Bye now!"

"G-goodbye," I managed to whisper.

After Trish closed the door behind me, I walked round the corner, bent down to pick up my cardboard box of Terriers, and, as the adrenaline shakes set in, vomited messily all over my shoes.

24

I sat in my hotel room and glared at my laptop. The next step was proving harder than I'd expected. The changes I had made to Logicurity's router had enabled me to connect directly to the Terrier I had secreted in their office. Using it as a sort of bridgehead, I was able from there to access their whole network. What I now needed to do was identify the 'Klaritee' server, which was the thing that stored the CCTV footage. Via my Terrier I could monitor every bit of information that went back and forth in their intranet, but I was stuck trying to figure out how to analyse it all to see what was Klaritee-related and what wasn't. What I wanted to do was relatively straightforward, and the sort of thing that most IT technicians could probably do in their sleep, but it happened to be outside my area of expertise: I'm a software nerd, and a cryptography nerd, but I'm not a *networking* nerd. I had a basic idea in theory of what I wanted to achieve, but I found myself stumped in practice. 30 different browser tabs charted several hours' worth of failed attempts and dead ends.

I forced myself to take a break. Normally in a situation like this I'd ask someone at work for help. But I could hardly send a message to Bled or Debi saying, "Hey, long time no see, I've just hacked into a security company's network to try to prove our mutual employer wrong, only I'm not smart enough to figure out what to do next... any pointers?"

So I tried something different: I went for a walk.

I'm not normally a fan of walking, particularly in London. I take up more than my fair share of space on narrow pavements, and hate having to negotiate impatient kids on scooters, aggressive dogs on leads, and hostile adults in general. Plus, as a means of getting from A to B it's neither fast nor energy-efficient.

But today I wasn't going from A to B. I took myself off down to Kennington Park, and pottered along a path around its perimeter for a little while.

I had to stop quite quickly, because my hips started hurting. And it was a bit cold, and I needed to pee almost as soon as I set out. So I wouldn't say it was exactly an *enjoyable* experience. But it turned out to be just enough of a change to get my brain ticking again. By the time I got back to my room I had three more ideas to try, of which the third actually worked, and soon I was monitoring a flood of network traffic as the various computers attached to Logicurity's network chattered to Klaritee and received replies. I made a mental note to try more of this 'exercise' lark when it all calmed down. Maybe there was something to it after all.

There was still plenty of work to be done. All the sensitive data was encrypted, meaning that while I could see that there were messages between Klaritee and various other computers, I didn't know what those messages were saying. I tried to access the Klaritee server directly myself, but immediately hit a login screen, for which I didn't know a password.

Fortunately, I was now back in the realm of software security systems and their circumvention, which was very much more my wheelhouse. I decided to use a technique known as a man-in-the-middle attack. When Logicurity employees tried to put their passwords in when they logged on to Klaritee, the router would divert those passwords via my Terrier, which would note them down for me before sending them onwards. Once I had an employee's password, I could simply log in to Klaritee as them.

As with Stableyard, first of all I had to lay my trap, and then I had to leave it alone and wait until someone fell into it. I spend a few hours getting it all ready, then I set everything running, making sure I would be notified if I got a hit, and logged out of the Logicurity network.

*

I had been so proud of myself for how long I'd lasted without checking AltMatch. It had been a full week, and, as part of my attempt to take myself 'off grid', I hadn't even checked my email to see if I had any notifications, let alone visited the site itself.

But in all that time I hadn't been able to stop thinking about Mary. I still couldn't make up my mind whether I believed she was real or not. That afternoon, with nothing to do but wait, I couldn't help myself. I checked my email.

As I'd expected – as I'd hoped? – there were several messages from her, sounding increasingly worried, the last of which was just a simple, sad plea for me to at least let her know I was ok. She sounded so upset that I couldn't bring myself to keep ignoring her. I signed in to AltMatch and hopped onto Instant. She was online.

THX1137: Hey

...

HarlequinCyanide: Oh my god!

HarlequinCyanide: Are u ok?

THX1137: I'm fine. I'm so sorry. I've had to be offline for a while.

HarlequinCyanide: What happened?

I paused. How was I going to handle this? I didn't trust her by a long shot, so I couldn't tell her the truth. But I also couldn't exactly *say* I didn't trust her. I also didn't want to lie to her.

Maybe there was a middle road.

THX1137: The hackers knew I was onto them and they basically told me if I didn't back off they'd kill me. I think they meant it. I think they had someone follow me in Boston, but I'm not sure.

THX1137: So I freaked out for a bit and basically went into hiding. I threw away my phone, moved into a hotel, paid for everything in cash.

THX1137: I've calmed down a bit now. I think so long as I leave them alone they'll leave me alone.

HarlequinCyanide: Oh my god! That's awful. Can you go to the police?

THX1137: No. For one thing, I've broken quite a few laws myself. But also, the police just want an excuse to close the file on this whole thing. The best explanation anyone can come up with is that I helped Pony Club pull it off, and I can't exactly prove that that's not true. So the last thing I want to do is start drawing attention to myself.

There. If it was Sandspidr on the other end of the chat then hopefully I'd just told him everything he wanted to hear. If it was really Mary, then at least I'd told her the truth. Well, part of it. But it didn't feel right. Labyrinth-related stuff aside, I hadn't told her any of the stuff I really wanted to say.

HarlequinCyanide: I'm so sorry. That sounds like really heavy stuff. Are you ok?

THX1137: I'm fine.

THX1137: Actually no

THX1137: I always say I'm fine. I'm not fine. I'm more stressed than I've ever been in my life. I'm not sleeping, I've got pretty constant heartburn, I don't know what I'm doing and every day I wake up hoping that the past few weeks were just a bad dream. This has been the most testing experience of my adult life and it turns out I'm not the sort of person who rises to the occasion.

HarlequinCyanide: *That sucks.*

HarlequinCyanide: *But also, like, thanks for being honest*

HarlequinCyanide: *I appreciate that. I think it's easy to hide behind a persona that you make for yourself, and it can be hard to reveal the bits of yourself that you maybe feel don't live up the persona. You know?*

THX1137: *I really do.*

Maybe it was because I was still stuck in a limbo state where I didn't know whether I could let myself believe she was real. Maybe it was because the events of the last few weeks had torn away what little shreds of dignity I still had. Whatever it was, I suddenly found it easy to say a lot of things I'd never normally say on AltMatch. I kept typing.

THX1137: *Ok, for the sake of continuing in that vein: I'm waaay worse to meet in real life than I come across on AltMatch. I sweat too much, I stammer horribly, and I'm paralysed with terror by the whole world. I _always_ say the wrong thing and I'm terrible at reading people, and the only time I ever say something funny or a propos is if I have half an hour to go away and think about it – which works on here but not in real life.*

...

HarlequinCyanide: *I'm severely agoraphobic, I find eye contact really hard, and even though I hate talking about myself I manage to make every conversation about me.*

HarlequinCyanide: *I cry most days.*

HarlequinCyanide: *I dye my hair to draw attention away from the fact that I've got a growing bald spot. Not that anyone ever really sees it, because I never leave home. These days I feel like I barely exist outside my job, and even with that I'm not really being me – I'm just pretending to be this confident customer service persona to get me through the phone calls. And all the while all I'm doing is waiting for the technology to improve enough that my job can be replaced by an AI in a few years, then I'll have nothing.*

HarlequinCyanide: *That tiny video message I sent you took me two hours to do because I got so flustered about the idea of you seeing my face that my mouth dried up and I kept having coughing fits. And it was still the closest thing I've had to a real human connection in years.*

HarlequinCyanide: *I flirt on here in a way that I never would in person. It's all play-acting to let me pretend to be something that I'm not.*

...

HarlequinCyanide: *Too real? Oh man, I just ruined this whole thing, didn't I?*

THX1137: *No! I mean, it's actually nice to know that I'm not the only one who's a bit... unfit for purpose? Sometimes?*

HarlequinCyanide: Bahahahha I'll remember that one. Yep, I'm unfit for purpose alright.

HarlequinCyanide: So... would you prefer to go back to pretending that you're some super-suave genius and I'm a manic pixie dream girl with a heart of gold and a dirty mind? Or shall we carry on as a pair of fat, broken weirdos?

THX1137: Tell you what. On weekends let's be our real selves, weeknights we'll be the fake projections of ourselves.

THX1137: Except on Wednesdays, when you can be super suave and I'll be a manic pixie dream girl.

HarlequinCyanide: Lol perfect!

THX1137: (That, by the way, is the sort of joke that the suave, fake online version of me can toss out off the cuff. In real life it takes me way longer to get there).

HarlequinCyanide: Oh well, I suppose I don't really mind if it takes you a long time to toss off in real life...

HarlequinCyanide: I guess old habits die hard, eh?

*

Mary and I kept chatting over the next few days. The shift between us wasn't tectonic, but the cadence of the conversation had changed. It was like we saw each other more clearly. We were more candid. She probed me about my weight and eating habits in a way I found uncomfortable, but I did my best to answer. And I... I realised I simply couldn't countenance the idea of her not being real. I just couldn't cope with it. So I set myself the rule that I wouldn't tell her anything about the hack and what I was doing about it, and other than that I put all inklings of mistrust from my mind.

I had never had anything like this before. I had occasionally made what felt at the time like an intimate connection, but there had always been a thick layer of make-believe. I was always projecting a persona of someone better than the real me, and I was sure the other person had been too. It was part of the fun. Even now it was hard to stop. But ultimately there was something more *real* about my relationship with Mary now. That was hugely important to me.

In the meantime, my trap wasn't getting any bites. No one seemed to be logging in to Klaritee from inside the office, and by Friday night I still had nothing to show for my elaborate infiltration of their system. It was frustrating, because no one was going to be logging in over the weekend, so I would now be unlikely to get anything until Monday at the earliest.

I did, however, get an email from Debi.

Colin!

Did you burn your phone? Not saying I blame you, but you could have told people before you did. It would have saved me a bunch of time leaving you voicemails and sending you messages.

I'm teasing.

I really hope you're ok. Everyone misses you. I know you know that, but I wanted to say it anyway.

Also, we're doing a BBQ at ours, Sunday at 1. Just the Bunker Buddies. It's been bloody awful at Paladin recently, we're all getting on each other's nerves, and I thought it would give us all a chance to be nicer to one another in a less stressful environment.

Come. I know the last time I saw you was a bit grim. It'd be nice to put that in the past.

X Debi

*

Saturday was a quiet day. Mary wasn't online because she had family visiting. I passed the time fairly mindlessly skimming content on Hacker News. There was a controversial article by serial startup founder Trey Masterson about how he'd bootstrapped his latest venture and how "capital is no longer a barrier to being an entrepreneur". The general consensus among the comments was that this was a bit rich coming from the founder of Quarc, the start-up that Finisys had bought for hundreds of millions of dollars. The deal had made Masterson rich enough that he had no business telling anyone that money was unnecessary. I paid attention at first because Quarc's sale was what had made Lena Mueller enough money to buy a £7.4m artwork from MDG in the first place. But there was no mention of her, or of the hack, so I soon lost interest.

I filled the rest of the afternoon by repeatedly changing my mind about whether to go to Debi's the next day. On the one hand, a barbecue with colleagues was very much the sort of thing I Do Not Go To, because I'm so intimidated by the idea

of 'hanging out' with people that I'm uniformly crap at social-
ising and no one benefits. But on the other, after all I'd been
through in the past couple of weeks, the idea that I could feel
intimidated by Bled, or Kayla, or even Rémy, was faintly pre-
posterous.

And then there was the thought of seeing Debi herself. I
was still upset at the way she'd so smoothly usurped my role as
tech lead. But really, could I blame her? She had been routinely
overlooked in the past, despite being phenomenally talented,
and credit where credit was due, she'd done incredible work
uncovering that timing attack vulnerability. That took talent,
which deserved to be rewarded, and arguably I was about to
be pushed out the door anyway, so why not take advantage of
the opportunity?

I missed Debi too. I missed them all, but she was the only
one of the Bunker Buddies I'd ever got close to thinking of as
a friend.

Except... did she actually like me? Or was it simply that I
was easy to boss around, which helped when she needed to
make up numbers? And really, truly, if I was completely honest with myself, did I actually like Debi? Or was it just that I
was attracted to her and craved the validation of her attention?

Late on Saturday night I came to a final decision: I wouldn't
go. I needed to stop following Debi around like a dog just because her *look* turned me on. I was getting nothing real out of
our friendship. And the rest of them... well, I'd probably never
work with them again, so what was the point?

I started drafting an email to Debi, but couldn't quite get the tone right. I couldn't seem to find a way of saying 'no' without making it sound rude. After ten minutes of false starts I deleted the draft and decided to give it another go the next day with the benefit of a night's sleep.

25

I woke up early on Sunday morning and, as normal, checked my phone before anything else. Inexplicably, I had a notification from my trusty Terrier: Someone had finally logged into Klaritee a couple of hours earlier.

I leapt out of bed. Ok fine, I flopped out of bed with more gusto than normal. As soon as I could jab my contact lenses into my eyes I pulled up my laptop and started to explore.

The user had the email address patricia.kearns@logicurity.com. It took me a second, then I realised: good old Trish. She had logged in at about 6am, and on a Sunday no less. Presumably some issue had come in overnight and it had got dumped on her, and she had accessed the network from her home computer. I decided I liked Trish. And she had tried so hard as well: her password was a proper, secure, random string of numbers and letters. Her professionalism was commendable. Hopefully she would never find out how I had taken advantage of her.

I used my Trojan Terrier to connect to the Logicurity network and opened up the Klaritee login screen. There was a bag of chocolate brioche buns on my desk, and I chewed on a few as I worked. I'd been playing fast and loose with my food supplies for weeks now, and was beginning to get the hang of not being able to eat whatever I wanted, whenever I wanted. I am ashamed to admit, though, that I was making up in quantity what I was lacking in diversity. I was quietly grateful not to have access to my bathroom scales to see how much weight I'd put on recently.

Trish's username and password let me in with no problems at all. With a few clicks I navigated to the archive for MDG, then I chose a date range, selected 'All cameras', and hit 'Download'. Cue a loading screen with a slow-moving progress bar as the server prepared my files, that was eventually replaced by a giant file download commencing.

The B&B's patchy wifi was a bit of a bottleneck. To kill time I allowed myself to take another sneak peek at my email inbox, and some of the messages I'd been ignoring so far. Evidently Big Sis had spoken to Mum about me, as a few days ago I had started receiving from Cyprus a flurry of over-excited, over-the-top emails, professing increasing angst over my well-being over a 48-hour period, before abruptly stopping.

Typical Mum. She'd decided to worry about me, and got more and more worked up – probably her agitation and her level of inebriation were closely correlated – before getting distracted by something else and forgetting all about me. That was what really bugged me: that for her, caring was an action, not a state of being. She'd do a bit of caring, and then she'd stop, and do something else. I wasn't any kind of expert on interpersonal stuff, but even I could see that that wasn't how it was supposed to work. Parenting is a long-term project, and you shouldn't get into it if you're only interested in short sprints. Why Mum had chosen to have children, and not just once but *three times*, despite being temperamentally completely unsuited to it, was beyond me.

No. Wait. That was being unfair. For one thing, at the time Mum hadn't known that she'd be raising us by herself. And anyway, what was it Little Sis had said? She only realised what Mum's life was like after she had children of her own. I was being a bit quick to cast stones. It was a habit: get angry with Mum every time she did anything. Find a way to find fault with her. That way I felt less bad about ignoring her. And I ignored her because... well, if I was honest with myself, I ignored her because I hated the fact that she still hadn't forgiven me for what I'd done to Little Sis.

No. Wait. Again, was I being fair? Did Mum really blame me? *How do you always manage to get everything so wrong, Colin?* That was the one thing she'd ever explicitly said about it, in the heat of the moment in the midst of the crisis itself. Since then everything had been expressed through looks, through awkward silences, through what was left *un*said. The blame that I was discovering in those empty spaces – was it really Mum who was putting it there?

This was a deeply uncomfortable train of thought. There was a thread here, and if I started pulling at it I wasn't sure where it would lead, or what it might unravel. Mercifully, before I could spiral too far in on myself, I got a notification that my download had finished. I let myself forget all about family issues and get back to the matter at hand.

To my delight, the footage was great quality: there was no audio, of course, but the picture was high resolution, and at a reasonable frame rate. There were twenty-three cameras in operation at the MDG premises, and as ill luck would have it, I eventually discovered that the three in the reception area were the last ones in the list, so it took me a while to get to them.

Three angles. What were the chances that one would give me what I needed?

The first just showed footage of the door opening and closing, and was no use to me.

The second was at the wrong end of the room. Moritz's desk was visible in the background, but it wasn't nearly close enough for me to make out any detail.

I paused for a second before opening the final file, and offered up a silent prayer to any passing patron saint of information security engineers. It was all riding on this.

I double-clicked the file, and immediately my heart sank. The camera was positioned so that Moritz's desk was front and centre in the frame, at a 45 degree angle. But his monitor was facing away from the lens. There was no way I'd be able to see what he had up on his screen. Even the mirror on the wall behind him was no use: the camera angle was too sharp, and the reflection I saw was of the surface of his desk, with his keyboard, mouse and stationery.

I watched the footage, disconsolate. Moritz went about his daily business, taking phone calls, chatting to colleagues, and doing an awful lot of very dull-looking printing and stapling at his desk.

I skipped forward, keeping tabs on the timestamp in the bottom right hand corner of the screen. Things got busier over the course of the morning, and Moritz had a couple of breaks where a woman with spiky hair took over at his desk for a few periods. At one point he went out, evidently to buy some lunch, because when he came back he sat at his desk eating some sort of salad from a clear plastic box. In the afternoon he dived into another mountain of paperwork, and then from about 4pm everything got quieter. A couple of times he got up and wandered around. He spent some time surreptitiously sending messages on his mobile.

Then, at a little after 5:30, the call came.

I watched him pick up the phone, arranging his face into a smile, as his mouth formed the words 'Hello, Maison de Gauguin'. He listened for a bit, said something like 'Yup' a few times, then frowned. A few moments later he started nodding, then he said something I couldn't interpret, and, wedging his phone to his ear with his shoulder, put his hands down out of sight where the keyboard was and turned his attention to the screen.

For the next few minutes he did lots of listening and a little bit of clicking with his mouse, and then a bit of typing. Occasionally he said something, and a few times he nodded, at one point dropping the phone as he did so. Then he did a long, slow bit of typing – that must have been the command that actually triggered the hack – and after a pause he slowly read out something – that must have been the Burncoin account private key that he could now see on screen. Then one more bit of typing (the command to clear the history so we couldn't see what was typed), and then he smiled, sat back, said a couple more short things over the phone, and then put the phone down.

That was it.

I watched the footage again, scrutinising the point where he executed the script. His lips moved as he typed. Maybe he was repeating the instructions he was given. But his face was angled down – he was a hunt-and-peck typist who had to stare at his keyboard to find the right keys – so while I could see movement in his lips, it wasn't clear enough to work out what he was saying. Besides, I kept getting distracted by the mirror behind him, which showed lots of other movements, from the reflection of his hands moving over the keyboard...

Hang on.

I watched the footage for the third time, and realised I had something. It wasn't clear, not by a long shot. I couldn't see the extreme left end of the keyboard, and of course his hands blocked a lot, but for the most part he typed with his middle fingers extended, and in the mirror I could see at least which area of the keyboard he was typing on. I could use that.

I knew that the last thing he'd typed was the phrase '*history -c*'. I re-watched that bit of footage to see whether I could match up what I saw with what I knew he had typed. Thanks to the camera angle I could see most clearly the keystrokes that involved him moving one of his hands to the right. So the 'h' and 'i' were largely obscured by his right hand as he typed them, and the 's' by his left, but the 't', 'o' and 'r' were all quite obvious, and because he reached over with his left hand for it, the 'y' was clear as day. I didn't see the space at all – the movement of his right thumb was evidently too subtle, but then got the dash and the 'c' pretty clearly, and the 'enter' key was unmissable.

Armed now with some understanding of what I could expect to see and what blanks I'd have to fill in, I turned my attention back to the main command.

It was long, that much was clear. There were a few slashes in it at the start. Then at least one dash, followed by a number. If I was going to decipher it all I'd need to go through it letter by letter. So I split the footage into 100 overlapping snippets. I worked my way through them, chucking out all the clips that didn't feature a clear, complete hand movement. Then I revisited what was left and marked the few obvious key presses. I was now pretty sure he'd typed 28 characters, of which I managed to definitively identify ten.

Then the hard work began. For each of the remaining characters I reviewed the relevant clip and, based on which hand moved and in which direction it tilted, I put together the set of keys it could be. Slowly, painstakingly, I worked my way through each character. Through inference and elimination, I built up a pretty solid guess at the whole command:

/usr/bin/openssl rand -hex 8

My heart started to sink. I rewatched the whole footage a couple of times, each time with more awful certainty: That was what Moritz had typed. Once I knew what I was looking at, the motion of his hands on the keyboard was unmistakable.

My stomach growled, and I thumped my laptop in frustration. The problem, you see, was that that particular command didn't *do* anything. It just printed on-screen a completely random set of letters and numbers. It was a trivial tool that people occasionally used to generate temporary passwords, nothing more.

That was it? They got Moritz to ask his computer to invent a random password, and read it back to them over the phone? How on *earth* could that be used to steal Burncoin from a different computer somewhere else in the building? It made no sense.

This, I realised, was the problem I had been up against from the get-go. The more I learnt about the hack, the less sense it made. I had assumed from the start that the hackers had a clear plan and knew what they were doing, but if that were true then I had to conclude that they were playing the game so much better than me that I didn't even recognise the moves they were making. And given how much I'd now learned about the hack then, even putting all ego and insecurities aside, we were getting to the point where that interpretation was stretching the bounds of credibility. But the alternative was that the hackers *didn't* have a clear plan, and were just making stuff up as they went along… in which case how the hell did they end up with the money?

God I was hungry. I'd long since finished the brioche buns, but I kept watching my hand slide towards the empty packet on my desk. It was making it hard for me to think straight. There was no room service in my B&B. Would any takeaways on Deliveroo be open yet? I realised that even though I'd spent a lot longer analysing the footage than I'd thought, it still wasn't quite lunchtime. I really wished my appetite would leave me alone, just for a little bit.

If the hack made sense, then I must be an idiot not to spot it. If I wasn't an idiot, then the hack didn't make sense. But of course, it *had* to make sense somehow, because they walked away with millions.

The ache in my stomach was no longer prepared to be ignored. Defeated, by everything, I got up, closed my laptop, and stomped out in search of some food.

26

I went to the barbecue.

There was no more work to be done on the MDG hack now. There were no more clues to examine, no more paths to follow. I had all the information I was ever likely to get right at my fingertips; I just couldn't decipher it. I felt utterly glum. So, since I'd never got round to declining, I decided I might as well go, as really *anything* was better than sitting round in my B&B room, hating myself for being too stupid to understand how we'd been hacked.

I picked up my rucksack (I kept my laptop with me at all times now), and headed to the underground. At the back of my mind I knew I was supposed to be keeping a low profile and staying out of public spaces as much as possible. But I barely cared any more. The hackers who weren't Pony Club either possessed such incredible powers of surveillance that they would find me as soon as I ventured into a tube station, in which case there was surely nothing they *couldn't* do, and trying to avoid them was pointless… or they didn't, in which case I was probably safe.

I noticed a couple of people stealing sideways glances at me as I got onto the train. A young man in his 20s and an older woman. I couldn't be bothered to be scared of them, couldn't be bothered to play the Gabardine Suit Game, so instead I simply stared back at them until they looked away. As far as I was concerned, if they were going to displace any of the stuff that was already on my mind they would have to do a hell of a lot more than just look.

*

Debi answered the door. She was back in black, wearing a sleeveless vest that showed off her arm tattoos and sporting her signature black cherry lipstick. I felt a rush of something that felt like nostalgia, or homesickness. I suddenly longed to be back in the Bunker, subtly leaning across to catch the delicious tendrils of exotic scent that she left behind every time she walked through the room.

Her eyes lit up when she saw it was me.

"You came!"

"Uh... yeah."

"I'm so glad. I've missed you."

"Well..."

We stood awkwardly for a second, me on the doorstep, her in the doorway.

"Listen, Colin, I just wanted to say, I'm... sorry about –"

At that moment Rémy emerged from the bathroom behind Debi.

"Yo Colin! What's up?"

"Hi Rémy."

Rémy thrust his way past Debi with an arm raised. Too late I realised he was coming in for one of those ghastly arm-clasp-cum-hugs. There was no way out of it, so I let it happen. I managed to avoid flinching too much. Debi caught my eye from behind Rémy and made a silly face. I half-smiled back.

"Man, you look like dogshit. Did you put on weight?" asked Rémy earnestly.

"It's good to see you too," I replied coolly, and Debi guffawed.

She led me through the house to the small, tidy back garden, where a not-yet-lit barbecue stood next to a table spread with assorted snacks. I was pleased to see that, alongside the inevitable raw broccoli and tahini pastes, there was some proper food: sausage rolls, crisps and a big bowl of oven chips. Perhaps this was a token effort towards reconciliation on Debi's part. Either way, today was an eating day, so I helped myself to a plateful before turning my attention to the other people in the garden. Bled was standing in the corner, and gave me a small wave when I caught his eye. He didn't come over, because Rémy had blocked his path, and appeared to be launching into a diatribe about... something or other. I couldn't make it out from here, and didn't care enough to get closer. Meanwhile Jason was trundling around, beset on either side by small children, muttering something about matches.

"Drink?" asked Debi, materialising at my elbow.

"Uh... do you have coke?"

"Ye-es... but it's wanky artisan cola. Is that ok?"

"Sure."

"So. What have you been up to?"

There was no way, I decided, of describing any of my adventures in brief, and I didn't have the energy to go into detail.

"Uh... this and that," I fudged.

"Yeah? You know, your sister rang the office. She sounded really worried about you."

"Oh, y-yeah. It was... a misunderstanding."

"Well it's good to see you. You know, it's been weird in the Bunker since you've been gone..."

Debi started off on some story about office politics involving Priyanka from the sales team and Brad, and I found my attention wandering. I had already nearly annihilated a whole plate of sausage rolls. I wondered if Debi had noticed. God I disgusted myself sometimes. I didn't even get any pleasure from the food. It was just a compulsion, a displacement activity that promised a fleeting moment of safe sensations to block out the awfulness of everything else. Pathetic.

And all because I wasn't a functional enough human being to be able to find *real* fulfilment in... No. No, Little Sis was right. I was mindlessly trotting out the same line I'd been telling myself for 20 years. Colin can't cope with real life, so Colin needs to hide from everything and try to fill the resulting emptiness with food. But fucking hell, in the past few weeks I'd travelled half way across the world to track down and confront a hacker, I'd social engineered my way into stealing data from a *security* company, and I'd embarked on the most profound, intimate relationship of my life with Mary (and yes, yes, we'd never even met, but *still*). Was there a tiny possibility that my starting point, my baseline assessment of myself, wasn't *entirely* fair? And if I was wrong about that...

I realised there was something happening in the back of my head, some thought about me, about Pony Club, about the whole damn mess. But I couldn't tease it out, couldn't articulate it yet. With an effort I turned my attention back to Debi.

"... and there's something really weird going on with Kayla and Brad. Ever since the Riga trip they've been antsy, but last week they could barely be in the same room without arguing."

"Is Kayla coming today?"

"No, she had to catch up on work. I think she's been finding it a bit overwhelming without you there. She and I haven't exactly... I don't think we've quite got into our stride with a working relationship. You know?"

"Hey Colin," said Bled, slouching over to me, as Rémy headed off in search of another drink. "So when are you coming back?"

"Uh... I don't know," I muttered, awkwardly. "I-I don't know if I'm coming back."

"We need you, though. We need someone to kick Debi's ass at riddles, she's winning every week now."

"Excuse me," said Debi, haughtily. "If you check the leaderboard you'll see it's been a long time since Colin's even come *close* to my arse. As it were."

I reddened, as much out of habit as anything else.

"You know we still haven't solved that fucking treasure chest one," continued Bled, oblivious. "I mean, fuck me. There's locked box, he can't open it without a key, he doesn't have a key, what does that even leave?"

And then it started to piece itself together in my head. Bled started saying something else, but I didn't really hear it, and I let myself cut him off.

"It's... obvious. It's really, really o-obvious," I said, my mind racing as I tried to grasp all the implications. "Uh, the box is locked and sealed. There's definitely no way of getting the treasure out of it, but the thief leaves with the treasure. So the only possible explanation... is that the treasure wasn't inside in the first place."

"Yeah, but the riddle–" began Bled.

"I'm not really talking about the riddle. I'm talking about... I'm... I'm sorry, I have to sit down."

"Colin? What's going on?" asked Debi.

"I need... I need some time to think. Do you have a room... a quiet room?"

"You can take the study," she said, gesturing into the house.

"I'm sorry," I said, getting up and grabbing my rucksack. "I just have to..."

I shuffled hurriedly out of the garden, leaving Bled and Debi looking thoroughly confused in my wake, and headed to the study. I'd apologise for my weirdness later, but for now... I pulled my laptop out of my rucksack and set myself up at the desk, which in an understated nod to Debi's style was adorned with a couple of Mexican Dia De Los Muertos-style skull ornaments, and what appeared to be a stuffed raven. I pulled up a text file and started to type. It was fairly unstructured at first, just an outpouring of ideas, but I found myself circling round again and again to a few key points. Not everything made sense yet, but I could see the beginnings of a new interpretation of events...

I got my phone out and messaged Little Sis. It wasn't really her I needed to talk to, but I didn't have Ruaridh's number, and besides, a message from me to him would carry more weight if it went through her.

Then I got up and poked through the door. Everyone was still out in the garden, and safely out of earshot. Good.

I went back into the study and called Kayla.

27

She answered on the second ring.

"Hey stranger!"

"Hi. Uh, I need your login details."

"Sorry, what?"

"I'm sorry. I really, really need your Paladin login. I need to sign in, and my access has been suspended."

There was a pause.

"Colin, I *really* can't do –"

"I think I've figured out the MDG thing. I just need to look through some of our documents."

"I... look, I'll tell you what I can do. Tell me what you're looking for, and I'll read you what you need down the phone."

"I don't *know* exactly what I'm looking for. I need to see the documents."

"I really want to help you Colin, you know that. But I mean, c'mon, you called me out of the blue. I can't just hand over my login."

"I'm not about to start making trouble."

"I know that, it's just... well, I actually *don't* know that. I don't know where your head's at at the moment, do I?"

"Ok…. ok…." I said, banging my knee against the underside of Debi's desk in frustration. "Then can… can *you* log in to Paladin's document server? And share your screen with me? I won't be able to do anything, you'll control everything, I'll just ask you to bring various files up on screen."

"Um…. ok. Ok, we can do that. When do you want to set it up?"

"Now. Right now."

"Oh Christ, I… you know what, fine. If it's important, it's important. Gimme five minutes, and I'll call you back."

"Thank you, I… just thank you."

"It's no problem. Speak to you in five."

Kayla was the absolute best sometimes.

*

It took a couple of tries to set up the screenshare – it always does – but soon I was chatting to Kayla on the phone while on my laptop screen I saw what was on *her* laptop screen as she connected to the Paladin network and navigated to the document server, which held an archive of files relating to all our different clients.

"Ok," said Kayla, "MDG, right?"

"Yep."

"Labyrinth development, or the Pony Club investigation?"

"Pony Club. Although it wasn't actually... never mind. Just click Pony Club."

"Ok... now where?"

"I need emails. The emails Labyrinth sends out whenever a Burncoin is sent or received. They get sent out from a dedicated email address to... some distribution list inside MDG. That was what alerted Todd to the fact that the money had left their account. It was on the list of things you requested from them when we started investigating."

"I remember."

"So it'll be, uh... S-scroll down... there. No, back up. That folder. Then, uh, click 'Download all'. When it finishes, double-click –"

"Colin, I know how to download a file."

"Sorry."

"Ok, here we go. So... this?"

"Yep."

Kayla had downloaded a document archive, and in a sub-folder marked "14. Notification emails" were a list of text files, each storing the details of an email sent by Labyrinth to the internal mailing list at ops@maisondegauguin.com. They constituted every email sent by our system in the month leading up to the breach, and they were organised by date.

"Open up the latest one for me?"

Kayla launched an email viewer, which showed:

From: labyrinth-notifications@maisondegauguin.com
To: ops@maisondegauguin.com

Date: Wednesday 12 April, 17:51
Subject: [LABYRINTH][NOTIFICATION] Burncoin sent
Hi!
You've sent some Burncoin!
BUO30,931 (approx £7,369,129) has left your wallet at 17:51 today.
Labyrinth

"Ok, now show me the previous one."
A similar email popped up on screen:

From: labyrinth-notifications@maisondegauguin.com
To: ops@maisondegauguin.com
Date: Wednesday 12 April, 11:28
Subject: [LABYRINTH][NOTIFICATION] Burncoin received
Hi!
You've received some Burncoin!
BUO30,931 (approx £7,369,126) has been deposited in your wallet at 11:28 today.
Labyrinth

"The amount in pounds is different between the two," said Kayla, flicking back and forth between the two. "Is that significant?"

"Oh. No. That's just changes in the Burncoin exchange rate over the course of a day."

"Oh. So what are you looking for?"

"I just need… hang on. Can you show me the most recent message before those two?"

"Sure."

Kayla clicked on another email. This time what we saw was:

From: *labyrinth–notifications@maisondegauguin.com*
To: *ops@maisondegauguin.com*
Date: *Tuesday 4 April, 09:36*
Subject: *[LABYRINTH][NOTIFICATION] Burncoin sent*
Hi!
You've sent some Burncoin!
BUO8.3 (approx £25,023) has left your wallet at 09:34 today.
Labyrinth

That was a notification of the last transaction that occurred before Lena Mueller's deposit. I stared at the message, willing myself to see the missing piece of the puzzle. I knew there was something wrong here. Something inside my head was yelling at me, trying to draw my attention to something, but I couldn't make it out.

"Uh… Show me the second email again."

Kayla switched back to the second email, and it was suddenly immediately obvious.

"Oh for fuck's sake," I murmured, and started to laugh my awful gulping, snorting laugh.

"What is it?" asked Kayla.

"It's a hyphen. Not an en dash. Show me the first email again? Yep. There it is. Both emails sent on the 12th April were sent from 'labyrinth *hyphen* notifications'. But that's not the address Labyrinth uses. We use 'labyrinth *en dash* notifications'. Bled set it up that week I was off with flu and his keyboard is... It doesn't matter. But those emails didn't come from our system."

"But they... I mean, look, they still came from an official MDG email address. So... you're saying Pony Club managed to hack the email system as well as Labyrinth?"

"I'm saying... I'm saying the hackers – uh, they weren't Pony Club by the way – they managed to hack the email system *instead of* Labyrinth. The reason the Labyrinth account was empty was that no money was ever transferred into it in the first place. The only reason we have evidence that money was there in the first place was these notifications, and these notifications are fake."

"But Colin, that's not the only evidence. Todd says he logged in to Labyrinth and saw the balance with the money."

"I don't believe him. No hack ever took place. And, uh, I can prove it."

"How?"

I took a deep breath.

"I stole a copy of the security footage from the cameras inside MDG. I saw the commands they got Mo to type into the computer. It was just gibberish. It was all a distraction."

"Wait... what?" said Kayla, after a short pause.

"Actually... m-maybe forget I told you that bit. But you've seen for yourself, these notifications aren't from us. Uh... Can you call Anil? Now? You can leave me out of it for now. Just say you've found this, and... and that you need him to strong-arm someone at MDG into auditing their email system and finding out who set up that email address."

"Have you ever tried reaching Anil on a Sunday? *He* calls *you* at weekends, not the other way round."

"Debi did it. Besides, this changes everything. He'll see how big this is."

Kayla sighed

"I'll... I'll try. But Colin?"

"Yeah?"

"You *really* owe me if this doesn't pan out."

"I know."

"Ok, I'll let you know what happens. Bye."

"Bye."

I put the phone down. A few seconds later, Kayla killed her screen share, and her desktop disappeared from my laptop screen, to be replaced with an annoying pop-up asking me to rate the video quality of my experience. I was just closing it when I heard a noise behind me.

"Detective Colin cracks the case, eh?"

It was Debi. I tensed. At that moment in time there were several bits of the whole thing that I hadn't worked out. Debi was one of them. I swivelled round in my chair and faced her.

"Uh, h-how much of that did you catch?"

302 | GILES K CAPERTON

"From a little bit before you admitted hacking a security company. A hyphen, you say, when there should have been an en dash?"

"That's right."

"And based on that, you're saying that Pony Club didn't hack MDG... at all?

"Not just on that. I've been working on this for quite a while."

Debi gave me a sad look.

"Oh Colin," she said, sympathetically. "I get it. I really do. It must really, really hurt that they hacked Labyrinth, and it must hurt even more not to know how they did it. But... don't you think this is a little far-fetched? I mean, we found a bunch of problems in our code, didn't we? Our tamper sweep *was* mis-configured, we *were* vulnerable to a timing attack. And sure, we haven't fully figured out how Pony Club could have practi-cally exploited them, but–"

"B-but Debi, *of course* we found a bunch of problems in our code. We find problems in code for a living. We spent sev-eral weeks single-mindedly hunting for problems in our own codebase, and never giving up because we were so sure that there was a critical flaw. It would have been amazing if we *hadn't* found anything. But, uh, just because we found them doesn't mean that the hackers found them, or that there was even a way to exploit them, let alone that they found that way."

Debi shook her head.

"Look, I know you're upset about all this," she said. "But you need to let this go. The system was vulnerable. There was a hack. It doesn't lessen you as a person just because you built a system with a flaw."

I grunted in frustration. I had a thousand thoughts whirring through my head at once, and right now I needed the space to work a few of them out, which was hard to do with Debi so intent on shutting me down.

Why was she so intent on shutting me down? Oh...

"Debi, I'm sorry. I-I know you really wanted to be the one to solve the hack, and... and I know it won't, uh, do wonders for you for it to come out that your theory was wrong, but–"

"Oh come on," she broke in with a scoff. "Do you think I'm that insecure? If I'm wrong I'm wrong and that's fine, I'll always own up to it. But Colin, you're grasping at straws, and it's not helping anyone. I need you to accept that it's time to let this all go, not because I've got something to lose, but because you're my friend."

"Am I really?"

I listened in horror as the words came out of my mouth. Debi gave me a cold, quizzical look of the sort that would normally stop me dead, but I didn't seem to be able to rein myself in now.

"I, uh, don't think I really am your friend. I d-don't think you care very much about me at all."

"Bollocks. You're in my house right now. I invited you *as a friend.*"

I blinked slowly.

"You invite me when you need to make up numbers, be-cause you know I'll show up, b-because I'm easy to push around. You wouldn't go out of your way for me."

"Colin, I go out of my way for you all the time. I make enough food to satisfy your ridiculous appetite, I try to put you among people you're not going to be threatened by, peo-ple like Holly who you might actually get on with – and don't forget I was the one who tried to set you up with her–"

"But you never even asked me what sort of person I might be interested in, it's not like–"

"Ok fine," said Debi, throwing her hands up. "That one was self-interested, I admit it. You know why I did it? Because I'm very happily married, and after a certain point I get sick of men like you perpetually mooning over me in the office. Ok? Because sometimes you're not very subtle when you stare at me, and I wanted to see if just *maybe* I could get you to transfer your attention to someone else. Alright?"

That shut me up. I felt myself go a bright crimson colour all over, and in the moments of silence that followed I became aware of just how much I was shaking and just how much I was sweating. I really wasn't good at this confrontation stuff.

"Now," said Debi slightly awkwardly, "We've both got slightly het up, and I think the sensible thing would be to take a little time out. I've got to stop my husband from setting him-self and our children on fire, and I'm sure you'd like to catch up with Bled and Rémy. Let's forget all about this for today, and maybe if you have the time next week we can have a sit down and talk some things through. Alright?"

I nodded in agreement and she started to shepherd me out of her study, but then I forced myself to stop. Things were not alright. And they were about to get even more uncomfortable.

"Debi, before I go… I want to talk about your riddle."

"Um, ok…?" said Debi, wrongfooted by the abrupt subject change.

"The point of it is that it tricks you into thinking the treasure is in the chest, right?"

"Ye-es…"

"But the treasure isn't in the chest. It was *never* in the chest. That's the twist."

Debi gave me a questioning glance. I could feel sweat dripping down my neck, and wanted nothing more to curl up in a ball, but I ploughed on.

"A-and that's, uh, a *bit* of a coincidence, because the same is true for Labyrinth. The reason we never figured out how the money could have been taken out was that, uh, the money never was taken out. It was never there in the first place. The hack was actually the bit where they faked it to make it look like the money had been transferred. So… how did you know?"

Debi put on an undecipherable expression, and folded her arms, but didn't reply. I found myself struggling against an urge to start apologising, so to keep it at bay I made myself keep going. I was committed now, so I might as well see it through.

"It… it seems an awful lot like you knew that the hack was a fake from the start. And I don't know why you'd make the whole thing into a riddle, unless… unless you wanted to taunt me with it, or... prove once and for all that you're more intelligent than me. So... I don't know if, uh..."

"So where's the treasure then? In the riddle?" asked Debi, her face hardening.

"Uh..." I said, uncertainly. "Well I suppose it's... in the crypt but outside the chest."

"Wrong! Try again. The first line of the riddle is: *The crypt is empty except for a treasure chest.*"

"So... maybe the treasure is outside the crypt?" I said, uncertainly.

"Wrong! Try again. *The thief enters the crypt empty-handed, and leaves with one item of treasure in his hand.*"

The sweat was now pouring down my back and pooling between my buttocks.

"I... uh..."

I tailed off. After what felt like a year, Debi spoke, slowly and deliberately:

"The chest *is* the treasure. It's made out of gold. That's the answer to the riddle. That's the only answer that works. I should know, because I spent hours trying to come up with something challenging enough to entertain my *friends.*"

I swallowed.

"Oh."

"So if it was a metaphor for your frankly pretty flimsy theory about Labyrinth, it's wouldn't be a very good one, would it? I mean, Labyrinth isn't made out of Burncoins, is it?"

"N...no," I whispered.

"Now, you just made a pretty unpleasant accusation, the sort of thing I wouldn't expect friends to say to each other. I'd rather hoped you trusted me a little bit more than that, and since you don't... I'd rather like you to leave my house now please."

She gave me a smile that could cut through tempered steel. I wilted.

"Uh... I'm so... uh, yes, I'll go... sor- sorry."

I fumbled to pick up my laptop and made a half-hearted attempt to get it back into my rucksack, but my fingers were jelly under Debi's frozen gaze, and I quickly gave up and just carried it separately. I crossed back into the kitchen and through the hall to the door.

"Hi Colin!" said Jason, cheerily, emerging from their sitting room.

"Uh... I... I have to... hi... uh, bye."

I didn't raise my eyes, so didn't get to see the expression on his face as I shuffled past him. But his opinion of me was the very last thing on my mind as I let myself out and onto the street.

I'd been wrong. I'd been so horribly, unforgivably wrong. I'd got carried away, I'd got too used to relying on hunches and guesses, and it had led me to making a completely baseless accusation and permanently wrecking a friendship that Debi had just started to patch up. Stupid, stupid!

I made my way back to the tube. I wanted to get out of there as soon as I possibly could... but even more strongly, I wanted to eat. A lot. There was a fried chicken place just next to the station. I went in and ordered the 'Family Bucket', and when it was handed over, spent a couple of minutes devouring the first few chicken pieces right there at the counter, before heading out and shambling through the tube barriers clutching my greasy cardboard tub.

I ate the whole way back into town, and then bought some more food the moment I got off the tube back in Oval. By the time I made it back to my room I felt very ill, but didn't care. The discomfort helped take my mind off the massive fool I'd just made of myself. I sat on the toilet for a while and felt sorry for myself. Then I lay on the bed and felt sorry for myself some more.

How do you always manage to get everything so wrong, Colin?

Debi wasn't involved in the hack. Of course she wasn't. I didn't know why I'd accused her. I had been so embarrassed when she said what she said about how I felt about her.

But if I was wrong about the solution to the riddle, did that mean I was wrong about MDG? It had seemed so clear, so *obvious* when I was sat in Debi's study: we'd assumed from the get-go that there must be a problem with Labyrinth, and lo and behold after enough digging we'd found one and assumed it was the explanation. We'd assumed that the hackers had stolen the money, and lo and behold we'd pieced together a semi-credible explanation of how they could have done it. We had assumed that I had fucked up, and lo and behold we'd created a narrative that seemingly confirmed that I had fucked up.

This, I realised, was the story of my life: I started from the base assumption that there was something wrong with me, and it meant that everywhere I went, I looked for – and inevitably found – evidence to reinforce that assumption. Then, for a brief second, I'd started to believe that maybe, just maybe, if you challenged the starting assumption, everything else could to make sense in a different way.

But I was wrong.

It was all too much to cope with. I curled up under a blanket and started binge-watching *Star Trek: Deep Space Nine*, forcing myself not to think about any of it any more.

A few hours later I took a break to order some food. While I was waiting for delivery I started considering next steps. If I had ever had a shot at redeeming myself, I had blown it. Fine. Time to give up and, somehow, move on. I had no idea how, though. Maybe I should ring Big Sis, and ask her advice. No, she'd just tell me again that I should give up and retrain as an accountant, which was a stupid idea... but... I mean, what *else* was really on the cards?

I spent a miserable hour researching accountancy qualifications online, and trying to persuade myself I could get interested in the differences between discounted cash flow and EBITDA multiples as forms of corporate valuation. It would be a living, I told myself. It was probably, on balance, better than starving to death.

Despondent, I was on the verge of signing up for an online course when I received a phone call from a very excited Kayla.

"You're not going to believe this. It was Todd! I rang Anil, and explained everything you said. He called MDG's chairman, and *he* called Yoo-Jin, their ops manager. She logged into their email admin and found the fake account, and it was *Todd* who set it up. So now the chairman, Gavin, has said he'll confront Todd about it first thing tomorrow, and he wants Paladin to be in the room. Anil wants to be there himself, with me, and Debi... and you! The way Anil was talking, if we finally manage to get to the bottom of this he'll have you back in the Bunker by the end of the day. Isn't that great? Everything will be back to normal!"

28

At 8:52am the next day I was back at MDG HQ. I walked into the lobby, instinctively glancing up at the ceiling-mounted security camera whose footage had proved so revealing. The receptionist (not Mo, who Kayla had said was physically recovered but not ready to come back to work yet) was a chirpy young woman, with just enough piercings to be unusual but not too many to seem unprofessional. She smiled and asked me who I was there to see.

"Uh... G-Gavin Baker, I think. The chairman. I'm here for a meeting. There's a group of us coming."

"Ok no problem. Take a seat and I'll let Sandy know you're here. She'll sort you out. Can I get you a coffee?"

"No thanks."

"Tea?"

"Uh... I'm fine. Thanks."

I sat nervously by myself for a few minutes. Then the door opened again and in walked Kayla, Anil and Debi. They must have travelled down together. Kayla gave me a smile and a little hand wave. Debi avoided eye contact. She was once again wearing a very toned down outfit, with just a few subtle nods to her normal goth style. Anil didn't appear to notice me, instead immediately announcing himself to the non-Moritz receptionist. He accepted the offer of a coffee, and only then strode over to the sofa where I was perching. I stood up as he approached.

"Colin," he said, without much emotion. He gave me a little nod, and reached out and clapped me on the shoulder, his eyes already sliding back to his phone screen. I utterly failed to disguise my natural flinch. Kayla gave me a sympathetic look.

We stood silently for a minute or so. Anil seemed to have no interest in making conversation, and we all followed his lead and played with our phones instead. Eventually a red-faced, grey-haired man appeared from within the building. Gavin. He was, by all accounts, a shrewd businessman, but people always said it slightly defensively, as if the presumption was that he wouldn't be. He had originally been a restauranteur who had dabbled in collecting art, but it turned out his real knack was creating exclusive-feeling spaces and getting pally with the rich and famous types who frequented them. Eventually he had realised there was money to be made flogging art to his patrons, and the business had evolved from there. He had the corpulent look of a life-long bon vivant, and a voice that exalted in an affluent Surrey upbringing.

"Anil! There you are," he boomed, plummily.

"Good to see you, Gav," said Anil, immediately losing the stern, taciturn demeanour he wore whenever dealing with his employees, and instead started adopting a tone much like

Gavin's own. I wondered whether we were watching the 'real' Anil put in an appearance, or whether this was simply him wearing a particular face for a particular client.

"So these are the boffins, eh?" said Gavin, gesturing loosely at Debi and me. "Well, come on, come on, let's get in. Time to put this whole thing to bed."

Gavin led us into the bowels of the building, to a large, empty conference room.

"We're in here. I think we're in here. Sandy love, are we in here?"

He didn't seem to be addressing anyone in particular, yet a moment later a glamorous-looking woman holding a laptop appeared from around a corner and replied: "That's right, Gavin. Got it booked for the morning."

"My hero. You all know Sandy, don't you?"

Anil and Kayla smiled and nodded. Debi and I didn't, but no one was paying us any attention. We all filed into the conference room and sat down. I had hoped to sit as far away from Debi as possible, but I got hemmed in by Kayla and ended up right next to her. Her expression remained completely impassive, and she didn't acknowledge me.

"Now look," said Gavin. "We've got a couple more people turning up, so I just want to make this clear now: Todd has my absolute faith. Absolute. But. We need to get to the bottom of this thing. Anil's told me that Todd set up these fake email accounts that are at the heart of it, but without knowing any of the context that's all meaningless to me. So we're going to have a civilised conversation, with everyone necessary in the same place at the same time, to unravel it all. Good?"

We nodded.

"Actually, Anil, there's a couple of legal things I wanted to catch up with you about, without..."

He tailed off as his eyes briefly drifted over the rest of us, as though we weren't worth wasting a breath on a description. "Take a walk with me?"

"Of course," said Anil, and he and Gavin sauntered out. Sandy hovered a few steps behind, leaving me, Kayla and Debi alone in the–room.

"So Colin," Kayla began enthusiastically, "In the car on the way over Anil was saying –"

"I'm, uh, really sorry Debi," I cut in. "I got carried away and I shouldn't have... I mean I should have trusted you and –"

"It's fine," said Debi, completely deadpan. "Let's not worry about that now."

"Uh... ok."

I caught Kayla's look of confusion.

"Sorry Kayla, it's... uh, you were saying...?"

"Ok. Um, I was saying this is apparently how Gavin operates – he likes to pull everyone into a room, and have one big meeting rather than lots of little ones. Obviously we'll need you to explain some of the details. And Debi's role is –"

"Debi's here to make sure what you say sticks to the facts and doesn't stray too far off into the realm of fantasy," cut in Debi, frostily.

"Uh... I'll just... pull up some things..." I mumbled, hunkering down behind my laptop, to give me some shelter from Debi's icy glare.

A few minutes later, Anil and Gavin returned. They were accompanied by a handful of MDG employees I'd not seen before, and two more faces I recognised: DI Otembi, and a scruffy-faced, hoodie-clad man who I took to be her colleague Ben.

"... simply that in future it would be more efficient for everyone involved if I was contacted directly, rather than arranging meetings via the deputy commissioner," Otembi was saying to Gavin, with barely-concealed frustration.

"Of course, of course," said Gavin, dismissively. "Nothing would give me more pleasure. Now, if you'd take a seat... Sandy, can you sort coffees for everyone? Great. Just need the man himself now..."

And then he was gone again. The new arrivals sat down. Otembi said an emotionless 'Hi' to the room, and then focused all her attention on her phone. Ben caught my eye and gave me one of those pursed-lip, raised-eyebrow upwards-nod smiles that's the universal primate code for "I'm not a threat." It's the standard greeting between two techies who find themselves in a room full of managers. I returned the gesture.

A few minutes later Gavin appeared one more time, this time with a friendly, if firm, arm around Todd Nash. Todd didn't seem surprised to see so many people in the room. I supposed he was used to this style of working. I thought back to the night of the hack, when he had seemingly corralled the entire company into the office in the small hours of the morning. Apparently this was just the MDG way. He said hellos to some people, waved at a couple more, shook hands with Ben – who I guessed was the only person he was meeting for the first time – and sat down.

"Right," said Gavin, taking a seat at the end of the table. "Thanks for coming in, everyone, and sorry for the short notice. The good news is, thanks to the tireless efforts of the crack team at Paladin, we've had a bit of a breakthrough about the Nua Nigel debacle. Now, first things first, Zoe, we'll need you to let the insurers know everything we learn from this, and Strawberry Capital too, because this might affect how quickly they get their payout. We'll need to keep Lena sweet if there's a delay, so... bung her some Moet or something. Get Hattie onto it, she always handles this sort of thing so well."

Zoe – one of the MDG ones I hadn't met before – nodded and made a note on her phone. Todd shuffled in his seat.

"Actually, Gavin, is this going to be a long one? I had said I'd take a call with the Singapore team upstairs in a bit. Sorry, I thought this was just a quick catch-up."

"Don't worry about Singapore. You can tell them it's my fault."

"Right, sure, ok. Er... Any chance I could go take a wee before we get stuck into –"

"I have every faith that you can hold it for as long as we need you to," said Gavin, firmly, and Todd, defeated, piped down. "Now. I'll stuff up the details if I try to explain them –

you know me – so over to the Paladin boffins for the... you know... tech stuff."

He made a dismissive gesture towards our end of the table. Anil looked to Kayla, who in turn looked encouragingly at me. Panic flared through my chest. The assembled company was looking at me expectantly. Oh God. Presenting to a room. I felt my bowels convulse alarmingly.

"I... uh...," I stuttered eventually. "There's an email addr- no, it's..."

I felt myself petering out. Then, to my utter amazement, Debi rescued me.

"If I may, I'll lay out the preliminaries, and get Colin to jump into the fine detail when needed," she said, speaking calmly, clearly, and warmly. "Now, as you all know, our understanding up until this point has been that £7.4m was deposited into Labyrinth on the morning of the 12th, and then a few hours later was stolen by Pony Club. We had believed they used what's known as a 'timing attack' to exploit a vulnerability in the Labyrinth code, and the culmination of their hack was a phone call through which they coerced Moritz Ortlauf into unwittingly handing over the master password that allowed them to transfer the money out. However, what we're exploring now is the *possibility* that the money wasn't actually taken from the MDG account in the afternoon, because it wasn't actually deposited in the first place, and the whole thing was an elaborate misdirection."

I felt a huge surge of gratefulness to Debi. She had explained things far better than I ever could, in a way that everyone would understand, without making any unnecessary accusations or giving anyone a reason to doubt her. I looked round the room, watching the others take this in. Otembi was pulling out her laptop from her bag while simultaneously muttering something to Ben, who was typing furiously on his own laptop. Todd, meanwhile, was largely impassive. I did notice that he was gently drumming his fingers on the arm of his chair. Was that a tell-tale indicator of stress?

"Talk to me about this evidence," said Otembi, without looking up from her laptop.

"Sure," replied Debi. "Basically the easiest thing is to talk about the lack of evidence that the money ever *was* in our account. The main reason we believed the transactions had taken place was the notification emails that were sent out, which we thought had come from Labyrinth. It turns out, though, that they didn't. On close inspection, those came from 'labyrinth *hyphen* notifications at maisondegauguin dot org', but emails from Labyrinth come from 'labyrinth *en dash* notifications at maisondegauguin dot org'."

Ben let out a snort, and then immediately blushed.

"I'm sorry, what?" said Otembi, looking up.

"En dash," repeated Debi.

"It's a punctuation mark that looks like a hyphen, only slightly wider," explained Ben, enthusiastically. "This is actually similar to a well-established phishing technique that scammers –"

"When did this come to light?" asked Otembi, cutting him off.

"Yesterday," said Kayla.

"And who discovered it?"

"Colin."

That brought Otembi eyes up from her screen.

"Colin, who's suspended and shouldn't have access to any of the relevant systems?"

Kayla started to stutter, "I was screen-sharing with him... it was a very limited interaction..."

"We'll come back to that later," said Otembi, ominously. "But we've got plenty more evidence that the money was deposited with MDG. For one thing, we've got testimony from Lena Mueller at Strawberry Capital that she executed the transfer. And if I'm not mistaken, Mr Nash, you logged in to Labyrinth and verified that the money had been received, right?"

Todd squirmed, just a little bit. Just enough to be noticed by the people watching him closely. Did he feel the net closing in?

"Well, yeah, I mean I looked on the website, but if that was faked, can you trust that?"

"Ah, but it was only the email notification that were faked," clarified Debi, "Not the Labyrinth web interface."

"Yeah, yeah, exactly," said Todd.

"Mr Nash," said Otembi. "So we're clear, because it sounds like rather a lot hinges on this, you're saying that on the morning of the 12th, you logged in to the website, and saw a notification saying that just over thirty thousand Burncoins had been received?"

Todd was silent for a second, then he said, firmly and emphatically, "Yes."

The words hung in the air like a challenge. DI Otembi looked across at Debi, with a shrug. Debi offered a very similar shrug in my direction.

Todd was lying. I was... well, I wasn't quite sure about it, but it seemed to make more sense than anything else. But I dearly didn't want to have to make that accusation. I had pushed myself beyond my comfort zone a lot in the past few weeks, but my innate social anxiety would only let me go so far. The idea of flat-out calling him a liar, in front of everyone, was more awkward than I could bear.

I studied his face. He didn't look like a criminal mastermind. He just looked as gormless as I'd always believed he was. And if he really was that gormless, then how could...

A thought suddenly occurred to me.

"T-Todd," I said, and then had to say it again because the first time the words got stuck in my throat as all eyes in the room turned back to me. "Uh... when you say you looked at the website... how did you access the website?"

"Access it? It was on my laptop."

"No, I mean, did you log in? Did you click on a link to get it?"

"I just clicked on it. You know, from the list in my inbox."

"Ok... so the thing that you saw, the thing that told you the money had arrived... Was that thing, uh, an email from Labyrinth?"

"Well, I thought so... but now you're telling me that it was fake."

"Hang on," said Otembi. "So what you're saying is that you received the notification email, and that's why you believed the money had been transferred."

"Yes."

"But just now you said you looked on the website. Not an email, a website."

"Yeah, but it's the same thing these days" said Todd, slightly condescendingly. "I go *to* a website to look *at* my emails."

Through clenched teeth, and in an almost complete monotone, Otembi continued: "Mr Nash... so you're saying that the website that you looked at wasn't the Labyrinth website at all... it was your email account?"

"Well... yeah, technically speaking."

"Remind me what your job title is?"

"Digital Director," said Todd confidently, not apparently noticing the expressions on the faces of his colleagues, Otembi, or Gavin.

"Just checking." Otembi looked back at Debi.

I breathed a sigh of relief. This wasn't the first time Todd had failed to understand the difference between a website and an email. My theory was still intact, and a confrontation had been avoided. The only problem was, it was harder and harder to picture Todd as the villain here. Could this really all be a carefully-composed front? After this display, surely no one would believe for a second that Todd had been the one to forge the notification emails. And without a culprit, would the whole theory fall apart?

I noted that Otembi, despite her initial reluctance even to be in the room, was now effectively chairing the meeting, while Gavin continued to sit back. We'd certainly aroused her interest.

"Fine," she said. "This email stuff is all well and good. But what about the phone call to Mr Ortlauf? The commands they had him type into the computer?"

"So it turns out they were harmless: they didn't actually do anything, and the stuff Moritz read to them over the phone wasn't the password, it was… just a random set of letters and numbers," said Kayla.

"Really? When did you learn this?" asked Otembi sharply.

"Yesterday," Kayla replied.

"And who discovered it?"

"Colin."

"Of course it was. So how do you know it was harmless?" she asked, looking straight at me.

"I, uh…" I fumbled.

"Colin unearthed a previously undiscovered data source with a record of the keystrokes Mo entered. Right?" said Kayla, coming to my rescue.

"Uh, right," I confirmed. I could see Ben knot his brows and draw a breath as if to ask a follow-up question, but Otembi responded before he had the chance

"But for heaven's sakes, *why?*" she asked.

"Well," said Debi, still adopting a carefully neutral tone, "according to this interpretation of events, it was a smoke-screen."

"Sounds pretty far-fetched to me," said Todd. "Why would they *pretend* to hack us?"

"Presumably to cover up what actually happened to the money," replied Debi.

"Well, if the money never came to us... I mean, does Lena still have it?"

"N-no," I said. "Uh... actually she never had it either."

Once again, all eyes swivelled to me.

"I, uh.... look."

I turned my laptop around and pushed it towards Otembi. On screen was an emailed reply I had received late the previous night from Little Sis.

Does this answer your question? xLS

---------- Forwarded message ---------

From: Ruaridh Morgan <r.morgan@lancastercapital.com>

Subject: FW: Quarc Acquisition

To: Daff <daphne@morganfamily.email.me>

Pass this on to the nerd. Ask him where he got the hunch? Tokyo fine, back late on Thursday. X

---------- Forwarded message ---------

From: David Chesham <d.chesham@lancastercapital.com>

Subject: RE: Quarc Acquisition

To: Ruaridh Morgan <r.morgan@lancastercapital.com>

Took some digging. Based on Finisys accounts and a little insider gossip to extrapolate other figures, so 70-80% confidence: £50 – £70m. Looks like Trey Masterson ran out of runway & it was a fire sale/ acqui-hire. Make it a Jaeger-LeCoultre? – Chez

---------- Original message ---------

From: Ruaridh Morgan <r.morgan@lancastercapital.com>

Subject: Quarc Acquisition

To: David Chesham <d.chesham@lancastercapital.com>

Last year Finisys bought Quarc. Got a tip it was much less than rumoured. Buy you a Rolex if you can tell me the real figure in 24 hours. Go.

"What am I looking at?"

"Uh, it's from my brother-in-law. He's a... he works in finance. I asked him to find out how much a company called Quarc got bought for. Strawberry Capital – Lena's company – led their early investment rounds. Everyone thought they sold for hundreds of millions, and Strawberry got very rich off it, but the details were kept quiet. If they really sold for only £50m Strawberry would barely make back their investment."

"But why does one deal matter?"

"B-because the rumour in the City is that the people who bankrolled Strawberry, Highgate Holdings, are going to pull their funding. Which would have been fine if Strawberry had plenty of their own money from the Quarc deal, but..."

"I see. And this came to light..."

"Yesterday."

"My Clayford, you seem to have had a very busy weekend." There was a slightly new note in Otembi's voice. She *almost* sounded impressed.

"So your theory is that Lena Mueller tried to buy a painting from MDG and, what, faked the hack to cover up the fact that she couldn't afford... oh. My apologies, everyone, I'm being very slow. Insurance. By making it seem like her money was stolen while held in escrow, she can claim the money *back* from MDG despite never having had it in the first place, and your reputation is so important to you that you'd ensure she got a payout from your insurers with the minimum fuss possible. This whole thing is an elaborate form of insurance fraud, and MDG is the patsy."

There was a moment's silence. Then Gavin turned to Zoe.

"Maybe hold off on the Moet."

Otembi started to put away her laptop.

"Well, thank you everyone. You've certainly given us some additional avenues of enquiry. I will of course need to take statements from everyone so that we have everything on the record, but we'll arrange all of that later. In the meantime I believe we need to speak more urgently to Ms Mue–"

"Just a moment, my dear," said Gavin, and Otembi bristled. "Enlightening as this has all been, we've still not discussed the main issue."

"Oh?"

"I mean, stop me if I'm wrong, Anil, but I thought we'd discovered who'd sent those emails, hadn't we? The ones with the... wrong type of hyphen?"

Anil nodded. "Kayla?"

"Right. Well, we know who created the account that the emails were sent from. Er, Yoo-Jin checked yesterday," said Kayla, nodding towards another of the MDG people I hadn't recognised. Yoo-Jin nodded back, and Kayla continued. I noticed her voice tightening. Grand drawing-room denouement this was not. It mostly just felt very, very awkward.

"So... yeah. Yoo-Jin checked, and the account was created... by Todd."

If I had been expecting gasps, or maybe an angry shouted denial, I would have been disappointed. There was just Todd, looking surprised and even a bit amused.

"Really? I don't remember creating an account like that," he said. "To be honest I don't think I've ever created an email account. I always ask you to do it, Yoo-Jin, don't I?"

I looked across at Otembi. She wasn't exactly reaching for the handcuffs.

"Well," said Kayla, "Whoever created the account was logged in as you. Did you give anyone your login details in the past few months?"

"No, not at all. I'm very good about that sort of thing."

"Are you sure? There's no possibility that someone else could have got your password? No one rang you up claiming to be, I don't know, from IT or anything?"

"No, absolutely not. Look, I'm really professional when I comes to my work account. Ever since I got scammed I've been really careful. I don't reuse passwords, I don't even write them down anywhere."

"Mr Nash... when you say you got scammed...?" prompted Otembi.

"Oh, yeah, *that*. God it was awful. It happened earlier this year. But don't worry," said Todd quickly, "it was personal, it was nothing to do with all this."

"I think we should be the judge of that. How did you get scammed?"

"Oh God, must I? It's *so* embarrassing. I mean," he gestured towards the end of the table with the Paladin team.

"Just tell them, Todd," growled Gavin.

Todd rolled his eyes.

"Ok, look, fine, I met someone on this dating app. Amanda's List. Her profile had all the same interests as me, we chatted, it felt like it was getting, you know, *interesting*, but we didn't meet because she was in Estonia. I tried to sort out flights to go meet her for a dirty w-... well, for a weekend visit. But I started getting emails in Estonian about visas from the embassy, so I gave her my password – to my *personal* email, before you ask – so that she could reply on my behalf, and then she must have logged in to the flight website and changed the flights so that it was one of her friends' names on the ticket, and then she just ghosted me. I only found out when I got to the airport. The whole thing was a con to get free flights for her friend."

"And you didn't report this?"

"Well, no. I was pretty embarrassed about the whole thing, to be honest. Plus... well, I emailed her a bunch of times after it happened, you know, demanding an explanation, and eventually she sent me back a really blunt thing basically saying she'd share a bunch of... well, look, we'd been chatting online for a long time, and of course she had some private messages, and... pictures. Of me. She basically said if I contacted her again she'd share all that stuff with my family on Facebook. So at that point I thought it would be best to forget the whole thing. But that's all it was."

"I see," said Otembi. "And how long ago was this?"

"Oh, you know, maybe three months ago."

"Yoo-Jin," said Debi. "Two questions for you. First up, when was the fake email account created?"

"Just give me a second," said Yoo-Jin, clicking around on her laptop. She frowned. "Oh. Um, 3rd of February. So... about three months ago."

"Second question: when people forget their passwords for their work email... how do they reset it?"

"Well, they.... Oh." Yoo-Jin took a breath and closed her eyes before continuing quietly "They can get an email sent with a reset link in it..." – she was practically whispering by this point – "...to their personal email account."

Simultaneously Ben and Otembi lowered their heads and pressed their palms into their faces.

"What?" asked Todd.

*

Things wrapped up pretty quickly from there. Todd, when he finally understood how he'd allowed scammers to set up the fraudulent emails, made a few plaintive bleatings about it not being his fault, not really. Otembi reiterated her desire to speak to him, Yoo-Jin, Kayla, Debi and me again to take formal statements. Anil started to fidget restlessly, and soon Gavin called the meeting to a close.

"Thank you for your time, everyone. I knew we could get to the bottom of this if we just put our heads together. I'd like my team to stay here, as we have a little bit of response planning to do. Yoo-Jin, could you run and grab Sandy for me? And let's also get Joy, Deneall, Lumpy, Clifford..."

The rest of us rose to leave. As we were filing out, Ben sidled up to me.

"Impressive work."

"Thanks. Uh... thanks."

"Listen, I don't know if you're going to go back to Paladin, but we're growing and... well, the pay isn't great – it's a government gig, after all – but... keep your options open?"

He handed me a business card, onto which he'd scrawled a web address. It looked like a careers site. Then he scurried off to catch up with Otembi, who was striding away towards the lobby.

"No," said Kayla, popping up from behind me. "You're coming back to Paladin. I need you in the Bunker with me. Give me the card. Give it to me."

"I, uh... I'm just... Look, I don't even know if..." I stuttered, and realised my fingers were closing round the card.

"Fine. You can keep it as a memento. But you know I'm not going to let you leave," she said stubbornly.

We came out to the lobby. Anil and Debi were dawdling behind us in conversation. Kayla took the opportunity to go to the loo. When Anil and Debi were done talking, Anil went up to the receptionist desk to ask for a taxi. I had a moment alone with Debi.

"Uh... thanks for, uh..."

I trailed off.

"No problem," said Debi, with an encouraging smile. "If anyone's going to embarrass me by utterly dismantling my theory about the hack, I'd rather it be me. Like Anil says, it's all about 'controlling the narrative'. Besides, you're a friend, and that's what friends do."

She paused for a second.

"And I was thinking about it, and you were right, I haven't always been a great friend to you."

"No, it's ok, I shouldn't have said... and *you* were right, sometimes I... uh..."

"Tell you what. Let's just draw a line under this and start again, shall we? As proper friends this time."

"Ok. I mean, y-yes. I'd like that."

Anil rejoined us just as Kayla returned from the bathroom. He led us out into the car park, out of earshot of anyone at MDG.

"Good," he said, as if in summary of the morning's events. "Thoughts?"

"Todd's an idiot," said Debi.

"Agreed."

"Colin's a genius, and we never should have suspended him," put in Kayla, a note of defiance in her voice.

"Well... possibly. But yes, you did well, Colin. We'll have to see about getting you back to work. Although, as I was saying to Debi, I think a reshuffle may be in order. You and Kayla make a good team, but Debi's recently shown herself to be a very safe pair of hands. We might see about splitting Foil in two, and hiring in the gaps. Maybe you two on existing client work and Debi on new accounts. Nothing promised. I'll chat to Brad. Ah, here we go."

A taxi pulled in to the car park. As we walked up to it, I heard Debi mutter to Kayla, "Bagsy you get Rémy."

When we reached the car Anil turned round to me.

"Colin, why don't you take the rest of the week off? It sounds like you've not exactly been relaxing these past few days, and I'm sure you'll be in and out of police interviews and the like. Kayla will call you about coming back once we've worked everything out internally. Yes?"

"Uh... y- yes. Ok."

He gave me one last curt nod, then got into the front of the car. Debi and Kayla climbed in the back, and they drove off, leaving me alone in the car park.

29

I went back to my flat, for the first time since I'd flown out to Boston. After so long bouncing around hotels, being back in a space that was *mine* was... well, actually it was a little underwhelming. My flat had always been my sanctuary, my safe space. But just at the moment I didn't feel quite so strongly that I needed one of those.

There was a pile of letters waiting for me. Mostly junk, and among it one stern note from my dentist telling me I'd missed my appointment and would be charged a no-show fee. I called them to reschedule and pay the fine, and only after I'd hung up the phone did I realise that I'd just arranged my own dentist appointment for the first time in my life. I felt proud of myself, and thought about messaging Big Sis to show off about it, and then was immediately ashamed at taking pride in something so pathetically small. Then I got angry with myself for shaming myself, and then I decided it was all far too complicated and sat down to watch some *Battlestar Galactica* instead.

I kept up the TV binge for the rest of Monday and all of Tuesday too. There were still a couple of things I needed to do, but I wasn't ready to address them yet. Instead, I set myself the challenge of being *just a little bit* healthier. So every couple of hours I made myself get up and do a couple of laps around my flat. And I restricted myself to one snack every half hour, and only three helpings of meals. It wasn't a big difference, but it was enough to make me feel like maybe – not yet, but when I was ready – I might be able to make a more meaningful change. If I wanted to.

I also sent Mum a message. Nothing much, just a short note thanking her for her concern, acknowledging that I'd found the last few weeks very upsetting, and assuring her that I was doing better now. Looking back though my message history I realised I mostly only ever sent one-word responses to barrages of texts from her. I'd never really established a tone of voice for communicating with her in writing. So my attempt to be a little bit more forthcoming now came out as awkwardly formal.

But still, I felt better for having sent it. I had been thinking a lot about that trip to Thessaloniki, and what it meant to Mum. It was a disaster for her, of course, and the start of the great family unravelling, but I'd started to realise that the Incident was only a small part of it. After Big Sis headed off to LAMDA, Mum was lost. Suddenly she was responsible for two moody children, and she had no one to help her. Those first few weeks had been rocky for me, but I'd never considered how difficult they'd been for Mum. We had just ignored her and sulked, and made it quite clear how much we wished

Big Sis would come back and take over again. It must have crushed her.

And that was what the trip to Greece was really about: it was her trying to prove that she could take charge, she could be fun, she could be *a mum.* But, in true Mum style, what started off as a grand gesture fell apart when it came to the implementation. She found it all too stressful, so she drank herself into oblivion each night, then spent the next day feeling hungover and guilty, which only made her drink more in the evening. And then one day her son woke her up from her alcohol-fuelled stupor to tell her that her youngest daughter had been hospitalised while she slept. She may have lashed out at me at the outset, but I couldn't help but wonder how much her treatment of Little Sis afterwards, and attitude to me, was powered by her own guilt.

And, perhaps ironically, I had started to suspect that my own habitual resentment of her, my instinct for finding fault with everything she did, was as much a result of *my* own feelings of guilt as anything else. A guilt that, ever since my stay with Little Sis, I'd started to feel less strongly.

*

On Wednesday afternoon I was called in to MPCCU headquarters to give my statement. Ben gave me another meek nod of greeting when he saw me. And Otembi was in the best mood I'd seen her in. She hardly rolled her eyes at me at all.

She started by giving me a brief update on how the case was progressing.

"Ms Mueller is cooperating fully. Once she realised how much we knew she capitulated pretty quickly. I suppose that's the venture capitalist in her: She took a massive gamble, but once she realised it hadn't paid off she adjusted her strategy accordingly. She's now cooperating as much as she can, to get herself in the least amount of trouble. Not that she's given us much to work with. She says she'd got to know some shady types on the dark web through a previous interest in privacy tech, and when things started to go down the tubes with Strawberry she started making enquiries about a little dirty dealing to try to rectify the situation. She eventually got introduced to someone who specialises in social engineering, who sometimes went by the handle 'Sicarius' – which is a type of sand spider, by the way. He made her a proposal, although she claims he never told her the details of how he would do it. She paid him an up-front retainer, in Burncoin of course, so we can't track him that way. And beyond that we don't have much to go on. But frankly, now that it's failed fraud rather than successful theft, we're happy enough just to get Mueller. She'll plead guilty, and we'll start a file on Sicarius in case he crops up again, although I somehow doubt he will. But before I can put this to bed I need your statement, so… where shall we start?"

I told them more or less everything, except for how I discovered what Mo had typed, of course. I skirted around the subject whenever Otembi's questions pushed in that direction, as I was very aware that I would get into a *lot* of trouble if I told the truth. I could feel her getting frustrated with me. Eventually, she came right out and asked me.

"Mr Clayford, on Monday your colleague Kayla suggested you had found a store of keystrokes from Mr Ortlauf's computer that allowed you to reconstruct what he had been told to type by Sicarius. When I asked her about it earlier today, she claimed she didn't understand any of the details, and was simply repeating what you had told her. I asked Ben how you might have found such a store, given that neither he nor your colleagues at Paladin did after an exhaustive search of the computer hard drive. He said he couldn't imagine how you would have done it. Will you please tell me now?"

I looked her in the eye, and swallowed.

"Uh… no," I said, in a strangled voice. It occurred to me that this was almost certainly the greatest show of defiance I had ever made. It didn't feel good at all.

She gave me an angry glare that lasted several seconds. Then she sat back and said, "You know, the last time we spoke on the phone, you were insistent that we should look at CCTV footage to see if Mo's screen was picked up on any of the internal cameras. And I rejected your idea, something I now realise was a mistake. It occurs to me that, if you'd had access to that footage, that might have enabled you to identify Mo's keystrokes, in a roundabout way. But you didn't have access to that footage, did you? Not legally, at any rate?"

I stared at the floor, and felt my cheeks go a bright red and sweat start to form around my temples.

"Well, then," said Otembi. "I apologise: I'm sure if I'd listened to you back then I would have saved you a lot of trouble. Trouble that I'm *sure* you will be very careful to stay out of in future. That will be all."

"Uh... not quite," I said.

"Oh? Would you like to put something else on the record?"

"I... uh, I know who Sicarius is. Well, sort of."

I told her, and she simply nodded and said she'd look into it. She didn't seem as impressed as I'd hoped she'd be, but maybe that was just her way. She thanked me for my time, and I stood up to leave.

"Oh, Colin? Ben tells me he talked to you about a role with us. I recommend you give it some serious thought."

*

Back in my flat I booted up my PC and logged on to Alt-Match. Mary wasn't online, but I opened up the Instant chat window anyway.

THX1137: Hi Sicarius.

THX1137: I tried emailing you, but it bounced. I guess you shut down your Sandspidr alias after you heard that Lena had been arrested?

THX1137: They know who you are, and they're coming for you. But while I still have the chance I just wanted to say one thing:

THX1137: Fuck you.

THX1137: Fuck you from the bottom of my heart. You must have felt so powerful, screwing around with me, lying to me, threatening me, and making me feel like I was so stupid. But I still beat you.

THX1137: That is all.

...

HarlequinCyanide: What?????

THX1137: Oh shit sorry!

THX1137: Ignore that. It wasn't meant for you.

THX1137: I was hoping to delete it before you saw it.

HarlequinCyanide: Er.... what?????

THX1137: I'm really sorry. Long story short, someone has been reading our conversations.

THX1137: I'm pretty sure it's someone who works at XOX Connections, the company who runs AltMatch. He's a scammer, and he's been using his access to user data as part of his scams. Basically he started looking for people at MDG and Paladin who were on their sites, and managed to find a guy called Todd on another XOX app, Amanda's List, and he set up a fake match to try to con him into giving him access to Labyrinth. Although in the end he couldn't find a way to get what he wanted directly, so he did a whole... well, it's complicated.

THX1137: But he also got really lucky, in that he could keep tabs on me throughout it all through my conversations with you. Basically every time I told you anything he saw it, which is how he managed to always seem one step ahead of me. I'm really sorry, for a long time I thought maybe you were part of the whole thing. I should have trusted you.

THX1137: Anyway, eventually I figured it out, and I know it's cheap but I really wanted a chance to tell him to go fuck himself, and this was the only way I thought I could get his attention.

...

HarlequinCyanide: Er... WHAT???

HarlequinCyanide: Bloody hell.

HarlequinCyanide: So can he read all of this too?

THX1137: Yeah, I think so. Sorry.

HarlequinCyanide: Then first of all, FUCK YOU Mr Hacker Man. You can fuck right off.

HarlequinCyanide: Bloody hell. This is so weird!!!

HarlequinCyanide: Also can we maybe switch to WhatsApp?

THX1137: Sure

THX1137: Or actually

THX1137: Would you like to meet up?

THX1137: In person, I mean?

...

HarlequinCyanide: Are you sure?

THX1137: Yes. I've actually never done this before, but I'd like to. With you.

THX1137: If that's ok?

...

HarlequinCyanide: Can we talk about this on WhatsApp? I don't really want to have any more conversations in front of Fuck-face McHackerdick.

My heart plummetted. I gave her my number, and she told me she'd message me, and then AltMatch notified me that she was now offline.

The next half an hour was sheer agony. I sat there, barely daring to move, my eyes glued to my phone. I wanted to eat, more than I'd ever wanted to eat in my life, but I refused to give in. *I'll eat when she responds*, I told myself.

Centuries later my phone pinged. I actually retched slightly at the sound, I was so on edge. It was Mary. I could feel pre-emptive tears welling up in my eyes as I opened WhatsApp.

I'm so sorry. I freaked out. I really don't see many people in real life. I don't go out very much. First of all, I want you to know that I'm so, so flattered to be asked. And I do want to meet up with you... It's just that I'm really, really rubbish in real life, and if you met me I'm scared you'd dislike me, and I'd lose what we have, and I really don't want to lose it. BUT I think it's got to the point where if we don't meet up I'm probably going to lose it anyway. I don't think we can go back to how we were now. I'm sorry, I'm making a hash of this, but I keep trying to write this better and keep deleting it and if I don't send you something to tell you how I'm feeling now I don't think I'll ever manage to send you anything at all. So what I think I'm trying to say is that if you want to meet up I will, and I'll do my best, but please, please forgive me for not being the person I am online.

It took me a couple of read-throughs before I was clear that she was technically saying 'yes', but when I finally convinced myself of it I allowed myself to let out a little whoop. I made it to the kitchen before realising I wasn't actually all that hungry any more. I was, however, absolutely vibrating with excess adrenaline, so I did a little lap around my living room, shaking out my hands to try to give it an outlet.

Eventually I settled back down on my sofa, and composed a careful reply. There was then a lot of back and forth, but eventually we agreed on a plan, and despite her initial extreme reticence, I got the sense that Mary was quite excited by it (although not nearly as excited as I was). I would go round to her flat, and we would watch some anime shows together, for exactly one hour, late afternoon on the coming Saturday. Neither of us wanted to be out in public, and I wasn't ready to let her into my home yet. We'd watch television so that we didn't have to chat much, to minimise awkward silences. There would be no physical contact of any kind, so that I wouldn't have to worry about flinching. There would be no food, as she wasn't comfortable eating in front of other people. The lights would be dim, because we were both self-conscious about how we looked.

All in all, it was probably the most elaborately constrained, destined-to-fail, ridiculous first date ever devised. But it was

342 | GILES K CAPERTON

also the first date I had ever been on, and I was so thrilled I even caught myself humming out loud.

At the end of the afternoon I finally pulled myself away from our chat. I had ignored a call from Kayla, and she'd left a voicemail. It was official: I was to be welcomed back to Paladin the following Monday. The Bunker Buddies were being split up. Debi was taking Bled and, along with a few new hires, would be forming a new team called Falx. Kayla and I would stay in the Bunker with Rémy, and apparently we'd get another team member just as soon as budget constraints allowed. Our first project would be the accounting system overhaul for J-Chem corporation.

Nothing about that filled me with any particular enthusiasm. The world was a big, new, exciting place, and none of the interesting bits seemed to be waiting for me in the Bunker. I thought more about the business card Ben had given me, which was sat on the shelf in my hall.

Then I picked up my phone. Many things were changing, but there had to be some constants too. It was a Wednesday evening, and that meant it was time for my weekly call with Big Sis.

CPSIA information can be obtained
at www.ICGtesting.com
Printed in the USA
LVHW041946051121
702546LV00005B/121